GRAND

The time D[...] [...] the majestic Grand Canyon had been the stuff of dreams and illusions—not the normal interaction of everyday life. But Dawn soon found that her love for Bryce had the power to turn the ordinary into the extraordinary and that true love is no illusion at all....

THE IMAGE OF A GIRL
by Billie Green

Archaeologist Mike Nicholson couldn't understand his fascination with the picture on the side of the ancient ceramic jar. True, the woman was beautiful, but she was only an image, after all, despite the way she haunted his dreams. Then Faith Bowen walked into view, and suddenly Mike had the strangest feeling that his dreams were about to come true.

FIESTA! by Barbara Faith

Annmarie Bannister was a dreamer, but never in her wildest dreams did she imagine herself getting involved with Diego Ortiz, a matador of all things! But, while in the beautiful Mexican town of Santa Catarina, Annmarie learned that love and adventure can go hand in hand.

Dear Reader:

What better way to relax during the summer than with a Silhouette Book. But you say the summer's busier than ever? You're so busy you don't have the time to even think about a "real" vacation? Or maybe you need a vacation from your vacation—too much packing and unpacking, and with the kids home from school you just don't seem to have enough time for reading pleasure...?

Well, Silhouette has the perfect solution—three *short* novels all with a vacation theme and, of course, romance. Barbara Faith, Billie Green and Joan Hohl, three bestselling Silhouette authors, have each written a wonderful story for this collection. So whether you're on the run, or just need some time to get away from it all, sit back, relax and enjoy—these stories were written just for you.

Sincerely,

Karen Solem
Editorial Director
Silhouette Books

SILHOUETTE SUMMER Sizzlers

Silhouette Books

Published by Silhouette Books New York

America's Publisher of Contemporary Romance

SILHOUETTE BOOKS
300 E. 42nd St., New York, N.Y. 10017

Silhouette Summer Sizzlers 1988
Copyright © 1988 by Silhouette Books

ISBN: 0-373-48214-0

First Silhouette Books printing July 1988

The publisher acknowledges the copyright holders of the
individual works as follows:

Grand Illusion
Copyright © 1988 by Joan Hohl
Fiesta!
Copyright © 1988 by Barbara Faith de Covarrubias
The Image of a Girl
Copyright © 1988 by Billie Green

Contents

GRAND ILLUSION

Joan Hohl

For Bruce and Jan and
Mick and Bill for their
patience with their sister's
propensity for research.

Dear Friends:

I have always been a dreamer. Faraway places, the other side of the mountain and what might be at the end of any road or path have always stirred my imagination. Being an eager as well as a happy wanderer, I consider myself fortunate for the opportunity to travel in connection with my work. And my work has taken me to many beautiful and interesting places, any of which I could have chosen for the setting of my contribution to the *Silhouette Summer Sizzlers*.

For example, imagine a vacation love story set in the languid warmth of Atlanta, Georgia, in June. Peach Tree Street, a prevailing sense of history and the soft drawl of the gracious citizens would add a dash of Southern hospitality to any story. Or, if you would, imagine our hero and heroine falling in love at some point along the Big Sur in California, with the rugged hills and the crashing Pacific as a setting. Then again, I might have chosen to set my story in any number of small communities along the New Jersey coast, which just happens to be my own favorite vacation spot. Since I love the ocean, it would seem to be the most logical location for a vacation love story.

Any of the above locations would have made lovely settings for a story in the *Silhouette Summer Sizzlers*. So why didn't I use any one of them? Let me explain. When my editor, Tara Hughes, called to ask me if I'd be interested in contributing a story for the *Silhouette Summer Sizzlers*, I felt both honored and inspired. The honor, of course, came from being invited to join forces with two delightful friends and very talented writers: Barbara Faith and Billie Green. The reason for my inspiration requires a short explanation.

For more years than I care to think about, my brother and sister-in-law, my sister and brother-in-law and my husband and I have discussed visiting Arizona and the Grand Canyon...someday. Someday when all the assorted offspring were finally out of school; someday when all the accumulated medical and dental bills were finally paid; someday when we could all arrange our schedules to coincide.

Someday came last summer. In loving and congenial company, I flew west from my Pennsylvania home to Arizona...and immediately fell in love. My vacation swiftly became a dedicated research trip. While my understanding companions stood waiting patiently, I happily perused magazines, books, pamphlets, brochures and anything else pertaining to wherever I happened to be at the moment. Our last scheduled stop was the Grand Canyon, and it was indeed the dessert following a lavish meal of scenery. Words cannot really describe the awesome impact of the Grand Canyon on the senses. Yet I had to try. I hope you enjoy *Grand Illusion*.

Chapter One

He was waiting for her.

Dawn wasn't certain exactly how she knew that the battered, dusty pickup truck belonged to Bryce Stone, but she would have bet her favorite thoroughbred that it did.

He was watching her.

Dawn's skin prickled as she felt his gaze crawl over her body. Controlling an urge to stiffen with resentment, she worked her lips into a friendly smile and closed the motel-room door behind her. She waited...and waited. When it became obvious that he wasn't about to come to her, Dawn gritted her teeth and began walking toward him.

He had parked the truck across four yellow-lined, vertical spaces in the motel lot. The truck-cab door was standing open and one long, jeans-clad leg was thrust outside, its booted foot swinging negligently. He was sitting indolently in the shaded interior, one arm draped over the steering wheel. His face was shadowed by the brim of a buff-colored Stetson. He was watching, waiting and...making her come to him.

Insolent plebeian!

* * *

Beautiful. Elegant. Classy. Bryce mentally ticked off the young woman's attributes as she walked toward him. A dry smile twitched the corners of his mouth as he thought of another, less complimentary word: *pampered.* As she drew nearer to the truck, Bryce swept her form with a second, more comprehensive gaze.

She was tall for a woman, even without the impractical spike-heeled sandals she was wearing. Bryce judged her to be about five inches shorter than his own height of six feet, four inches. And every inch of her was perfectly proportioned. Her legs were long. Bryce's insides clenched as he skimmed his narrowed gaze from her slim ankles to her elegant thighs, which, regretfully, were concealed but blatantly outlined by designer jeans that clung to her body like a wet swimsuit. She was wearing a tailored, man-style shirt that effectively enhanced her femininity and her rounded, up-thrust breasts. Her shoulder-length chocolate-brown hair gleamed with red highlights in the bright September sunshine and made his fingers itch with a desire to play with the shiny strands. Her facial features were aristocratic and assembled into a perfection that very likely stopped traffic...as well as a man's breath. Oh, yeah, Bryce mused wryly, this gal was accustomed to having her every whim indulged.

Spoiled brat.

"Mr. Stone?" Dawn watched for a response, a flicker, anything on his expressionless face. There was nothing, not a hint of what might be going on behind those harshly etched, austerely set features. The man had an aura of toughness—both physical and psychological toughness. From behind their narrowed lids, his dark eyes stared at her with an unsettling cold steadiness. Implacable strength radiated from him, enveloping her in an invisible but almost palpable chill.

"Yes, ma'am." He raised a hand to the broad hat-brim to tilt it slightly. His manner wasn't particularly respectful.

The chill creeping along Dawn's spine intensified at the sound of his low, disinterested voice. Resentment broke through her control, sending her temper to flash point. With an action that never failed to intimidate, Dawn angled her chin and examined him—from the narrow tips of his dusty boots to the curled brim of his hat—with an aloof, disdainful expression.

"I am Dawn Kingsley." She extended her hand in a cool, regal manner.

Bryce Stone was obviously not impressed, with either her name or her haughty expression.

"Yeah, I heard." Moving with slow, insulting laziness, Bryce eased his long body from the truck. Dawn was on the point of lowering her arm when he finally reached out to grasp her hand with his. "Chad over at the service station said you were asking about me." His broad, long-fingered hand swallowed hers, giving her an unusual sensation of feeling small and dainty by comparison.

"Yes." Drawn up to her not inconsiderable height of five-eleven, Dawn only needed to tilt her head slightly to meet his drilling stare. She felt the impact of his cold gaze to the tips of her manicured toes. Absolutely refusing to feel intimidated, Dawn disengaged her hand and transferred it to a side pouch on her large shoulder bag. Withdrawing a slip of paper, she waved it gently and held it aloft. "I wasn't sure where to find you," she explained, smiling faintly. "All I was given was your name and the name of this town, Tusayan."

"'Given'?" His expression altered a shade; one eyebrow arched in question. His gaze didn't waver by as much as a flicker.

Beginning to feel warm, which she blamed on the unrelenting sunlight, and uncomfortable, which she attributed to his rudeness, Dawn shifted her gaze to skim the area with a dismissive glance.

"Not much of a town, is it?" Dawn had deliberately infused a note of scorn into her tone, hoping to get a reaction from him, as she scanned the length of the highway and the assortment of buildings that bordered it. Her ploy failed. Bryce remained implacable.

"Given?" He repeated the one-word query in the exact same inflectionless tone as before.

Dawn's temper flared alarmingly. Gritting her teeth, she forced a frigid coolness into her voice. "Yes. A mutual friend gave me your name."

"What mutual friend?"

Three whole words! The man had actually spoken three whole words to her! Wryly telling her fluttering heart to be still, Dawn fought an urge to laugh in his face. "Bruce Clayton," she replied, with what she thought was commendable restraint. "I believe you acted as guide for him last fall on an expedition to photograph animals."

"Umm."

Dawn exhaled a deep sigh of impatience. Old long-in-the-legs-and-short-in-the-response was really beginning to annoy her. "Might one ask if there is a meaning to that ambiguous 'umm'?" she asked with sweetened sarcasm.

"There's a meaning to everything," Bryce replied in a bored tone of voice. "But the only one I'm interested in is the meaning behind Clayton's reason for giving my name to you."

"The obvious reason, of course," Dawn retorted. "Bruce recommended you as the best guide in Arizona, if not the entire West." Her tone hinted that she was beginning to have serious doubts concerning Bruce Clayton's judgment.

"Why?"

"Why?" Dawn stared at him blankly. "Why what?"

It was Stone's turn to sigh heavily. "Why did he recommend me, and what do you need a guide for?" His lips tilted into the semblance of a smile as he swept her body with a cool glance. "You want to take photographs of animals?"

"No! Of course not." Dawn started to shake her head, but on consideration stopped abruptly. "Well, in a way," she admitted hesitantly.

"That certainly clarifies everything," Bryce drawled. "But do you think you could be just a tad more specific?"

Dawn was back to gritting her teeth. Bryce Stone had to be the single most irritating man she'd ever had the misfortune to run across. It was a pity she needed his services, she mused as she glared at him. Nothing would give her more pleasure than to tell this insufferable tall man to take a hike in the desert and leave his water bottle at home. With thoughts of the desert and water, Dawn realized how very warm and dry she was. Deciding that with any luck at all there might be a restaurant or diner nearby, she injected a conciliatory note into her tone.

"Ah...umm...do you think we might find a place to sit down?"

"Don't blame you." Bryce shot a look at her feet. "If I was wearing those spiked excuses for footgear, I'd ache to sit down, too."

That did it! She had plunked down her credit card to the tune of two hundred and seventy-five dollars for the sandals she was wearing, and to have this...*cretin*...refer to them as excuses was absolutely the last straw! Dawn's temper danced perilously close to the edge of her control. She opened her mouth to administer a blistering retort, but closed it again as she remembered how much she needed him.

"In that case, is there a place where we could sit down?" Dawn swallowed the taste of gall along with her pride. "A place where I could order something cold to drink?"

"Sure." Bryce shrugged and nodded at the building behind her, the very one she had so recently exited. "There's an excellent restaurant in the motel." His lips curved into that infuriating wry smile. "A bar, too. In case you want that drink to be on the stiff side."

Dawn longed for the opportunity to show him the stiff side of her hand. Instead she offered him a stiffly polite smile. "Then, let's go, if you don't mind?"

"No, I don't mind." Flicking his hand, Bryce motioned for her to precede him. "You hit it lucky, honey. I have nothing better to do this afternoon."

Dawn glared at him over her shoulder. "How complimentary of you," she said bitingly.

A smile pulled at his lips. "You want compliments?" His dark eyes gleamed as he made a slow inventory of her face and slender form. "You are a beautiful woman with a sleek, inviting body," he said with blunt appreciation of her attributes. His smile mocked the sudden shock in her eyes. "Is that more what you had in mind?"

"You . . . I . . ." Dawn raked her mind fruitlessly for a suitably annihilating reply. Never had she felt so flamingly angry. "How dare—" That's as far as he allowed her to go.

The insulting clod actually had the nerve to laugh in her outraged face!

"Save it for someone who might be impressed, sweetheart," Bryce drawled in that same bored tone. "I'm not," he added, moving on impatiently. "But if you want to talk to me, you'd better get it in gear." He nodded at the motel. "Either you make some quick tracks or I cut out of here." He shrugged. "The choice is yours."

Egotistical, overbearing, arrogant . . . Dawn was so furious she couldn't even think straight. But one tiny section of her mind remained lucid enough to remind her how very important he was to her project. Fuming, she spun around and strode toward the motel entrance.

"Hey, Bryce, what's up?" The desk clerk raised a hand in greeting as they entered the lobby.

"Not much, Ted," Bryce replied laconically. "The lady's thirsty." He indicated Dawn with a barely perceptible nod.

Ted ran an appreciative eye over Dawn in exactly the same annoying way he had earlier when she'd checked into the motel. "Take your pick," he said, gesturing vaguely. "The restaurant and the bar are practically empty." He swept another glance over Dawn and grinned. "I go off duty in a few minutes. Maybe I'll join you and the lady."

Dawn stiffened. Deciding she'd had about as much as she could take of leering men for one day, she opened her mouth to protest. She wasn't quite fast enough.

"Maybe you won't." Bryce's voice was mild but his eyes were cold. "We've got business to discuss."

A flush tinged Ted's cheeks. "Ah...right. I wouldn't want to intrude."

Bryce smiled and nodded. "See you, Ted." Cupping Dawn's elbow, he ushered her toward the restaurant.

"I've already eaten," she said tersely. "The bar will be fine."

Bryce shrugged and changed direction. "Wherever."

Dawn bristled but kept pace with him. She couldn't remember ever reacting so strongly to any man. Bad vibes, she told herself. Her eyes narrowed as she slid into a booth in the dimly lit bar-lounge. She had felt an instant antagonism for him. Bryce Stone churned her up, and that could prove difficult later. Watching him slide into the seat opposite her, Dawn felt a strange coiling sensation in the pit of her stomach. Yes, she thought, dealing with him could prove very difficult.

"What would you like?"

Startled out of her thoughts, Dawn blinked and glanced up. "What?"

Bryce gave her a dry look. "Janice is waiting to take our order."

Dawn frowned. "Janice?"

"Our waitress," he said, inclining his head slightly toward the uniformed woman standing by the booth. The girl was Navajo, young and pretty, with beautiful soft, dark eyes. "What would you like to drink?"

"Oh!" Dawn offered the patiently waiting girl an apologetic smile. "White wine on the rocks, please."

"I'll take mine with a head on it, Janice." Bryce gave the young woman a smile that took Dawn's breath away. Staring at him in bemusement, she was only vaguely aware of the woman's dry reply.

"So what else is new?"

The rich sound of Bryce's laughter sent a tingle down Dawn's spine. The change in his appearance was almost shocking. Laugh lines crinkled at the corners of his eyes. His white teeth gleamed in contrast to his tanned skin. He looked relaxed and easygoing, the complete opposite of the cold-eyed, granite-faced man of seconds ago. Dawn was on the verge of deciding she could like this man, after all, when the waitress walked away and he returned his attention to her.

"Okay, lady, what do you want from me?" Bryce asked bluntly.

Dawn's nerves contracted with renewed tension. Resentment shivered through her. Wondering what it was about her that turned him off, she raised her chin and met his relentless stare. "I want to hire you," she answered with a coolness she was far from feeling.

"For what?"

"To guide me into the canyon," Dawn replied in a reasonable tone.

Bryce stared at her in amazement. "The Grand?" His tone reflected his expression.

"Well, of course," Dawn said impatiently. "Is there another?"

"Lady, there are one whole helluva lot of canyons in Arizona," Bryce said flatly.

Dawn's temper snapped and so did she. "I know that! But I wouldn't be here, in Tusayan, if I didn't want to see the Grand Canyon, would I?" She drew a sharp breath. "And don't call me lady!"

Bryce's lips twitched. "Why not?" he asked innocently. "Aren't you one?"

"Yes, damn you!" The gritted words were out of Dawn's mouth before she could catch them. Appalled at herself, she drew a deep, calming breath. She never lost her cool, never. To lose it now, to this man's casual baiting, was almost unendurable for her. "I must apologize," she said tightly. "I didn't mean to swear at you."

"Yes, you did." Bryce shrugged. "But that's okay, I earned it." Lifting his hand, he pulled the Stetson from his head and dropped it onto the seat. Returning his hand to his head, he raked his fingers through the flattened waves of his thick dark hair. "Look, I'm sorry, too. Suppose we start again?" He arched his eyebrows questioningly and smiled encouragingly. "Okay?"

Dawn was again mesmerized by the masculine beauty of his smile. Resisting the sensation of warmth stealing through her, she eyed him coolly and nodded. "All right, Mr. Stone, we'll begin—"

"Bryce," he interrupted softly. "The name's Bryce."

Dawn hesitated a moment before giving in to his unspoken invitation. "Bryce," she repeated.

His lips curved into a smile of satisfaction. "And may I call you Dawn?" he asked.

Her defenses beginning to crumble, Dawn took a deep breath to gather her strength and steel herself against his appeal. Made cautious by his abrupt change of attitude, she eyed him warily but nodded in agreement.

"Good." His smile deepened and his dark eyes gleamed. A warning voice within urged Dawn to run.

Too late. The waitress arrived at the booth with the drinks they had ordered. Oddly breathless, Dawn observed Bryce closely as he bantered with the young woman.

On his guard, Bryce Stone was merely fascinating. Relaxed and charming, he was devastating. And yet there was something about him, some element that made him completely different from any man she had ever met. Watching his eyes, Dawn searched her mind for a definitive word to describe that element.

Basic. The word leaped into her mind. There was a basic quality about him that spoke of another era, an era when men strode the earth like conquerors, taking whatever they desired from the land and the females who inhabited it.

The analogy sent a tingle shivering down her spine. Dawn was acquainted with the modern-day sharks of the business world; her father was one of them. But Bryce didn't fit the mold of the ulcer-ridden, stress-jangled men of the latter part of the twentieth century. He was too self-contained, too earthy, too essentially male. Dawn felt everything feminine inside her responding to his masculine allure. The sensation was much too basic; it bordered on the primitive, creating dark urges deeply hidden beneath an acquired layer of civilizing sophistication. The feeling scared the daylights out of her.

Dawn didn't like the sensation. Trying to deny the tingle of awareness spreading through her from merely looking at him, she raised her chin. Her attention returning to reality, Dawn smiled faintly and wondered what Bryce had said to the waitress to bring a blush to her cheeks as she served the drinks. Then, assuring herself that she really didn't care, Dawn lifted her wineglass and tilted it slightly toward him.

"Your health . . . Bryce."

Chapter Two

The barely concealed note of cynicism in Dawn's voice captured Bryce's attention. His chest heaving in a silent sigh, he eased around to face his companion. A grim smile played at the corners of his mouth as he gripped the handle of his frosted mug.

"And yours—" Bryce paused deliberately before adding "—Dawn." He took a long swallow of the cold beer and, settling more comfortably on the booth seat, examined her features in detail.

The exercise was not without its rewards. Up close, Dawn Kingsley was even more beautiful than he'd originally thought. Her nose was slender, her cheekbones high, her jawline firmly delineated. Her eyebrows were a shade darker than her auburn hair and arched delicately. Her eyes were hazel, a leafy green highlighted by flecks of brown and gold.

The kind of eyes a man could happily get lost in, Bryce reflected, accepting the sudden tightening of his body. The same way a man could happily lose his fingers within the red and brown strands of her silky hair. But it was her mouth that commanded his most intense scrutiny. His throat going dry, Bryce decided that tasting Dawn's mouth would be like tasting honey-coated ecstasy.

Suddenly compelled by a hunger that was baffling in its intensity, Bryce leaned forward. The flaring light of wariness in her eyes and an almost imperceptible tightening at the edges of the mouth he was craving brought Bryce back to reality.

Impatient with himself for allowing his imagination to get the upper hand over his common sense, however briefly, Bryce reacted in a very human manner by speaking impatiently to her.

"Suppose you tell me why you want to go into the canyon."

Every nerve in Dawn's body was quivering. Fully aware of her appearance, she was not unaccustomed to admiring stares from men. She had been visually dissected and undressed countless times, as recently as a few minutes previously in the motel lobby by the brash young desk clerk. And though she resented the long, appraising looks, Dawn told herself she should be used to them. She wasn't. Yet her reaction to Bryce Stone's narrow-eyed assessment of her was surprisingly different from her usual impatience and annoyance. Her body quivered. She felt tingly. Her skin prickled, growing hot and then cold. She ached inside…deep inside. It frightened her. It threatened her in a way she didn't understand. Responding to the warmth spreading inwardly, Dawn froze outwardly.

"Research," she answered shortly and succinctly.

Bryce frowned. "What sort of research?" One eyebrow tilted quizzically. "Are you a naturalist? An archaeologist?"

Dawn shook her head. "I'm a novelist."

Once again Bryce Stone had the temerity to laugh at her. "A novelist!" he exclaimed.

"Yes, a novelist." Dawn's tone dropped to subzero. "I write fiction."

Bryce's lips curved into a wry, knowing smile. "And you're a contemporary of Bruce Clayton's."

Dawn stiffened at the tone of derision in his voice. "What does Bruce have to do with it?" she demanded, confused and suspicious.

"What does Bruce Clayton have to do with anything?" he countered. "At least, anything useful?" The lines bracketing his mouth deepened and his lips pursed, as if from a sour taste. "From what I learned of Clayton when he was here, he is nothing more than a parasite, living off the money his grandfather earned, while filling the emptiness of his life with jaunts around the world, keeping score on how many women he can con into his bed and dabbling in the occasional photographic expedition." He quirked one eyebrow. "Is playing at writing the way you fill the hours of your life?"

Dawn's temper finally escaped her control. "Playing!" she repeated, incensed. "How dare you imply—"

Bryce cut her off ruthlessly. "I'm not implying anything, I'm saying it outright. Research." He made a snorting sound as he picked up his hat. "Sorry, sweetheart, but I don't have time for bored little rich girls looking for kicks in the canyon." His laser stare pinned Dawn to her seat. "Hell," he muttered, "I wouldn't have time for you if I didn't have another damn thing to do." Pushing his half-finished beer aside, he moved to slide out of the booth.

"Wait a minute!" Without thinking about what she was doing or why she was doing it, Dawn reached out to clasp his wrist. An unfamiliar feeling of fear slithered through her when his glance sliced to her fingers. "Please, hear me out," she added in an equally unfamiliar, pleading tone of voice.

Bryce slowly raised his eyes, sending another trickle of fear through her as his gaze tangled with hers. "Make it good, beautiful," he said with a tone of warning.

Dawn detested being called "sweetheart" and "beautiful" and "honey" but felt too rattled by him to object. She used the seconds required for him to settle himself into the booth again to gather her thoughts. She began to speak the instant he leveled a prompting look at her.

"First of all, let me assure you that I never *play* at anything," she began.

Though Bryce didn't reply, his expression said much about the skepticism he was feeling.

Keeping her composure, Dawn ground her teeth before continuing. "Even if I did indulge, the absolute last thing I'd play around with is my work."

" 'Work'?" Bryce made no attempt to conceal his incredulity.

"Yes, work!" Dawn retorted. "I work for a living, Mr. Stone, exactly like you and most other people do."

"Sure."

Dawn literally saw red. Sheer fury engulfed her. The gold flecks in her eyes glittering with the anger shimmering through her, she inspected his lazily lounging body narrowly. Who was this man to disparage her? What did he do other than to guide the occasional hunting party? He was impudent as well as insolent!

"I have four novels to my credit, Mr. Stone," she said tightly. She held up her hand, thumb and forefinger separated by less than an inch. "The last book came that close to the bestseller list."

"I'm impressed," Bryce drawled in a tone that belied his assertion.

"You should be," she snapped. "And I'll tell you something else, Mr. Stone—" Dawn's voice was low and fervent "—I want one of my books to make that list so badly I can taste it, and I think the book I'm working on can do it for me." The combination of anger and intense emotion had dried Dawn's throat. She paused to take a sip of wine. Bryce used that moment to insert a dry comment.

"A writer has to sell a book before it can make the bestseller list."

"No kidding?" Dawn replied tauntingly, no longer even trying to hide how very obnoxious she thought him to be. "Well, for your information, I *have* sold the book," she went on sweetly. "And for a generous advance." Dawn quoted a figure that finally succeeded in drawing a reaction from him.

"What?" Bryce Stone stared at her in blank amazement.

Dawn sipped her wine and looked superior. "You heard me."

Bryce gazed at her for several seconds, then his expression of surprise changed to self-mockery. "Go get 'em, sweetheart," he said encouragingly, tilting his beer mug in a salute. "I honestly hope you make it to the list."

The sincerity of his tone sent a rush of pleasure surging through Dawn that was baffling in its intensity. Strangely afraid to examine the feeling, she avoided self-analysis by plunging into speech. "Thank you. I hope I do, too," she said candidly. "But, in order to lend authenticity to the story, I must research the canyon."

"Why?" The skeptical note had returned to his voice.

Dawn sighed. Why me? she asked herself tiredly. Shaking her head, she picked up her glass and frowned when she saw that it was empty. Wondering why the waitress hadn't returned to the booth, she said wearily. "I'll explain, if you'll find your friend Janice and order another glass of wine for me."

"Not until you've eaten."

Dawn glanced up sharply. "I assure you that I can handle more than one glass of wine, Mr. Stone."

His response was short and to the point. "Maybe so, but we'll have dinner first, just to stay on the safe side."

"Dinner?" Dawn repeated, frowning.

Bryce almost succeeded in hiding his amusement. "In case you haven't noticed, it's after six." He flicked his hand to indicate the lounge. "The night crawlers have begun to wriggle."

Her frown deepening, Dawn glanced around in surprise. The number of people crowded into the previously empty lounge explained the waitress's inability to get back to the booth. The crush of thirsty humanity unnerved Dawn, not because crowds bothered her but because she hadn't been aware of their presence. The realization that she had lost track of time, place and everything else while engaging in a verbal duel with Bryce Stone gave Dawn a funny feeling in the pit of her stomach. Choosing to blame the uncomfortable sensation on hunger, Dawn shot a questioning look at him.

"Did you say 'We'll have dinner first'?"

Bryce nodded.

"Where?"

"In the restaurant right here in the motel," he replied, shrugging.

"At whose expense?" Dawn asked politely.

A slow smile worked its way to his lips. "I'll bow to women's lib for once and allow you to pick up the tab." His teeth flashed in a grin. "Besides, you're the one with the hefty advance."

Chapter Three

The meal was delicious. It was the company that Dawn was uncertain of. She felt disoriented by his lightning changes from abrasive to beguiling and back again.

Bryce played the role of charming companion throughout dinner, entertaining Dawn with humorous anecdotes of his trials and tribulations with greenhorn photographers.

"Why do you continue to do it?" she asked, toying with her small after-dinner liqueur glass.

Bryce shrugged. "It gives me an excuse to occasionally walk away from my real work and spend time simply poking around the wild places."

Dawn's eyebrows arched. "Real work? I assumed guiding was your real work."

"Just as I assumed that you were a dilettante, like your friend Clayton," Bryce drawled.

"You're still unconvinced that I'm not," Dawn replied, matching his drawl.

Bryce gave her his wry smile. "Damn straight," he agreed. "And you have your work cut out for you if you're hoping to convince me otherwise." His tone took on a chiding edge. "So maybe you'd better get at it."

Renewed irritation with him made Dawn's skin prickle. Silently cursing his chameleonlike personality, she drank the last of her liqueur and set the glass on the table with controlled force. The act elicited a knowing smile from Bryce, which succeeded in irritating her even more. Reminding herself that he was necessary to her plans, Dawn drew a deep breath in preparation for launching into an explanation. The waiter appeared at their table before she could utter the first word.

"Will there be anything else, sir?" the man asked Bryce politely, completely ignoring Dawn.

Dawn glared at the waiter and silently accused him of being a chauvinist. She had always detested the feeling of being invisible while automatic respect was accorded to her male escort. And in this case it was worse; she was paying the bill!

Bryce shook his head. "No, I don't think so." He slanted an amused look at her. "Dawn?"

Dawn was fuming, and Bryce knew it. The realization that he could read her so easily intensified her irritation into a slow, simmering fury. "No, thank you." The smile she managed for the hapless waiter didn't hide the anger in her eyes.

Bryce, however, appeared to be enjoying himself immensely. His dark eyes glowed with mocking humor. "You may give the check to the lady," he instructed the waiter as he smiled benignly at Dawn.

"Yes, sir." Having obviously picked up the tension humming between them, the baffled waiter shifted a wary-eyed glance from Bryce to Dawn as he made out the check and carefully placed it on the table in front of her.

Dawn signed the check and retrieved her room key from her purse to prove she was staying at the motel. The waiter edged away from the table with a murmured "Thank you, ma'am."

Dawn muttered the correct response, then stared narrowly at Bryce. "I'm willing to pay anything—" she began, only to be silenced by a slicing motion of his hand.

"We can't talk here," he said, ending the movement of his hand with a wave at the doorway to the restaurant, where a dozen or so people were waiting to be seated. "I have a hunch the management would appreciate the table."

During the minutes required for them to vacate the restaurant and cross the lobby to the motel entrance, Dawn fought an inner battle between anger and frustration. She was beginning to feel certain that Bryce Stone was toying with her and, in the end, would turn down her offer, no matter how well she presented it.

The autumn night was clear and cool. The dark sky appeared like a canopy spattered with millions of twinkling lights. The three-quarter moon bathed the land with silvery illumination. The soft breeze carried the sharp scent of piñon and juniper trees.

Ever the writer, Dawn came to an abrupt halt just outside the plate-glass doors. Quivering, she closed her eyes and inhaled deeply, drawing in the feel and taste and smell of new surroundings, unaware and uncaring of the contemplative gaze of the man observing her through narrowed dark eyes.

"You've never been West before?" Bryce asked quietly as he settled the Stetson on his head.

A faint smile played over Dawn's beautifully shaped mouth. "Las Vegas, Los Angeles, San Francisco," she answered, shrugging. "There were always lights and noise and people. It was never like this, never this glorious, scented stillness, this ensnaring sense of peace and tranquility."

"You like it?"

Dawn's smile faded. "It could become addictive. I might even succeed in convincing myself that I could work better in an atmosphere such as this," she admitted wryly, "if I didn't know that it's all an illusion."

"Are you absolutely positive it is an illusion?" There was challenge in Bryce's tone.

Dawn met his challenge with cynicism. "Can you convince me that it's not?"

Bryce smiled with lazy confidence. "Probably, if I felt so inclined, which I don't." His smile quirked tauntingly. "Besides, the plan was for you to convince me—remember?"

The tension within Dawn returned in full force. Growing taut, she glanced around. Her gaze settled on his truck, still parked illegally with the cab door standing wide open. Wondering why on earth it hadn't been ticketed or even stripped, she returned her pensive gaze to him. "I suppose we can sit in your truck to talk?"

Bryce was shaking his head before she'd finished speaking. "No, the truck's grimy." His gaze drifted the length of her body. "You'd ruin those designer jeans." His shoulders lifted in a helpless shrug. "I guess we'll have to go to your room."

Dawn stiffened noticeably. "Guess again," she said tightly.

Bryce didn't laugh; he sighed. "Look, sweetheart, you're the one who wanted this conversation, not me."

"I didn't want it to take place in a motel room!" she exclaimed.

Impatience flashed in his eyes. "What the hell are you afraid of?" he demanded. "Do you actually think I'll go mad with lust and attack you?" His brief burst of laughter was insulting. "You should live so long."

Dawn was livid. "You overbearing, conceited—" That's as far as he allowed her to go.

"Forget it, okay? I'll give you the name of another guide." His shoulders moved again, betraying the impatience rippling through him. "Hell, all you have to do is call Bright Angel Lodge and make a reservation for one of the mule trips into the canyon. All the trips are guided by experts." Hands resting lightly on his slim hips, Bryce stood tall, glaring at her.

Dawn returned his glare and blurted out, "I don't want to go with a bunch of tourists from the lodge and I don't want the name of another guide! I want you!

The instant the words were out of her mouth Dawn realized they were true. She didn't know exactly why it was so important for him to guide her, and she didn't particularly want to examine her reasons too closely, but instinctively she knew it was imperative that he did.

Unfortunately Bryce didn't recognize the importance at all. He deliberately chose to misunderstand the last part of her statement. His attractive lips curved into a sensuous smile that had the power to melt bones...Dawn's bones. "Now, that can be arranged," he murmured in a soft, suggestive drawl.

Disgusted with her own suddenly weak limbs, and taut with anger, Dawn raked a disdainful glance over his rangy body. "You should live so long," she retorted, tossing his words back at him scathingly, denying the excited rush of heat spreading through her.

Bryce laughed. "You're a cool one, I'll give you that." She heard reluctant admiration in his tone. "Okay, beautiful, I'll listen to your argument." His amusement vanished and he was suddenly all business. "But it will have to be in your room, and it better be good."

Dawn's throat went dry. "Ah...shouldn't you shut the door on your truck?" She was biding for time; Bryce knew it as well as she did. "The interior light's out, which probably means the battery is already dead."

He spared a disinterested gaze for the dusty vehicle. "The battery's not dead; I turned the light off, and the truck's not going anywhere—'' his lips tightened ''—unless you decide that my services aren't worth an explanation.'' His restless movement told her clearly that he'd be long gone if she didn't make up her mind, and quickly.

His grim tone sent an apprehensive shiver down Dawn's spine. Without demur, she started walking toward her room. Bryce was one step behind her. Was she out of her mind? she demanded of herself, nervously digging through her purse for her room key. Other than the recommendation from a casual friend, she didn't know a thing about Bryce Stone. For all she knew, he could possess the base instincts of an animal and might pounce on her the minute they were alone! Her fingers trembled as she inserted the key into the lock on the door. The room was even darker than her thoughts.

More nervous than she could ever remember feeling, Dawn groped for the wall light-switch, gasping sharply when her hand made contact with warm, hard fingers. Deep male laughter flooded the room along with the light from the table lamp.

''You're as jumpy as a native at a ceremonial rain dance,'' Bryce observed as he sauntered into the room. He gazed at her dispassionately when she hung back, hovering just inside the door.

Eyeing him warily, Dawn stepped into the room. ''If you don't mind, I'll leave the door open.'' Trying to appear cool and composed, she tossed her handbag onto the bed.

Bryce exhaled impatiently and dropped into the only chair in the room. One dark eyebrow slowly inched up. "Do you realize how silly this is?" he asked, glancing indifferently from her to the door.

If there was one thing Dawn hated more than being called beautiful, sweetheart or honey, it was being accused of acting silly. "I beg your pardon?" She tilted her chin defiantly.

"You should," Bryce drawled. "Your attitude casts doubt on my honor." He waved a hand negligently at the open doorway. "Correct me if I'm wrong," he said wearily. "But didn't you request this meeting to convince me to guide you into the canyon?"

"Yes, but—"

"But, hell!" Bryce retorted. "Didn't it occur to you that if you succeeded in persuading me to take you, we'd be alone down there?"

"Of course it occurred to me!" Dawn exclaimed indignantly. "But . . ." Her voice trailed away as she glanced at the bed.

Bryce grimaced as his gaze followed hers. "Oh, for God's sake," he muttered, shaking his head. "I certainly wouldn't want to shatter any illusions, honey, but I feel I must tell you that a bed is not a prerequisite for seduction." His hand moved to indicate the room and the phone resting on a table by the bed. "Believe me, you are one helluva lot safer here, surrounded by four walls and with a telephone close at hand, than you would be at the bottom of a mile-deep canyon, surrounded by nature and its lure of the senses." His lips flattened into an uncompromising straight line. "Now shut that damn door!"

Though Dawn had never responded well to orders, the sharp crack of his voice impelled her to obey. Her back stiff with resentment, she walked to the door and slammed it shut. The sight of the satisfied smile that flickered on his lips didn't do a thing to improve her disposition.

Planting her hands on her hips, Dawn glared at him. "Okay, the door's closed. Are you ready to listen?"

Bryce grinned. "Have a seat and take your best shot, sweetheart," he invited expansively. He raised his hand to tilt the Stetson to the back of his head, telling her silently that he didn't expect to be there long enough to warrant removing the hat.

Since he was seated in the only chair in the room, Dawn was given the choice of standing or perching on the end of the bed. Gritting her teeth, she strode to the foot of the bed. She began speaking before her bottom made contact with the mattress.

"As I already told you, I need to go into the canyon to do research for the novel I'm working on."

"Why?"

Dawn's fingers curled in to grip the bedspread. "It's important to a section of my story," she said tightly.

Bryce stared at her expressionlessly. "As I pointed out before," he said, glancing at the phone, "all you have to do is call Bright Angel. There are regularly scheduled mule trips into the canyon every day."

Frustration sharpened Dawn's voice. "And, as I pointed out to you before, I don't want to go on a scheduled trip!"

"Why?"

Dawn's legendary cool shot to red-hot. "Simply because they *are* scheduled—with every minute accounted for!"

Unperturbed by her outburst, Bryce stretched his legs and settled more comfortably in the chair. "What's wrong with that?" Coming so swiftly after his lazy action, his hard tone was startling.

Dawn bolted up to pace the floor around his long legs. "You don't understand," she cried, dragging her fingers through her hair. "I'm not on a vacation. I don't want to be distracted by a group of chattering tourists while being led like one of the mules through a routine schedule." Her hand dropped limply to her side as she came to a stop inches from his boots. "I need to experience the solitude and silence of the canyon. I need time to take notes." Her patience snapped. "Dammit! I need to absorb the canyon's unique ambience."

Bryce looked mildly interested. "The Grand does have plenty of ambience," he admitted.

"Then you'll guide me?" Dawn asked eagerly.

"No."

If Dawn hadn't sucked in her breath, she probably would have wasted it screaming at him. Instead, she forced herself to bargain with him. "I'll pay double your usual rate," she said, controlling her quavery voice with sheer willpower.

"Sorry." Bryce shook his head and treated her to one of his wry smiles. "I'm not for sale."

"But your expertise is!" Dawn exploded.

"Maybe so," Bryce conceded. "But not to you."

Dawn stared at him in utter bewilderment. "I don't understand. Why not to me in particular?"

Chapter Four

Staring into Dawn's angry, gold-flecked eyes, Bryce felt a hard knot form in his gut. Though he remained silent, he could have answered her question with four succinct words: *because I want you.*

Damned fool, he cursed himself harshly. You knew what was happening from the moment she walked toward the truck. You felt it happening. You want her too much for your own good, he told himself.

The change in Dawn's tone drew Bryce from his thoughts. A frown scored his brow as he realized that she was pleading with him.

"Will you listen, please?"

Bryce focused his attention on her. "Listen to what, more arguments?"

"No!" Dawn peered at him. "Haven't you heard a word I said?"

He sighed. "'Fraid not, honey. Sorry, I wasn't paying attention."

"Oh." All the fight seemed to go out of her as she backed away and slowly sat down on the edge of the bed. "I see."

Dawn's look of defeat was Bryce's undoing. Positive he was making a mistake, yet somehow compelled to see the light of battle flash in her eyes again, he said mockingly, "Did I miss anything important?"

Dawn's head snapped up and her fascinating eyes glittered. "I asked you if I could tell you a bit about my book."

Bryce was hard put to hide his amazement. Damned if the woman hadn't actually snarled at him! He frowned, merely to keep from laughing. Yeah, he thought, savoring an inner warmth of satisfaction. That's the way Dawn should always look—challenging and fiery and prepared to take on the world should the need arise. Bryce didn't question why he felt so strongly on the issue of Dawn Kingsley's personality, he simply accepted the fact that he did. And, though he didn't particularly want to listen to a verbal synopsis of her book, he accepted the fact that he would, simply to enjoy the sight of her a little longer.

"Okay," Bryce finally answered, swallowing a sigh. "It probably won't change a thing, but you may tell about your story."

Dawn stared at him in wide-eyed surprise for some moments—during which Bryce was forced to fight an urge to spring from his chair and take her in his arms—then she began speaking very quickly, as if afraid he'd get bored and allow his thoughts to wander again.

Watching her, wanting her, Bryce listened attentively to her soft voice weaving a story about two Arizona families and the love that bound them together and the hate that was tearing them apart. Despite his initial reservations, Bryce found himself caught by both the allure of Dawn's voice and the twists and turns in the intricate plot of her story.

Since a pivotal section of the book concerned the frantic search for a young woman lost in the Grand Canyon, Bryce could understand Dawn's need to re-search and experience the location firsthand. Bryce could appreciate it but, as he'd warned her, his un-derstanding didn't change a thing. He still considered her a member of the quasi-sophisticated, overin-dulged, bored—and boring—*useless* generation. As far as Bryce could see, the only elements that set Dawn apart from the rest of her small cadre of contempor-aries were her ability to tell a truly captivating story and the astonishing fact that *he* was interested in her to an intense degree of physical pain.

It was the realization that he was actually aching for Dawn that kept Bryce from weakening to the point of agreeing to guide her into the canyon. Accustomed to, and comfortable with, a much more traditional type of female, Bryce was determined to deny himself the pleasure of Dawn's company for any extended length of time. He'd had experience with women from her stratum of society. Hell, while in the youthful throes of lust disguised as love, he had even married one, to his everlasting regret. In his opinion, these young li-onesses devoured a man, then left him wounded and bleeding to go on to other unsuspecting prey. It really was hellish, Bryce mused, intently observing her gorgeous mouth as she described the conclusion of her tale, but Dawn Kingsley was definitely not his style.

"Well, what do you think?"

Bryce felt a tug of compassion for the uncertain tremor hidden in Dawn's controlled tone of bravado. "I liked it," he replied with blunt honesty. "It has all the ingredients of a bestseller—suspense, adventure, romance."

Dawn nodded her head slightly. "Thank you."

Her solemn response weakened his resolve. Bryce silently applauded Dawn's attempt to appear unaffected by his opinion. But he'd caught the flicker of gratitude in her fabulous eyes and the uneven movement of her throat when she swallowed. He'd been moved by her vulnerability. Dawn's work was obviously very important to her; he could relate to that.

Bryce was tempted, sorely tempted, to do all manner of stupid and delightful things, starting with agreeing to guide her into the canyon, and ending with...

Stunned into silence by the thrill she'd felt on hearing Bryce's approval, Dawn stared at him, unaware of the mute appeal in her eyes as she waited for his decision. Expecting rejection, she jumped up gleefully when he relented.

"All right, I'll take you into the canyon." Exhaling harshly, Bryce heaved himself from the chair, hands extended to halt her sudden impulsive rush toward him.

"Oh, Bryce, thank you! You..." Dawn lost her voice, or more accurately, the shock of sensation that flashed through her when his hands grasped her arms made speech impossible. "You won't be sorry," she finished in a bemused murmur.

Bryce frowned as his gaze dropped to his hands. "I'm sorry already," he muttered, glancing up to meet her eyes. "So I'm warning you now...don't make me any sorrier." His features settled into grim lines of determination. "I want your word that you will do exactly as I say, the instant I say it, without argument or complaint."

Repressing a shudder caused by the steely sound of his voice, Dawn replied immediately. "You have it." Somehow she managed to endure the drilling stare he leveled at her. She sighed in relief when he nodded sharply before releasing her.

"Okay." Turning abruptly, Bryce strode to the door. "You hang loose here, close to the phone," he ordered, tugging on the Stetson's brim to settle the hat into place low on his forehead. "I'll get in touch with you after I've made the necessary arrangements."

Annoyed by his directive and its clipped tone, she raised her chin and started toward him. "Wait a minute!" Dawn's voice had an imperious ring. "I don't see why—" Her protest was cut short when he turned to stare at her with hard, narrowed eyes.

"Is that what your word's worth?" he demanded too softly. "About ten seconds of lip service?"

Dawn suddenly felt small and not too bright. Aware of a flush warming her cheeks, she lowered her eyes and shook her head. The fingers that caught her chin to raise it were hard but careful not to bruise. The dark eyes that captured hers glittered with angry impatience. Imprudently, Dawn reacted as she always did when she felt threatened; she glared at him defiantly. Everything about Bryce was cold—his voice, his eyes, the dismissive glance he ran over her body.

"I should have followed my gut feeling and walked away from you at the beginning. You're too used to having things go your way, lady. You're an imperious, demanding, arrogant woman," he went on relentlessly, ignoring her outraged gasp. "Your act may work with the Bruce Claytons of this world, but I'm having none of it." Grasping the doorknob, he twisted it with controlled violence and pulled the door open. "I'll say this just once more," he said impatiently. "If you want to go with me, you will follow orders. Now make up your mind."

Dawn flinched at the tone of his voice. She was trembling with fury—fury and another emotion she couldn't quite define, but it felt too much like respect to be tolerated. Never had any man dared to speak to her the way Bryce Stone had, not even her father, a man Dawn had always believed to be tough and unyielding. Feeling insulted as well as humiliated, she was on the verge of telling him to go to hell when he barked another command at her, restoring her perspective and common sense.

"Now, Dawn!"

Pushed to the wire, Dawn realized she had no real choice. Her work was too important to toss aside merely to salve her injured feelings. Hating the taste it left in her mouth, Dawn lowered her eyes and ate humble pie.

"All right," she mumbled.

"All right, what?" Bryce snapped. "And look at me when you talk to me!"

Dawn's head jerked up. "All right, you're the boss," she said succinctly, staring directly into his eyes.

"Believe it." Leaving her with that hard-bitten advice, Bryce stepped outside and slammed the door shut.

Dawn did not enjoy a restful night of refreshing slumber. Her active imagination was too busy devising intricate plots of revenge to be meted out against Bryce Stone to allow any deep sleep to claim her mind. Fitfully tossing and turning, she contemplated various legal and illegal acts to perform upon his person. Outright murder was out, of course, she decided regretfully, flopping onto her back. So was seduction...since the mere idea of sharing intimacy with Bryce held far too much appeal.

It was too easy to imagine her body melting against the strength of his; too alluring to envision the heat of his mouth playing with hers; too enticing to even toy with the thought of his broad hands stroking her soft, willing flesh.

Frowning at the anticipatory shiver skipping dangerously along her spine, Dawn advised herself to stay on the track of revenge and off the seduction trail. It would be in her best interests to let her imagination savor thoughts of immersing Bryce in a caldron of boiling oil, she mused muzzily, or even tossing him into the roiling Colorado River, than to indulge in dreams of sensuous retribution.

The birds were twittering a welcome to the approaching new day when Dawn, sadly relinquishing her wildly improbable schemes of revenge, surrendered her consciousness to sleep.

Some miles from the motel, in the spacious bedroom of an adobe house plastered a smooth, stark white, sleep was an illusive hope for Bryce Stone.

Stripped down to briefs, Bryce paced the sparsely furnished room, alternately cursing himself for ignoring his gut instincts, and railing against Dawn for presenting a challenge he couldn't ignore.

"You're losing it, Stone," he muttered, moving away from one window and circling the king-size bed to get to another window on the other side of the room. His lips curled into a grimace as he stared sightlessly into the night. "You're so far gone you're even beginning to talk to yourself." Snorting with disgust, he spun to retrace his steps around the foot of the bed.

Bryce disliked making mistakes and, to his way of thinking, the mistake he'd made in weakening to Dawn's plea had been a beauty. She was trouble walking on two fantastically long legs, the kind of trouble Bryce didn't want or need. And there was no way he could see himself spending time alone with her in the canyon without giving in to the desire that was heating his blood and body.

Merely thinking about Dawn's legs set his heart thumping with an erratic beat and sent his imagination on a flight of erotic fancy. Every muscle in Bryce's body clenched as he envisioned her long legs curling around his passion-taut hips.

"Damn!" Expelling the curse on a harsh breath, Bryce turned sharply and flung himself onto the bed.

Lying rigid, his hands clenched into fists at his sides, Bryce drew deep breaths and forced his mind away from temptation by minutely reviewing the arrangements he needed to make for the trip into the canyon. Not once did Bryce so much as consider canceling the trip; he had told Dawn he'd take her and, come hell or high water, he would not renege.

Dawn's namesake was hovering on the horizon when Bryce drifted into an uneasy sleep.

Dawn slept until late in the morning, and wouldn't have wakened then if someone hadn't slammed the door of the room next to hers. Feeling listless and mentally hung over from her restless night, she called room service to order coffee and juice, then dragged herself from the bed to the shower. By the time room service delivered her order, Dawn was alert, dressed and ready to face the day...and possibly even the phone call from Bryce Stone.

Chapter Five

*H*e's *changed his mind.*

Dawn froze in midpace as the thought occurred to her. She whirled around to glare at the phone, willing it to ring; it didn't.

Hanging by the thumbs over a snake pit!

The image of Bryce suspended above a hole crawling with hissing serpents brought a cold little smile to Dawn's normally soft lips. Her narrowed gaze fastened on the innocent beige phone and she resumed her pacing of the claustrophobic confines of the motel room.

Dawn had regressed to devising methods of torture for Bryce sometime around midafternoon. It was now past the dinner hour, and since the only things she'd put into her stomach were a glass of juice and too much coffee, Dawn was feeling a little light-headed and very mean. During the intervening hours of restlessly pacing, she had rejected the ideas of enough poison to make him sick but not actually knock him off, an oversize dose of castor oil and a sound thrashing with a bullwhip—even though she rather relished the picture they created.

But hanging by the thumbs... The thought splintered when Dawn caught sight of her grim expression in the mirror above the dresser. Coming to an abrupt halt, she stared at herself in wide-eyed amazement, momentarily appalled by the path she'd allowed her unbridled imagination to skip along. Then, trying to envision herself actually performing any one of the atrocious deeds, Dawn laughed out loud.

Laughter released the tension tearing at her nerves. Tilting her head, Dawn grinned at her reflection.

"Loosen up, you nit," she advised herself wryly. "If you had half a brain in your head you'd tell Mr. Bryce Stone to take a flying leap off the canyon rim, then call Bright Angel Lodge and make reservations for the next available mule trip going into the canyon!

The hazel eyes staring back at her from the mirror grew thoughtful as she mulled over what she'd just said. Though she'd left her home in New Jersey with high hopes of securing the services of a private guide to take her into the canyon, Dawn knew she could do her research while in the company of other tourists. So why was she driving herself to distraction—not to mention ridiculously imagined plots of revenge—over one bossy, abrasive, insultingly arrogant trail guide? she asked herself indignantly.

Raising her chin, Dawn nodded sharply to her image and turned away from the mirror. Purposeful strides brought her to the phone. She grabbed the telephone directory. Her finger was on the reservations number for Bright Angel and she was reaching for the phone when it rang, startling her so badly that she jolted up, sending the directory flipping to the floor with a muted thunk. Biting back an unladylike curse, Dawn snatched the receiver from its cradle.

"Yes?"

There was a pause for an instant, as if the caller had been startled by her sharp tone, then Bryce said impatiently, "What's your problem, lady?"

"I'm hungry," Dawn retorted, "among other things."

"Haven't you had dinner?"

Dawn gritted her teeth at the baffled sound of his voice. "No, I haven't had dinner," she replied evenly.

"Why not?"

"Because I was ordered to remain by the phone!"

"Oh, for God's sake," Bryce muttered. "Have you ever heard of room service?"

"Have you ever been told to go to—"

"Careful, sweetheart," Bryce cut in on a note of warning. "I don't take kindly to being cursed."

"And I don't take kindly to being confined to my room for an entire day," Dawn retaliated.

"So leave it."

Completely forgetting that she had decided to tell him to jump, Dawn grew silent as she examined his lazily drawled advice. Was Bryce trying to tell her something? she wondered. Was he going to back out of their deal? The sound of his voice interrupted her thoughts.

"Dawn?"

"What?"

"Did you hear what I said?"

Dawn sighed and steeled herself for what she feared was coming. "Yes, I heard you. I was trying to figure out what you meant."

"I meant exactly what I said," Bryce replied. "I'm in the bar. Leave the room and join me. They make a good steak sandwich here. I'll order one for you, if you'd like. Then, while you eat, I'll brief you about the arrangements I've made."

"Order the sandwich," Dawn responded eagerly, assuring herself her sudden giddy feeling was caused by hunger and not relief. "I'll be there in five minutes." Without waiting for a reply she cradled the receiver and dashed for the bathroom and her makeup case.

Six and a half minutes later Dawn slid onto the booth seat opposite Bryce, who glanced at his watch and grinned.

"Amazing. I had resigned myself to at least a twenty-minute wait."

Since Dawn had allowed herself the barest application of makeup before dashing from her room to the bar, she covered her breathlessness with a slow shrug. "I detest being late," she informed him between casually drawn deep breaths. "Besides, I told you I was hungry."

"I swear I ordered the sandwich." Bryce held his hands up defensively.

"I hope you ordered a drink for me as well." She sighed. "I haven't had anything since before noon and I'm parched."

Bryce looked pained but refrained from reminding her of room service. "I did. White wine on the rocks, right?"

"Umm." Dawn nodded, and mentally kicked herself for feeling ridiculously pleased that he'd remembered.

The steak sandwich proved to be every bit as good as Bryce had claimed. While savoring each bite of the tender beef liberally stuffed into a crunchy roll, Dawn listened attentively as Bryce gave her a brief outline of the arrangements he'd made.

"Since I forgot to ask you how much time you needed to do your research, I ordered enough supplies for a four-day trip," he told her. "Will that be sufficient?"

Dawn stopped chewing on the last bit of her sandwich to stare at him in shock. Four days! A thrill shot down her spine. At best she had hoped for two days. Sufficient? Four was terrific! Remembering to chew, she finished, swallowed, and offered him a controlled smile.

"Yes, I'm sure that will be fine."

In a state of excited anticipation, Dawn barely heard the rest of Bryce's outline until a sudden sharp question caught her attention.

"I hope to hell you brought sturdy boots and riding clothes with you?"

"I did my preliminary research, Mr. Stone," she said, giving him a hard stare. "And even if I hadn't, I'd have known what kind of clothes to pack. I've been trail riding before."

Bryce looked skeptical. "Yeah? Where?"

"In the mountains of Pennsylvania and New York."

"They are hardly the Grand Canyon." He dismissed the eastern mountains with a wave of his hand.

"Granted," Dawn conceded. "But sturdy clothes and boots are still required."

Bryce knew when to give in and how to do it with humor. "Your point, and if I'm keeping score correctly, you're one up on me." An attractive smile curved his lips.

Dawn returned the smile. "Are we in some sort of match?"

Bryce laughed. "Are you serious? Honey, we've been scoring points off each other since we met." His eyes gleamed with amusement. "Hell, can't you smell the sulfur from the sparks we strike off one another?"

Recalling the plans for revenge against him that had occupied her mind, Dawn was tempted to tell him that while she didn't smell the sulfur, she did detect the faint sound of hissing snakes. Deciding to be prudent, she nodded instead.

"You definitely have a talent for riling me, sweetheart," he said, grinning at her.

"Really?" Dawn arched her eyebrows. "You merely infuriate me."

Bryce's grin vanished and his eyes darkened. "You do realize that we'll both be damned lucky if we come out of that canyon unscathed?" he asked softly.

Dawn's throat went dry and her pulse went crazy. "Wh..." She paused to slide her tongue over her suddenly dry lips and swallowed convulsively when his gaze fastened on her mouth. "What do you mean?" she asked in a hoarse whisper.

"I think you know very well what I mean." Bryce raised his gaze to her eyes. "I can see it in your eyes. There's an attraction between us that we're going to have to deal with sooner or later, and you know it."

"No." Dawn's denial was little more than a breathy whisper.

"Yes."

Beginning to feel cornered by the inevitable truth of his assertion, she shook her head fiercely. "We hardly know each other. I'm not sure I even like you!"

"I know what you mean." Bryce sighed. "Ain't it a bitch?"

His words struck her like a blow. Unbelievably hurt, Dawn resorted to sarcasm. "Ain't it just?" Somehow, from somewhere, she dredged up a taunting smile. "And I've got a news flash for you, Stone. It's gonna get a lot worse, because I have no intention of dealing with anything except my research, sparks or not." While commanding his gaze with a direct stare, Dawn slipped her trembling hands into her lap, out of his sight.

Bryce was quiet for several seconds, his intent gaze probing her eyes so deeply that Dawn imagined she felt her soul cringe. Then he smiled, slowly, sensuously. "This trip's sounding more and more interesting," he observed in a dry tone of voice. "Tell me, Dawn, how do you intend carrying out your *intentions*?"

A dash of poison.

A dose of castor oil.

A bullwhip.

A snake pit.

Dawn rejected as too revealing the immediate replies that came to mind. Her instincts warning her to remain cool and remote, she twined her fingers tightly together and gave him a superior smile. "I could decide to tell you to take a hike, and go into the canyon with a tour from Bright Angel."

Bryce shrugged. "That's right, you could."

"But I won't, simply to prove a point," she continued as if he hadn't spoken. "Instead, we'll go as planned, and I'll smother your imaginary sparks by ignoring you . . . as much as possible."

"Not imaginary, and you know it." Bryce shook his head slowly. "And ignoring me will be impossible— you know that, too."

A shiver of anticipation told Dawn that he was right; a sinking, drowning sensation had her praying that he was wrong. He had to be wrong! The silent cry sent an icy feeling of near panic to her chest and throat, contracting muscles, cutting off air.

Suddenly Dawn had to move, had to be outside, had to *breathe*! Lifting her chin and tossing back her hair, she slid along the seat and stood. Looking down at Bryce gave her a sense of control that lasted long enough for her to deliver a stinging exit line. "I find this conversation both offensive and boring. So, if you'll excuse me?" Without waiting for a response, she turned and walked away from him.

"Dawn, wait!"

She was halfway through the lobby when she heard him call her name in a tone of quiet command. Putting her assertion into practice, Dawn ignored him and quickened her step. She began to run the instant the lobby door shut behind her. Bryce caught up to her as she was trying to insert the room key into the lock on the door.

"Dammit, Dawn! Will you listen?" Clasping her arm, Bryce turned her to face him.

"No!" Dawn cried, slipping her hands behind her back to continue fumbling with the key. "I won't listen to more threats of—"

"Threats of what?" Bryce cut her off impatiently. "Force?" He gave a short but genuine burst of laughter. "I never use force, and even if I had ever considered it, force certainly won't be necessary in this situation. Proximity will do the trick."

"No!" Dawn shook her head sharply to enforce the denial, and felt a flood of relief on hearing the soft but unmistakable sound of the key turning the lock.

"Yes, Dawn."

There was the sound of an emotion in his voice that confused her, instilling in her an amazing conviction that he was desperately trying to avoid the inexorable by attempting to scare her off. Rejecting the idea as ridiculous, Dawn nudged the door open and took a careful step back.

"Wait." Bryce's fingers flexed convulsively into her soft flesh.

It was as if...as if the contraction of his fingers was in direct opposition to his considerable willpower! Dawn thought with a sense of incredulity. With a flash of insight, the realization hit her that Bryce was a man in conflict with himself. And if Bryce was desperately trying to avoid the inexorable, he was fighting an inner battle similar to the one that raged within her. The knowledge induced a measure of calm in Dawn, calm and something else—acceptance of the inevitable?

Unwilling to explore the depths of her emotions, Dawn shook off the sensation with a shrug of her shoulders.

"Why should I wait? It's getting late and—" Once again her words were interrupted by his.

"It's not too late to change your mind and go into the canyon with a scheduled tour," he reminded her— as if she needed reminding! "Would you prefer to do that?"

Yes! She clamped her lips against the immediate response. Without knowing why, Dawn felt certain that she had to prove herself, her courage, her worth, her integrity as a person to Bryce Stone. Lifting her chin, she met his riveting stare.

"No." The word contained a wealth of conviction.

Loosening the fingers coiled around her arm, Bryce raised his hand to her face and gently brushed his knuckles over her cheek. A sigh—of longing? of regret?—whispered through his lips when she trembled in response to his touch. "I'm afraid that this expedition is going to result in a lot more than research for your book. I only hope that neither one of us emerges from the canyon regretting those results."

Slowly, slowly, Bryce lowered his head to hers. The door was open, Dawn could have escaped to the safety of her room, yet thoughtlessly, mindlessly, her pulses drumming, she raised her parted lips to meet his. The anticipated contact did not happen. Dawn could feel his breath misting her lips, could feel the heat of his mouth and could identify her own hot, hungry need to taste him, when Bryce suddenly jerked his head up and stepped back.

"You do a lousy job of ignoring a man," he muttered raggedly. "I'll be here at seven tomorrow morning. Be ready." With that last parting shot, he turned and strode away.

Fighting tears of anger and frustration, Dawn backed into the room and quietly closed the door.

Bryce was right and she was only fooling herself by believing she could ignore him.

The thought settled in Dawn's mind as she double-checked the clothes she had packed in a soft nylon bag and then prepared for bed.

Her lips burned for the taste of his. Her breasts ached for the touch of his hands. Her body throbbed a demand to be filled by his.

Dawn was shaking from the inner turmoil by the time she crawled into bed. In an attempt to allow herself enough calm to be able to sleep, she lay still and silently reminded herself of long-held beliefs.

At the end of an affair with a man she had believed was a soul mate, but who had eventually proved to be a soul destroyer, Dawn had immersed herself in her work to the point of exhaustion. The purging through work had two lasting effects on Dawn: one was tangible, the other was less concrete. The tangible result was the money she'd earned from her writing marathon. For the first time in her then twenty-two years, Dawn was financially free of her father, a ruthless shark of the business world who raised thoroughbred horses as a hobby. The second effect concerned her future self-preservation. Determining never again to allow herself to be vulnerable to any man, Dawn had deliberately repressed her previously outgoing personality. Meticulously, she'd built a facade of a haughty, sophisticated, aggressive woman. And the facade had kept the sharks at bay and her emotions secure, until Bryce Stone stepped out of his truck and into her life.

Until Bryce Stone.

The thought revolved in Dawn's mind until unconsciousness blanked it out.

Chapter Six

Bryce was not in the best of all possible moods. Two nights of soul-searching restlessness interspersed with brief snatches of sleep had taken their toll on his temper and appearance. In a word, Bryce looked and felt awful.

Why did she have to reveal that flash of courage?

The question had tormented Bryce throughout the long night. As long as he could believe that Dawn was the shallow, self-centered, spoiled type of woman he disdained, he had succeeded in quelling his conscience by rationalizing that she deserved everything she got—even if that "everything" turned out to be more thrills and chills in the canyon than she'd bargained for.

Dawn's proud display of courage had badly undermined Bryce's rationale, leaving him vulnerable to his conscience. In consequence he'd spent the dark hours in conflict. Since the battleground of his conscience was unfamiliar terrain for Bryce, he had begun by engaging his inner antagonist confidently and—as conscience utilized the superior weapon of logic—ended by arguing defensively.

He wanted her.

He was running the risk of hurting her.

She had begged him to take her.

Into the canyon—not literally.

Her kind can always be had—and they always take much more than they give.

Generalization. Categorization. Bad example.

But she needs to be taught a lesson!

By whom—an embittered teacher?

She's nothing more than a spoiled brat!

The brat has courage.

Yes—dammit!

Every time Bryce had drifted into slumber he'd been awakened again by a fresh attack from his better self, urging him to give up his plans for the expedition and leave Dawn exactly as he'd found her.

And conscience might have won the internal war by the time Bryce tumbled from his rumpled bed—if he hadn't touched her, if he hadn't come within a hairbreadth of kissing her, if he hadn't felt the claws of a voracious hunger for her raking at his body. In the end, conscience was silenced by the unprecedented need governing Bryce's actions.

Bryce wanted to be with Dawn to the exclusion of every other consideration.

End of argument.

"Good morning." Dawn's already low spirits nosedived as Bryce grunted in response to her hesitant greeting. The shiver that brought tiny goose bumps to her skin had nothing to do with the crisp early-morning air. Standing at the open door on the passenger side of the truck, she clutched her nylon bag closer to her chest and cleared her throat. "Ah…what should I do with my bag?" Immediately aware of her poor choice of words, Dawn steeled herself for the obvious retort when Bryce slanted a glance at her.

"Put it to bed."

Dawn was beginning to frown when understanding clicked in her mind, translating his reply to "Stow it in the back of the truck." Since he obviously wasn't going to climb out of the cab to do it for her and his tone indicated a decided lack of patience, Dawn hastened to comply before scrambling into the truck beside him. The instant she pulled the door shut, she felt the tension vibrating from his taut body. Buckling up, she sat very still and held her breath as he slammed the stick into gear and tore out of the parking lot and onto the highway.

Since she had seen most of the small town the day she arrived in Tusayan, Dawn shifted around on the bench seat to study Bryce's profile. The grim set of his firmly delineated jaw goaded her edgy temper. Having awakened unrested and irritable, Dawn had lectured herself on the necessity of maintaining a congenial attitude if she hoped to survive her trip into the canyon with Bryce. His grunting, growling rebuff of her tenuous attempt at being reasonably pleasant tested her patience.

Envisioning four long days of being grunted at and growled to, Dawn told herself she could do one of three things. She could play his game of silence interspersed with monosyllables. She could rant and shout, if only to get his attention. Or she could attempt to tease him out of his black mood. Dawn opted for the third choice, simply because she hated the silence and was too tired to rant and shout.

"Are you always this chipper in the morning?" she asked brightly.

Bryce shot a narrow-eyed look at her. "If you wanted 'chipper,' you should have hired a bird."

He looked so harsh, so forbidding, and yet Dawn couldn't contain the laughter that sprang to her lips. Shoulders shaking, she stared at him and thought she detected a slight twitch at the corner of his mouth.

"It doesn't take much to amuse you, does it?" This time when he spared a glance from the nearly empty highway his eyes were open and gleaming.

Dawn smiled and lifted her shoulders in a helpless shrug. "I'm a pushover for dry, rim-shot one-liners and off-the-wall, oddball humor."

"Don't tell me, let me guess." There wasn't a hint of a growl left in his voice. "You fall apart for the Henry Youngman type of stand-up comics and convulse at Mel Brooks and Monty Python movies."

"Guilty." Dawn's breath caught when he glanced around to smile at her.

"And me."

Dawn laughed and stared at him in surprise. "You enjoy Mel Brooks and Monty Python movies?"

Bryce nodded. "And dry, rim-shot one-liners from stand-up comics." He offered Dawn another smile with the admission.

A warm feeling trickled through her at the realization that they had more in common than a mutually strong physical attraction. It was a small thing, perhaps, and probably of no long-term importance, but Dawn savored the warmth just the same.

The truck ate up the miles as they tentatively discussed bits of comedy routines and pieces of movies they had either appreciated or detested. The tension inside the truck's cab had all but disappeared by the time Bryce brought the vehicle to a stop at the toll booth at the south entrance to the Grand Canyon National Park. A contemplative frown drew Dawn's eyebrows together as, lowering the window, Bryce stuck his arm out and flipped open a small leather identification folder.

"Mornin', Bryce." Barely glancing at the folder, the guard grinned and waved them through.

As Bryce pocketed the folder, then put the truck into motion, Dawn suddenly recalled their first conversation and Bryce telling her that guiding was not his real work. Her frown was replaced by surprise.

"You're a park ranger!"

Bryce slanted an amused look at her. "No."

"But you do work here?" Dawn waved her hand to indicate the park.

"I work for the National Park Service." He glanced around at the tranquil, forested grounds. "I was assigned to this park because I was born in this part of the state. I grew up exploring the terrain."

"But what do you work at?" Dawn asked impatiently.

"Fossils."

"I beg your pardon?"

Bryce laughed. "I'm a paleontologist, Dawn," he explained. "I look for, study and classify fossils."

"Oh." Of course Dawn knew what a paleontologist was. It was just that Bryce Stone didn't fit the image that attached itself to the title. In truth, he looked exactly like her idea of a saddle-tough, rugged trail guide.

"Finally found a way to shut you up, did I?"

Dawn was immediately suspicious. "Are you putting me on?"

His smile was sensuously suggestive. "Come up to my lab sometime and I'll show you my...fossils."

He'd done it again. Laughing, she started to toss an earlier remark of his back at him. "You should—"

"Live so long," Bryce finished for her. "Are you telling me I probably won't?"

Her smile was slow and teasing. "You're a fast study, Stone."

"Yeah, I know," he said sourly. "But mostly with dead issues...like fossils."

Startled by his lightning-quick change back to moodiness and confused by his cryptic statement, Dawn fell silent. Tension returned, dispersing the companionable warmth. Dawn greeted her first sight of scattered buildings with a sigh of relief.

"What are all these buildings we're passing?" she asked, too curious to remain silent.

Bryce's voice assumed the impersonal drone of a tour guide. "The one we passed at the first right turn was the National Park Service's operation office. The one we passed at the second turn was the Fred Harvey General Offices. We are now approaching—"

"Fred Harvey," Dawn interrupted in a musing voice. "Wasn't there a Fred Harvey who built hotels along the Santa Fe railroad route?"

"Very good." Bryce commended her. "And, if you'll look to your right as I make a left, you'll see the one-hundred-room hotel the Harvey Company built here in 1905, named El Tovar in honor of the Spanish explorer, Pedro de Tovar, who led the first expedition into Hopi Indian country in 1540."

"You're a fount of information," Dawn said in a dry tone, craning her head to get a better look at the imposing, turn-of-the-century style building. "I'd like a closer look at it."

"Don't strain your neck," Bryce advised her. "You can look your fill when we get back from the trip. I reserved a room for you."

Dawn jerked around to face him. "You did! That's wonderful! But why?"

Bryce shrugged. "In case you wanted to include the area in your research."

Dawn did, and since she hadn't mentioned it to him previously, she was touched and warmed again by his thoughtfulness. "Thank you," she said, offering him a soft smile. "I did want to poke around a bit but I never thought about booking a room."

"You should have," Bryce chided her gently. "There's a lot to see here along the south rim." He returned her smile. "And you're welcome."

Suddenly feeling very young and very unsophisticated, Dawn glanced away just in time to catch a corner of another building. "What's that?" she asked, craning again.

"Bright Angel Lodge," Bryce answered. "And we've almost reached our destination."

Dawn whipped around. "And that is?"

"The corral where we'll collect our animals and gear."

He parked the truck in a parking lot and they walked to the corral—Bryce toting Dawn's bag. Excitement curled along her nerves and fluttered in her stomach as they approached the animal enclosure. A black-haired, dark-skinned man leaning against the rail fence watched their progress. When they got to within a few yards of the man, a flashing white smile altered his etched features.

"Yo, Bryce." The man clasped the hand Bryce extended.

"How's it goin', Sam?" Bryce grasped his hand firmly before reaching back to draw Dawn to his side. "Dawn, this is Sam Surefoot Davis. He works for me now and again." He grinned at Sam. "Sam, say yo to the paying customer, Dawn Kingsley."

"Hello, Sam." Not quite certain what to do, Dawn offered her hand and a smile.

Sam accepted and returned both. "Yo, Dawn." His teeth flashed, his hand was gentle.

"You're Indian, of course."

"With a name like Surefoot, what else?" Sam grinned. "Havasupai nation."

"He thinks he's Tonto," Bryce inserted wryly.

Sam looked pained. "I don't believe Tonto was Havasupai."

"Don't let it keep you up nights."

"A girl . . . maybe. Tonto . . . forget it."

Beginning to feel as if she'd been caught in a cross fire or in the middle of a stand-up routine, Dawn shifted her bemused gaze from one man to the other. Bryce brought the banter to a conclusion as he started toward a waiting string of mules.

"Okay, Cochise, let's head 'em up and move 'em out."

Sam looked even more pained at the trite Hollywood Western phrase. "Cochise wasn't Havasupai, either," he groused, following the grinning Bryce. "He was Apache and you know it."

Bryce shrugged. "Sure, but I do enjoy ruffling the feathers of your headdress." Abruptly he became all business. "Let's do a check here."

Telling herself that she should be getting used to Bryce's sudden mood shifts, Dawn trailed after the men to the pack animals. Pondering the complexities of the man she had hastily dismissed as an arrogant, insolent plebeian, she studied the enigma known as Bryce Stone as he methodically moved from one mule to the next, and heard not a word of the murmured conversation between him and Sam.

The enigma was dangerous to her. Dawn had at last recognized and identified the threat he posed to her assiduously maintained facade. The threat to her position of emotional security was not the physical attraction they had immediately felt for one another. Dawn knew she was capable of controlling her physical response, regardless of the power of the allure. The danger was in the emerging facets of character of the man himself.

The normal sounds of everyday activity swirled around Dawn. Employees went about their business; tourists in groups large and small, some attired casually for a stroll along the canyon rim, others in hiking clothes and carrying containers of water, strode briskly toward the various walking trails. Laughter and murmured conversations and the raised voices of friends calling to one another blended into the background music from the trees soughing and rustling a response to the caress of the crisp fall breeze.

For the first time ever while on a new research site, Dawn was out of tune with her surroundings. She did not see. She did not hear. She did not absorb. Every nerve, every cell, every working particle of Dawn's mind was centered on the character of an enigma. Her inner computer assimilated the information that had been fed into it over the previous few days, then pulsed out conclusions on the subject in rapid succession.

Intelligent.

Confident to the point of arrogance.

Thoughtful.

Humorous.

Reserved.

Truthful.

Honest.

Dawn began to quiver as the conclusions pulsed through her, defining the threat the enigma Bryce Stone presented to her. Dawn was confident of her ability to control the lure of sensuality. She was equally certain that she could not withstand the allure of truth and honesty.

Alerted by her own thoughts, Dawn blinked and focused her eyes on Bryce. Every instinct for self-preservation she possessed urged her to escape while there was still time. She took one step back, then froze as Bryce raised his head to capture her with his level gaze.

"Ready to experience the Grand?"

Time had run out. Dawn was caught in the dilemma of her own making. Squaring her shoulders, she smiled and walked to his side.

"Yes."

There were four mules in the string, two bearing carefully packed equipment, and two saddled for riders. Bryce helped her to mount the second animal before swinging into the saddle of the lead mule. Sam smacked his palm against the mule's rump to get it started, then raised his hand in farewell.

"Have a good trip. I'll be here when you get back."

"Right, Sam." Bryce waved, then settled deeply into the saddle. "See you."

Excitement and anticipation merged with the feelings of trepidation inside Dawn, pumping adrenaline into her system. Her eyes grew wide with awe as the plodding animals drew near to the rim, giving her her first glimpse of the canyon.

The eight-mile-wide canyon was spread out before her eyes in all its morning mauve and brown, purple and sand-colored splendor. A writer, with a command of superlatives, Dawn was nevertheless reduced to one descriptive word: "Magnificent!"

"It ain't half bad," Bryce responded wryly in understatement, then, as if to prepare her, announced, "Here we go."

The animals started down the canyon trail and Dawn knew another dimension had been added to her dilemma: the canyon was not only magnificent; it was a mile deep.

Sitting astride a mule moving along a switch-back path that wound its way down the wall of the Grand Canyon, Dawn belatedly developed a chest-constricting, throat-closing fear of height.

Chapter Seven

At home in the saddle, Bryce shifted around to glance at Dawn and felt alarm spear through him. Her body was rigid. Her eyes were wide. Her face was pasty white. Her expression revealed stark terror.

"Damn—" Bryce bit off the expletive. Why in hell hadn't she told him she suffered from acrophobia? An equal measure of concern and impatience could be heard in his raised voice.

"Dawn, are you all right?" Bryce was calling himself all kinds of stupid names even as the question passed his tight lips. It would have been obvious to any fool that she was anything *but* all right; Dawn was literally frozen to the saddle with fear!

"I...I'm...fine." Dawn's lips barely moved as she replied in a reedy, hesitant voice.

Bryce swiveled in the worn leather, his narrowed gaze sweeping the path bordered on the inside by a sheer cliff and on the outside by a sloping drop to the path below. The path was not very wide but he knew that if he had to, he could turn the animals and lead her back to the rim and safety. He glanced over his shoulder to call out to her once more.

"Do you want to go back?"

"No!" Though Dawn's mesmerized, wide-eyed daze remained riveted on the base of the yawning canyon, the refusal burst from her lips with strength and determination.

An emotional mixture comprised of sympathy, compassion and admiration welled up in Bryce's chest. Dawn was petrified, and yet she obstinately refused to quit. She would not be defeated by fear.

Damned if she doesn't remind me of myself! Bryce mused, breathing deeply to clear the emotion constricting his throat before calling to her again.

"Look at me, Dawn." When her fascinated gaze remained fixed, Bryce raised his voice to bark a harsh command. "Dammit, Dawn! I said, look at me!" Bryce felt his admiration for her expand when, straightening her spine, Dawn tore her eyes from the canyon to glare at him resentfully. She was trembling, and yet she tilted her chin proudly.

"Don't swear at me, Stone."

Damn! The woman did have courage.

Dawn saw a wisp of a smile curve Bryce's lips. Interpreting it as a reflection of his smug satisfaction, she clenched her teeth and silently vowed that, if only to thwart him, she'd die before she gave in to the irrational fear gripping her.

"I want you to follow my instructions," Bryce called calmly.

Follow his instructions! She'd see him in he— Dawn's furious thought was curtailed, and she instantly felt ashamed of herself for misjudging him, as he continued in the same even tone.

"Fasten your gaze to the center of my back. Don't look down, don't glance out and don't worry about the path in front of you. The mule knows the way." The faint smile whispered over his lips again, only this time Dawn recognized the smile as one of encouragement and—could it be possible?—pride in her. Bryce inadvertently answered the question in her mind when he added, "You're doing fine. You've got guts. You'll make it. Remember, keep your eyes trained on the center of my back as if you were attempting to stare a hole in it."

Contrite, Dawn lowered her gaze to his broad back as he returned his attention to the path. After several minutes of staring at his gently rocking torso, she felt a subtle lessening of the tension in her body. The panic constricting her chest and throat eased slightly, allowing her to breathe at a near-normal rate. Dawn was still frightened, but she was no longer gripped by immobilizing terror.

Unfrozen except for the stare that clung tenaciously to Bryce's back, Dawn closed out the surrounding terrain by focusing her concentration inward to examine her extraordinary reaction to the awesome grandeur of the canyon.

Dawn had never before felt a fear of heights but, she acknowledged wryly, she had never crested the rim of a mile-deep canyon before, either. Odd, the things people could discover about themselves quite by accident. Inside the leather riding gloves she was wearing, her palms were clammy with a sweat that had been induced by fear, as were her forehead, the back of her neck and, of all places, her ankles. In direct contrast to the moisture on the surface of her body, her throat, nostrils and eyes felt hot and dry. Her mind felt numbed by shock and she was cold and trembling.

Dawn hated every symptom indicating acute acrophobia, but there wasn't a blessed thing she could do about it except grit her teeth, persevere and keep her gaze glued to the reassuring width of her guide's back.

It was a long, harrowing journey down the inside wall of the canyon. Dawn's pulse fluttered with every step the mule took, and leaped alarmingly each time the animal's hoof kicked a stone and sent it skittering over the edge of the path. But at last it was over; they had arrived at the rest house located near the Colorado River.

Slumping in the saddle, Dawn closed her eyes and gulped deep breaths of air. She didn't witness Bryce's agile leap from the back of his mule, but suddenly he was there, his hands gentle as he lifted her from the saddle and into the safe haven of an embrace.

Shaking violently, Dawn clasped her arms around his waist and clung to the solid strength of his body as tenaciously as her gaze had clung to his back.

"I'm sorry, Bryce, so sorry. I swear to you I didn't know...I...I..." Dawn's voice failed, defeated by the sobs that broke from her throat. Ashamed of herself and the tears racing down her pale cheeks, she buried her face in his shirt.

"Shh, it's all right," Bryce murmured. His arms tightened, crushing her trembling body against his. "I know. I understand." He held her until the harsh sobs had subsided and she was weeping softly, then he brought his hand to her chin to tilt her face up to his. His dark eyes were tender and glowed from within with the light of pride in her accomplishment. "At first I was angry, believing you had known what to expect but had arrogantly decided to brave the canyon in defiance. But then I realized that your surprise and shock were too intense to be other than a first-time experience with acrophobia."

"I...I made a fool of myself," Dawn sniffed. "I'm sorry."

"No." Bryce smiled and shook his head. "You were magnificent."

Stunned by his praise, Dawn stared at him in wonder. On approaching the canyon rim, her writer's imagination had latched onto the word *magnificent* to describe the panoramic, breathtaking beauty of the Grand Canyon. That this particular man had used the exact same adjective to describe her was the highest praise Dawn could ever imagine.

As Bryce slowly lowered his head, Dawn immediately changed her mind. No. The highest praise imaginable would be the sweet bestowal of this man's mouth. Without hesitation, Dawn parted her lips in readiness for his.

His kiss was incredibly sweet, incredibly tender, incredibly... incredible. His lips did not pressure; his tongue did not test. Bryce was making no demand; he was bestowing a reward for a job well-done. It lasted only seconds and yet, within that brief span of enchantment, Dawn felt her personal world shift on its axis, creating havoc with her senses, undermining every one of her preconceptions. Deep inside, in a tiny section hidden away and carefully guarded, Dawn felt a stirring of renewed life. The amazing part was that the awakening didn't frighten her at all.

Dawn was shaking again, more intensely this time than she had been before when reacting to the effects of the terrifying descent down the canyon wall. She was shaking with need—complex and basic. Suddenly Dawn needed to fulfill many needs: emotional needs, psychological needs, physical needs. Bryce misunderstood the cause of her tremors.

"You're exhausted," he said, lifting his head to examine the evidence stamped on her tear-streaked face by the relatively short journey into the canyon and the longer distance she'd traveled inside. "Come into the rest house and sit down while I rethink my plans."

Lowering her revealing gaze from his beautiful, exciting mouth, Dawn allowed him to assist her into the simple, rustic way station. Pondering his last statement, she sat down gratefully and quietly gathered the remnants of her shredded composure.

Bryce didn't sit down. While Dawn rested, he paced the floor. When he came to a stop in front of her, he pulled the Stetson from his head and raked his fingers through his matted dark waves.

"I had made reservations for us to stay the night at Phantom Ranch," he said abruptly, sliding the hat onto his head. "Do you know what that is?"

Her composure regained, Dawn looked at him solemnly and nodded. Intrigued by its name while doing her preliminary research, Dawn had hoped to see the ranch-lodge where accommodations were offered for the tourists taking the two-day trip into the canyon from Bright Angel.

"I think we'll have to give Phantom a skip." Bryce placed his hands on his narrow hips and waited, as if expecting an argument from her. A day before, a few hours before, Dawn would have fulfilled his expectations. Now, what seemed eons later, she was merely curious.

"Why?"

Bryce was startled but recovered quickly. He shrugged. Dawn smiled faintly at the realization of how endearingly familiar that shoulder movement had become to her. He frowned. Her smile grew soft; Bryce looked so forbidding when he frowned. Bryce gave up and smiled back at her. Dawn began to tremble.

"Why are you looking at me like that?" he asked.

"Like what?"

"All trusting and . . . and . . ." Bryce broke off and shrugged.

Dawn smiled again. "Because I do trust you, Bryce. I'd trust you with my life." Her smile teased, just a bit. "As a matter of fact, I believe I just did."

"Dawn." Bryce whispered her name and took a step toward her. Then he stopped with such obvious reluctance, Dawn felt a tingle skip over the surface of her entire body. "Ah..." The hat was yanked off; fingers plowed through dark strands of hair. "You asked why I decided not to stay over at Phantom."

"Yes."

Bryce narrowed his eyes to study her for a moment. "But you don't mind." It was an observation, not a question. Dawn answered anyway.

"No, I don't mind."

His eyebrows drew together in consternation. "It's not important to your research?"

His concern for her work knocked the pins right out from under the last of Dawn's so carefully structured reserve. Her smile was a reflection of the woman hidden behind the facade.

"No, Bryce, it's not necessary to my research. I had wanted to see it, but..." Her shrug was an imitation of his.

His inner struggle was mirrored on his face, revealing to Dawn his desire to allow her to experience whatever she wished of the canyon. The fact that there was a struggle told her he had a solid reason for denying her wish. The reason interested her.

"Why did you decide to rethink your plans?"

Bryce rubbed the back of his neck. "To get to Phantom, we have to cross the Colorado on a high, narrow suspension bridge," he explained. Then he exhaled deeply. "Honey, I don't think you should attempt it."

Considering Dawn's stomach muscles had contracted at the mere mention of the words high and narrow, she readily agreed with him. "Okay," she said, unconsciously echoing his usual laconic response.

Bryce smiled but spread his hands in a cautioning gesture. "There's more. In fact I've revised the entire trip."

Since he hadn't outlined his plans in the first place, Dawn couldn't dredge up a lot of disappointment. She was merely curious.

"Are you going to tell me or surprise me?" Her teasing tone contained not a hint of the haughtiness Dawn had used so effectively the day before.

The strain eased from his expression, leaving one devastatingly attractive man. His stance was loose, his voice confident. "After spending tonight at Phantom, I'd planned to double back to the Tonto Trail, but I don't think you're up to that, either, seeing as how it's a mini-version of the one we just came down," he said, nodding when she winced. "Exactly." Bryce sighed. "Honey, I sure as hell hope you don't have a phobia about water."

Dawn's eyes grew wide as saucers. She had secretly longed for a raft trip down the river, if only a short one, but hadn't dared mention it. "I don't," she answered firmly. "Why?"

"Because if you're game, we'll take a ride down the river and I'll show you one of my secret, special places."

Forgetting her traumatic trip down the canyon wall, and her fear and her exhaustion, Dawn sprang to her feet. "I'm game! I'm ready!" She laughed as he started with surprise. "When do we leave?"

Laughing with her, Bryce grasped her hand to lead her from the rest house. "As soon as we unload the mules and inflate the raft." He glanced up as he stepped outside. "And we'd better get it in gear or we'll lose the light before we make our destination."

Dawn hadn't the vaguest idea where their destination was, nor did she care; if it was special to Bryce, it was special to her. She did have one question, though.

"What about the mules?"

"We'll leave them here," Bryce said, jerking his head in the direction of a small corral off to the side of the rest house. "I've left animals here before. They'll be all right." Giving her hand a tug, he led her to the small animal that had borne her safely down the trail. "Climb aboard."

Dawn stared at him in confusion. "But I thought we were going down the river?"

"We are." Bryce smiled but motioned for her to mount. "But first we must get to the river."

"But I can see it from here!" Dawn protested.

"That's right." Bryce gave her a dry look. "You want to tote this gear down to below the rapids?"

"Oh."

"Yeah."

Grinning, Bryce walked to the lead mule. Her own smile a little sheepish, Dawn remained silent, her fascinated gaze intent on the white water swirling around the boulders in the river.

It was not a lengthy ride. After helping Dawn dismount, Bryce again checked the position of the sun, then immediately began unpacking the animals with an economy of movements.

In the end, Dawn was very little help to him for, as she took the second bundle he handed her, she made the mistake of looking around, then up for the first time since they'd gained the base of the canyon.

With her feet planted firmly on its floor, the breathtaking sight of the Grand Canyon did not fill Dawn with fear; it enthralled her. The midafternoon sunlight had subtly changed the coloration of the plateaus, buttes and mesas within the yawning canyon walls to deep purple, dark brown and, where the sun's rays struck directly on certain layers of strata, bright pinkish red.

Tilting her head back, Dawn looked up, way up to the canyon's rim. "My God!" she exclaimed in a reverent tone of voice.

"Pretty impressive, huh?" Bryce asked softly.

Dawn shook her head. "It's much more than impressive," she murmured, her wide-eyed gaze slowly drinking in the beauty and sheer grandeur of the canyon. "It's . . . it's . . ." Once again Dawn found herself at a loss for words. "It defies description."

"It also gets very, very dark," Bryce said briskly, breaking the spell. "We've got to haul it, sweetheart."

"Oh! Yes, of course." Dragging her gaze from the mind-boggling wonder of nature, Dawn glanced around. Another, softer "Oh!" rounded her lips when she realized how much he had accomplished while she'd been caught under the spell of the canyon.

Not a sound had penetrated her dreamlike state, yet the raft had been inflated, loaded and positioned on the riverbank, inches from the water. A flash of embarrassment brought a blush of pink to Dawn's pale cheeks.

"I was no help to you at all. I'm sorry," she murmured, not at all surprised but still impressed by his efficiency.

Bryce shook his head. "There's nothing to be sorry about," he said, turning to the lead mule. "I get paid for doing the work." He indicated the canyon with a sweeping hand motion. "And you were doing exactly what you came here to do . . . experiencing the canyon." He slipped a booted foot into a stirrup and swung into the saddle. "Now go put on a life preserver, wait by the raft and contemplate experiencing the river. I'll be back as soon as I've taken care of the animals."

Obeying without question, Dawn turned and walked to the raft. Excitement coiled within her as she stared at the swiftly moving water. There was a hollow feeling deep inside. Of course, it was midafternoon and she hadn't eaten a thing since bolting down a breakfast of coffee and toast before six that morning. Smiling wryly, Dawn wondered if the sensation was caused by intense anticipation or plain hunger, but either way, she didn't doubt for an instant that the river ride would prove to be the experience of a lifetime.

Chapter Eight

The ride *was* absolutely exhilarating. Clinging to the handles on the sides of the large raft, Dawn gulped air into her lungs, then laughed aloud as Bryce successfully negotiated the last of the small section of rapids. Her body was soaked. Water trickled from the ends of her hair. She was starving. Dawn had never felt better or enjoyed herself more. A masculine echo of her laughter came from behind her as the raft skimmed along on the river.

"Like that, did you?" he shouted.

Dawn glanced over her shoulder to grin at Bryce. "I loved it!" she exclaimed. "Shooting those rapids was fantastic! Will there be more?" she asked eagerly.

Bryce shook his head. "'Fraid not. We're almost there."

"Where's there?"

Since both his hands were employed with the raft, Bryce indicated a point in the distance with a sharp nod. "See that break up ahead?" Dawn scanned the bank and nodded when she spotted the indentation in the shoreline. "That's a creek that feeds into the river. Our destination is along that creek." A few minutes later he shouted, "Hang on!"

The raft rocked wildly from side to side as Bryce steered it toward the creek, then began to shudder as the mighty Colorado appeared to lift the craft and fling it into the narrow tributary. After the rushing roar of the river, the creek was placid and peaceful in comparison . . . placid, peaceful and deeply shaded.

Suddenly chilled, Dawn gazed up at the high, jagged cliff walls looming above the creek, and then farther up to the narrow opening between the rims of the cliffs to the patch of sky, which was growing dark with the approach of night. Her body was jolted as the boat lurched. She gave a startled cry and twisted around to ask Bryce what was happening. She was just in time to see him leap from the raft.

"Hold on, Dawn," he ordered, dragging the raft halfway out of the water and onto the gently sloping creek bank. His chest heaving from exertion, he extended his hand. "We have arrived," he said between gasping breaths. "Everybody out of the bus."

Grasping his hand, Dawn made her way carefully to the end of the raft, then jumped to the ground beside him. "Is this your secret, special place?" she asked, peering through the fading light at the surroundings.

"Yes," Bryce grunted, panting as he dragged the raft completely out of the water. "Home away from home. What do you think?"

Beginning to shiver from the wet cold, Dawn wrapped her arms around herself for warmth and flashed a bright smile at him. "I think it's terrific," she answered truthfully, returning her delighted gaze to the broad expanse of earth that sloped upward to a wide-mouthed, high-ceilinged shallow cave in the base of the cliff wall. "D-d-do many tourists c-come here?" Dawn clamped her teeth together to keep them from chattering and swung around to look at him.

Head tilted back, Bryce was gazing at the sky. "None at all," he answered absently. Lowering his head, he bent to begin unloading the raft. "I think we'd better set up housekeeping in a hurry. It's going to be dark soon."

Afraid to unclench her teeth for fear that he'd hear them clattering together, Dawn silently moved to help him. Her hand brushed his as she reached for a bundle, and Bryce jolted up as though he'd been shot.

"Dammit, Dawn, you're freezing!" he exclaimed. "Come on, we've got to get you warm." Giving her no time to protest or even respond, he grasped her arm and practically ran her up the bank and into the cave. "Stay in here, out of the night air, until I've built a fire," he ordered, releasing his hold on her.

"With what?" Dawn asked, frowning as she scanned the area. Except for a stone-encircled hole in front of the cave, the sandy earth was smooth and uncluttered all the way to the creek. There wasn't a branch or twig in sight.

"I keep a cache of firewood," Bryce answered from the rear of the cave, some twelve or so feet from the entrance. Turning toward the sound of his voice, Dawn strained to see him in the dim recess. Bryce was crouching as the cave narrowed at the back to little more than three feet in height. Shaking with cold, she hugged herself tightly as she watched him back up until he could stand erect.

"I'll have this going in a minute," he said, kneeling beside the stone-ringed hole. Bryce dumped a handful of twigs into the pit, then pulled a plastic bag containing shredded paper and matches from his sodden denim jacket pocket. Moments later he carefully placed larger pieces of firewood on the flames licking at the paper and twigs. He was issuing orders as he rose to his feet. "Come stand close to the fire and get out of your clothes." He was sprinting away as her head snapped up.

"What?"

"You've had a long, rough day." Bryce called from the raft. "You're tired, wet, cold and hungry." He came striding back to her and dropped her nylon bag on the ground next to her. "And unless you feel up to dealing with hypothermia, get out of those wet things and into something warm and dry." Spinning around, he was off again. "Now, Dawn!"

Realizing that under the circumstances modesty was ludicrous, Dawn pulled at her suede jacket. Something solid tapped against her hip and she frowned. Then, remembering the small camera she'd slipped into a pocket that morning, she sighed and dropped the wet garment to the ground. Dawn had wanted to get pictures of the canyon as they descended into it. She had wanted to take pictures of the river. And she had completely forgotten the camera tucked in her pocket.

A faint smile curved Dawn's lips as her numb fingers fumbled with her shirt buttons. She had been too frozen with fear to think of anything but staying on the mule while coming down into the canyon, never mind handling a camera. And that wild ride on the river hardly lent itself to taking snapshots, either.

With a shrug, Dawn tossed her shirt and bra on top of her jacket and pulled a large sweatshirt over her head. Shivering violently, she plopped onto the ground to tug at the laces of her ankle-high walking boots. His arms laden with their gear, Bryce strode by her as she yanked the second boot from her foot.

"I'll change back here, then get supper going."

Dawn didn't reply; she couldn't. A thickness lodged in her throat. Bryce had done all the work and had taken care of her while doing it. The terse sound of his voice betrayed his weariness. Dawn grimaced as she scrambled to her feet.

Some independent, self-sufficient person you are, she told herself scathingly. You allow him to do all the work, while you play Miss Modesty! Anger at her actions warmed her from the inside out. The snap popped on her jeans and the clinging wet denim was dispatched impatiently. Digging into her bag, she grabbed lacy panties, baggy sweatpants and heavy boot socks and quickly pulled them on.

"What can I do to help?" Dawn raised her voice to reach Bryce at the back of the cave. Her question was met with a short silence. When he finally answered, his voice held an unmistakable note of admiration.

"I didn't bring the water bottles up. You can go get two of them out of the raft."

Motivated by mixed feelings of shame and pleasure, Dawn was moving before he'd finished speaking. Bryce was busying himself by the fire when Dawn returned with two of the four large plastic water containers Sam had packed with their supplies. Bryce glanced away from his work to smile at her.

"How are you feeling?"

Dawn lowered her eyes with unaccustomed shyness. "Fine. Warm. Famished." She raised her gaze when she heard his laughter. He'd changed into worn denims and a soft chamois shirt. He had rolled the shirt sleeves to midforearm and Dawn caught the play of muscle and tendon as he wielded a knife, slicing a canned ham into thick pieces. Salivating, she decided he looked every bit as appetizing as the meat sizzling in the frying pan. The thought brought warm color to her cheeks.

"You can pour water into the coffeepot." Bryce studied the flush on her cheeks before nodding at a blue agate-ware pot set to one side of the fire. "We'll eat in a few minutes."

The meal was simple but utterly satisfying. Ravenous, Dawn cleaned her plate of ham and baked beans, and even sopped up the juice with the crusty roll he handed to her. The aromatic coffee brewed in the old pot was the best she had ever tasted. Replete, she held out her cup for a refill and heaped praise on the cook.

"That was delicious." A teasing smile curved the lips she licked. "I don't suppose you'd consider relocating to the East Coast and hiring out as a houseman, would you?" A tremor of excitement shivered through her as, smiling slowly, Bryce stretched out on the ground next to her and propped his torso up with his forearm.

"Oh, I don't know," he said softly, angling his head to give her a hooded look. "It would depend on the fringe benefits offered." He looked lazily relaxed and sexy as the devil.

Dawn suddenly had trouble breathing. "Ah... hospitalization?" she asked too brightly.

Bryce smiled and shook his head, refusing.

Dawn cleared her throat. "Two weeks' vacation with pay?"

His smile turned wry. "I get a month now."

"A month. Umm, I see. Well, then, ah..." Dawn raked her mind for more ridiculous, deliberately obtuse suggestions. Bryce laughed out loud and rolled to his feet.

"Since your mind is obviously asleep," he taunted, "I think you'd better follow its example." With the same economy of movement he'd exhibited before, he neatly arranged their sleeping bags side by side. As he turned back to her, a teasing but still-sexy smile played over his lips. "Maybe you'll be able to think of a more tempting offer by tomorrow morning."

Dawn would have loved to continue sparring with him, but her tired mind simply wasn't up to it. Yawning, she glanced at the debris from supper. "What about the dishes?" she mumbled, smothering another yawn behind her hand.

"We'll both think about that tomorrow." Holding the sleeping bag open, Bryce gave it a little shake. "Come on, sweetheart, in you go."

Dawn was long past argument. She crawled into the sleeping bag fully dressed, then removed her sweatpants and socks under cover and tossed them in the direction of her nylon bag. Too tired to as much as notice the hard ground beneath the sleeping bag, she snuggled down and closed her eyes. Dawn never heard Bryce whisper a soft good-night.

Dawn was in an unfamiliar place. She was strolling along, a grim smile of satisfaction on her lips. Life was far from perfect, but it had its perks and rewards. Then she felt a presence, a strong presence, warming her, filling her with a deep longing for something. Frowning, she glanced around. The sky was blue, the sun was shining and the earth was friendly. What could be missing? Then she heard laughter—soft, sensuous, alluring—and she knew what was missing from her barren world. Then the laughter began to fade and she cried out in despair for it to wait for her, only for her. She was running, trying to catch the laughter, when the rim suddenly appeared. Dawn couldn't stop. She couldn't stop running! And then the earth fell away and she was plunging down, down into an abyss. As she plummeted toward the void, Dawn opened her mouth and screamed a plea for the laughter to help her.

"Dawn! Honey, wake up!"

"Bryce!" Dawn's eyes flew open as she jolted up. He was there, beside her, drawing her into his strong, protective arms. The dream still more real than reality in her mind, she shuddered and clutched at the laughter and the man, which were one. "I was falling, falling," she cried, gasping for breath. "The ground suddenly fell away.... There was no bottom, no end."

"It was only a dream. Dawn, I have you. You're safe. It was only a dream."

Slowly the urgent sound of Bryce's voice broke through the terror gripping her imagination. Trembling, breathing harshly, Dawn searched for strength and found it in his warm lips.

There was an instant of startled hesitation, then his mouth claimed hers with a power and force that demolished the remnants of the nightmare clouding her mind. Dawn knew nothing; nothing except the burning heat of Bryce's mouth, the flame of his scorching tongue, the fire ignited in her body wherever his hands touched and caressed.

His kiss deepened until Dawn thought she'd go mad with excitement and pleasure. She shivered with anticipation when his hands slid beneath her sweatshirt, then she gasped with delight as his long fingers stroked her arching breasts. Desire coiled through the lower part of her body, throbbing a demand for release and fulfillment.

Obeying the demand without thought or question, Dawn tugged at him, at his clothes, with trembling fingers. Bryce eased the kiss but kept his lips against hers.

"Dawn, are you awake, sweetheart?" His voice was raw with need, his breathing was ragged. "Do you know what you're asking of me?"

"Yes." Dawn's voice was little more than a low moan. "I need you. I need the laughter that's in you." She had managed to yank his shirt halfway up his back. Sighing, she flattened her palms against his heated skin. "Please, Bryce," she whispered, smoothing her palms over a ridge of taut muscles. "Please, give me your laughter and your strength."

Bryce shuddered as he swept away the last of their clothing. In the sketchy light cast by the flickering fire, Dawn's skin glowed like the sheen of fine porcelain. Her hair was a dark, tangled mass spread out on the beige lining of the sleeping bag. Her eyes gleamed with blatant arousal. Her parted, kiss-reddened lips glistened.

Arched over her, Bryce fought an inner battle against a voracious need to plunder and lay claim to this woman who had somehow managed to demolish every one of his misconceptions.

He needed her! Bryce was shaken by the knowledge of never before experiencing so deep a need as he felt for Dawn. And she was his for the taking. Not only was she willing; Dawn had sobbed a plea for him, his strength, his laughter.

The desire in Bryce escalated, stabbing into him like a naked, jagged blade. But still he hesitated, cautioning himself against taking a gift offered in trauma. *Laughter.* The word pierced the red haze of desire clouding his mind. The last thing he wanted to do at that moment was laugh—cry maybe, but not laugh.

Then his entire body went taut with pleasurable shock as, with a murmured plea, Dawn encircled his hips with her long, elegant legs. How many times had he fantasized about lying in the embrace of Dawn's beautiful legs? Bryce couldn't remember, and then it no longer mattered.

Speaking softly of his need for her, he lowered his body to hers. Dawn was warm, ready, hungry for him. Like a starving man offered a banquet, Bryce feasted on her sweet lips and, as he slid his tongue into the honeyed depths of her mouth, he slid his body into the velvet depths of her warmth.

The very last coherent thought Bryce had before giving himself to the glorious wonder of Dawn's responsive body was that hopefully, he'd feel like laughing tomorrow.

Dawn was falling again, but this time, locked body and soul with Bryce, the fall was ten times more exhilarating than the ride down the Colorado. Her blood rushed ten times faster. The roaring in her head was ten times louder. Having Bryce inside her was ten times, ten hundred times, more thrilling than anything she could ever have conceived of in her fertile imagination.

His hands danced over her body, leaving a delicious shiver wherever they touched. His mouth followed the trail blazed by his hands, turning the shiver into a searing flame. The measured movements of his taut body tightened the spiraling coil of tension within her. His murmured words, indistinguishable yet understood, mesmerized her mind.

Never, never had Dawn wanted, as she wanted to be one with this man of truth and honesty and laughter. Her lips sought his with unabashed greed. Her hands stroked his heated skin with unashamed intimacy. Her body arched wantonly to the increasing cadence of his.

Clinging to Bryce, moving in unison with him, Dawn released every inhibition and gave herself wildly to the man and the moment. First she was soaring, higher and yet higher. Then, cresting the absolute end of everything, she was free-falling, clinging, shuddering and gasping his name. Her cry bounced in an eerie echo off the night-shrouded canyon walls.

Moments later, as Bryce followed her over the edge, his victory cry joined with hers in the narrow canyon.

Her body sated, her mind serene, Dawn sighed and stroked his quivering back. She would have been content to spend the rest of the night as one with the man who had given her her first taste of genuine repletion, and sighed a protest when Bryce carefully moved to lie beside her. It seemed perfect that the first sound she should hear from him after the beauty of their experience was the comforting sound of his soft laughter.

"You must rest," Bryce murmured, smoothing a tangled tendril of hair from her cheek.

Dawn snuggled close to his warmth and tasted his tangy skin with her tongue. "I am resting," she whispered. She smiled as his chest muscles rippled with his laughter.

"You won't rest for long if you do much of that," he said in warning.

"But I like tasting you," Dawn protested, skimming his flat nipple as she repeated the performance.

"I like it, too," Bryce admitted in a husky voice. "Too much. But you're exhausted and you must rest." Holding her with one arm, he groped for the edge of the sleeping bag to draw it over both of them. "Sharing this thing will be a tight squeeze."

"I like it," Dawn muttered, already half asleep.

"I like it, too." Bryce brushed his lips over her hair and drew her body closer to his. His warmth and his strength and his humor cradled her body and emotions. "Now, go to sleep."

Sighing with contentment, Dawn obeyed immediately.

Chapter Nine

I'm afraid I owe you an apology."

Her fingers clenching around the fork in her hand, Dawn glanced at Bryce sharply. "An apology?" she asked in a carefully controlled tone. "For what?"

Bryce met her stare with the clear-eyed honesty she now knew was an integral part of his character. "For making a snap, first-sight judgment on what type of person you are," he replied. "Then acting on that judgment by giving you a rough time."

Relief left Dawn feeling weak. She had been teased from sleep a few minutes before by the mouth-watering aromas of fresh coffee and sizzling bacon. Noticing her attempt to struggle into her clothes unobtrusively, Bryce had thoughtfully turned his back to her to give her some privacy. While she finished dressing he'd portioned out the bacon. So far, their only words to each other had consisted of an exchange of good-mornings. When he mentioned owing her an apology, Dawn had immediately feared that he was referring to their night together.

Dawn bit into the roll he'd warmed by the open flames and offered him a tenuous smile. "You were rather beastly, you know."

Bryce grimaced. "Don't remind me." He refilled their cups with the steaming coffee before continuing in a flat tone. "I thought I had good reason for my attitude."

Dawn popped the last bite of roll into her mouth and followed it with a careful sip of the hot coffee. "What was the reason's name?" she inquired bravely.

Bryce stiffened and turned to gaze at the murmuring creek wending its way through the narrow canyon to the Colorado River. Watching him, aching for him, Dawn cradled the cup in her hands and moistened her suddenly dry throat with another sip of the hot brew. She knew she had hit a nerve. All she could do was wait and wonder whether he'd answer or ignore the query entirely. Bryce began speaking as he slowly brought his dark-eyed gaze back to her.

"Her name was Margaret—not Maggie, not Meg— *Margaret*. I was twenty-four, she was twenty-seven." A bitter smile twisted his lips. "Margaret was a very independent, self-sufficient, arrogant woman. And she impressed and excited the hell out of me." His smile curved into the more familiar wry slant. "I quickly fell...in love and all over her."

"Bryce," Dawn murmured when he paused. "If you'd prefer not to talk..." She was silenced by his soft laughter.

"I figure it's long past time I talked about it," he said in a rough tone. "Maybe if I'd gotten it out of my system, I wouldn't have been so quick to pin her label on every woman who as much as vaguely reminded me of her.''

"She left you?''

"No." Bryce shook his head. "I left her, after one week of wedded bliss and six months of married misery." His smile soured. "You see, Margaret didn't only want equality; I would gladly have given that. No, Margaret wanted domination, and that I wouldn't give her. Hell, at twenty-four I was still caught up in the illusion of male supremacy."

"She did a number on your ego," Dawn guessed.

Surprisingly, Bryce grinned. "I dented hers a bit, too."

Dawn began a laugh that faded to a sigh. "And you thought I was like her?''

"I thought you were exactly like her," he answered with brutal honesty.

"Then why didn't you tell me to kiss off the day we met?"

Bryce arched an eyebrow. "You want the right answer or the truth?"

Dawn replied firmly and at once. "The truth, please."

"Because, even as I dismissed you as a spoiled brat, you excited and impressed the hell out of me and I wanted to fall all over you." Her expression drew a burst of laughter from him. "So, of course, I denied myself and made you pay for it by hassling you every chance I got."

Dawn wasn't amused. Instead, she felt slightly sick. "I see," she murmured, setting her cup aside. "And last night when I threw myself at you, you decided that, still excited if no longer impressed, you'd fall all over me and hassle me in a different but much more effective way."

"That's not true."

Dawn raised her chin. "Isn't it?"

Bryce didn't hesitate. "Is the same thing true in your case?"

Dawn stared at him a moment in utter confusion. "I don't understand. What are you getting at?"

His smile was patient. "Tell me you didn't label me as some sort of macho desert rat the first time we met." His smile broadened as a flush crept into her cheeks.

Dawn swept her tousled hair back with a casual brush of her hand. "Arrogant plebeian," she corrected him coolly, then chuckled.

"And last night," Bryce said over the tinkling sound of her laughter, "when you gave yourself to me so sweetly, so hotly, had you decided any man would do to take your mind off the dream, even an arrogant plebeian?"

"No!" Dawn cried out as if wounded.

Bryce shrugged his shoulders. "There's your truth."

Yes, there it was. Dawn lowered her gaze to the crackling fire. She had felt the searing pain of rejection and had responded true to form by taking offense. She had accused Bryce unfairly of taking advantage of the situation and her. Would she never learn that not all men were sharks? she asked herself. Had Bryce learned that not all women were Margaret? Dawn looked at him as the tagalong question swam into her mind.

Suddenly, like all new lovers down through the ages, Dawn was consumed with a need to know everything about him. Bryce was watching her with an odd expression on his face. Hopeful? Expectant? Drawing a deep breath, she decided to find out.

"There has been no one since..." Dawn let the faint movement of her shoulders finish the question.

Bryce understood her thoughts at once. "There have been several...all nice, quiet, unassuming women, and none of them serious." The light of sudden realization leaped into his dark eyes. "Funny," he went on in a musing tone, "I seem to have deliberately chosen to spend my time with women who projected an attitude of near subservience to men yet, though I liked them, I never felt a sense of...of communion." His lips slanted into that wry smile Dawn was coming to love.

"What does that tell you?" Dawn asked, feeling a sense of excitement beginning to unfold inside.

Bryce sighed. "That I'm not as bright as I thought I was," he replied candidly. "It now occurs to me that I haven't found any more satisfaction with the potential slave than I did with the determined master." The light in his eyes grew brighter. "It also occurs to me that I've met an equal." His voice went low and rang clear with the note of truth. "Last night, in your arms, your body, your self, I experienced a satisfaction I had no longer believed it was possible to attain."

Dawn was forced to restrain an urgent impulse to leap over the fire and into his arms. Her eyes glistening with a sheen of tears, she stared at him in delighted astonishment. "Thank you, that...that's the nicest compliment I've ever received."

"It's true." Bryce's lips had a gentle curve. "And what about you? Did your reason for labeling me have a name?"

Dawn felt her body begin to stiffen and she made herself relax. She had never discussed him or the traumatic effects she'd suffered as a result of their disastrous affair. But Bryce had offered her truth, could she offer him less? Knowing the answer, she drew a breath and launched into a brief, edited, explanation.

"His name was John and I believed I was in love with him. He had been handpicked and carefully groomed by my father as a replacement for him as head of his company, when or if my father ever decides to retire. He was and still is ambitious, a hard worker and every bit as ruthless as my father—a fact I didn't fully understand until it was too late to escape unscathed." Dawn wet her dry lips. "We were together six months, during which I watched him maneuver and perform with the deadly smoothness of a killer shark." A tiny smile formed on her lips. "Given I was my father's daughter, John not only expected me to tolerate his questionable business practices but to assist him in all the ways a woman could. I refused; John insisted. I told him to go to hell." Dawn shrugged. "The experience left me suspicious of self-contained, arrogant men."

"That has to be the understatement of the century," Bryce observed dryly. "And has there been no one since . . ." He quite deliberately repeated her earlier words.

"No one," Dawn stated flatly. "Until last night."

"You're kidding!" Bryce exclaimed. Then, noting her expression, he said softly, "You're not kidding."

"No, I'm not kidding." Dawn sighed. "I seem to be attracted only to self-assured, strong men and, afraid of being burned again, I usually stay away from the flame." Her use of the term "usually" was a giveaway. Dawn knew it. Bryce knew it, too.

"Until now," he said, rising to circle the fire to her.

Dawn stood up to meet his advance. "Yes, until now." She faced him with her head high. "I'm glad I persisted in talking you into guiding me. It gave me the opportunity to learn that all strong, self-assured men are not unscrupulous sharks."

His smile sensuous, Bryce brought his hand to her chin to raise her face to his. "I feel at this point that I must confess that had I not wanted to guide you, you couldn't have talked me into it no matter how persistent you were." He lowered his head to hers slowly. "I feel I must also tell you that there are many differences in men, even among the strong, self-assured ones."

His lips were almost touching hers. Dawn could barely breathe, never mind think. She said the first thing to jump into her mind. "Name one."

Bryce drew a soft moan from her by gliding his tongue along her lower lip. "Some of us are sexier," he murmured an instant before he captured her mouth under his. With his lips fused to hers, Bryce lifted Dawn into his arms to carry her the few feet to his sleeping bag. Once there, he proceeded to prove his claim.

Dawn woke around noon feeling ravenously hungry, deliciously lazy and uncomfortably warm. Shoving her hair off her face with one hand, she clasped the top of the sleeping bag to her chest with the other and sat up.

"Hello." Covered by a pair of faded, low-slung, cutoff jeans and his gorgeous tan, Bryce was on one knee beside the fire, preparing lunch.

"Hello." Sniffling delicately, she tried to identify the aroma teasing her senses. "What are you cooking?"

Bryce grinned a challenge. "Come see."

Feeling a flush climb from her throat to her cheeks, Dawn let go of her hair to wiggle her fingers at him. "Turn around." The swath of hair flopped over her face again and she exhaled sharply to blow it aside.

Laughing, Bryce made a production out of turning his back to her. "If you weren't so damn prudish," he called over his shoulder, "I'd suggest a bath before lunch."

"A bath?" Dawn sat up straighter. "Where?"

"Wake up, woman," he chided. "Where else could we bathe but in the creek?"

We? Dawn eyed him warily. "We?" she voiced her thought. "You mean we should bathe together...naked together?"

His bark of laughter echoed off the canyon walls. "Of course, together, and of course, naked." His tone warmed. "We've been together and naked before."

The thought of how very naked and together they'd been sent a thrill racing through Dawn's body. Her hungry gaze caressed his muscular back, his slender waist, his slim hips and his long, well-shaped legs. She knew his body intimately, had felt the taut muscles beneath his smooth skin and had embraced his tight buttocks with her thighs. She had experienced the joy and wonder of his body sheathed deeply within her. She had shared everything of herself with him. Why not share nature's flowing bathtub with him?

Calling, "Okay, last one in does back-scrubbing duty!" Dawn flipped back the cover and raced toward the creek.

"Hey, no fair!" Bryce bellowed, shucking his cutoffs. "Besides, you forgot the soap!"

Their bath turned into a romp. Laughing and splashing like children, they engaged in a furious water battle. Then, laughing and splashing like adults, they took turns soaping one another's bodies until their laughter dwindled to soft murmurs. A hunger of a different kind finally drove them from the water....

Dawn ate a lunch of crusty overfried corned-beef hash and enjoyed every morsel of it. The canned hash was followed by canned fruit cocktail that tasted to her like ambrosia. After they'd cleared away the lunch dishes, Dawn and Bryce stretched out in the sun, she in a lacy bra and bikini panties, he in the worn, thin cutoffs. Dawn had never felt so relaxed and content before in her life.

"I really should be taking notes," she said at one point, yawning daintily.

Bryce slanted a roguish look at her lounging body. "You want to take notes on sunbathing in your lingerie?"

"Clever, Stone," Dawn retorted. "You know very well what I mean." She roused herself to sit up and glance around at the looming canyon walls and the sparkle of sunlight dancing on the water. "I should be jotting down my impressions of all this." She raised her arm and made a sweeping gesture encompassing the narrow canyon.

Bryce sat up beside her. "And what is your impression of all this?" he asked interestedly.

Dawn clasped her arms around her drawn-up legs and rested her chin on her knees. "Quiet, solitude, peace," she said softly. "Mostly peace."

"As with most things in nature, the peace is an illusion," Bryce murmured. "Beneath the surface forces are in conflict. A large animal pounces on a smaller animal for food to survive. Growing things struggle for water, air and sunlight to live. The canyon itself continues to lose ground to the cutting edge of the river. Life is a continual struggle, made worth the fight by the illusion of peace."

Turning her head, Dawn laid her cheek on her knee and gazed at him. "You make it all sound so fruitless."

Bryce smiled gently and shook his head. "Not at all," he denied her assessment. "If the struggle for life was fruitless, the animal would never know the satisfaction of repletion, growing things would never burst forth with flowers and leaves and food, the waters would die and never carve out a canyon, and humans would never experience the wonder of love." His smile slanted wryly. "No, Dawn, life is never fruitless. If we're paying attention, it teaches us balance. To appreciate light we must experience darkness. In the darkness this canyon is a hole in the ground. In the light it's ... grand."

"You're a philosopher!" Dawn exclaimed in awe.

Bryce laughed softly. "Honey, every breathing person who bothers to think is a philosopher." He gave her an arch look. "Actually, what I am is a paleontologist, and believe me, life is a struggle."

"Which reminds me that I am a writer," Dawn said, sighing dramatically. "And I have research to do."

Bryce suddenly looked suspiciously innocent. "Are there any love scenes in this story of yours?" he asked in a bland tone.

Dawn walked right into his trap. "Yes. Why?"

Leaping up, Bryce swept her into his arms and began running toward his sleeping bag.

Laughing, Dawn clung to him and cried, "What are you doing?"

"I'm going to help you research the love scenes for your book. You can do the other, less interesting research by yourself tomorrow."

Relaxed and playful, Bryce revealed another, youthful facet of his character to Dawn. There was a teasing, robust quality to his lovemaking that she found irresistible. And there was his laughter—warm, sensuous, free. Her spirit soaring with his, Dawn was pleasurably exhausted when, near sundown, she curled close to his body and closed her eyes. Dawn was totally content; wide-awake, she had captured the laughter that had eluded her in her dream.

Locked together, spoon fashion, inside his sleeping bag, Dawn and Bryce slept straight through the night and never even minded missing supper. Bryce woke her at sunrise by murmuring in her ear.

"You are well named, my Dawn."

Feeling fully rested for the first time in years, Dawn smiled and turned in his embrace to curl her arms around his neck. "How so?" she asked, staring in fascination at her own tiny image reflected in his dark eyes.

Bryce tasted her sleep-softened mouth before responding. "You broke over the edge of my horizon and chased the shadows from my world."

Stunned speechless by his words, Dawn gazed at him unabashedly as a rush of tears ran down her face. "I . . . Bryce, I . . . that's beautiful . . . thank you."

"You're beautiful." Bryce smiled. "And you're probably starving." With a burst of energy, he tossed back the cover. "Come on, morning girl, bath first, then breakfast." He sprang up and extended his hand to her. "And, if you do a good job of scrubbing my back," he said, his eyes gleaming as he drew her to her feet, "I'll even help you with your research."

Dawn's day was filled to overflowing with the wonder of Bryce. Breakfast alone was a source of wonder to her. In his now familiar, economical way, Bryce produced a satisfying meal of cooked oatmeal sprinkled with brown cinnamon-sugar, bits of canned apple, and milk made from a packet of powdered milk. The coffee was hot, dark and delicious.

Replete and feeling exceptionally good, Dawn gave him an arch look as they finished cleaning up the campsite. "Were you satisfied with your back scrub, fossil finder?"

"Fossil finder?" Bryce showered her with sparkling laughter. "I love it!" Grasping her around the waist, he planted a quick, hard kiss on her lips. "And I loved the scrub, so go get your notebook and we'll get to work."

It didn't take long for Dawn to discover that she was in the company of a man who was a veritable fount of information about the canyon. Following a barely discernible path along the shoreline of the creek, they headed toward the Colorado River. As they walked, Bryce not only answered her every question, he offered bits and pieces of interesting information she hadn't even thought about. Since Dawn paused frequently to jot down salient facts, their progress was slow.

The first time she paused it was to gaze in appreciation at the multicolored layers of rock forming the canyon walls. "What is it composed of? Limestone? Sandstone?"

"Yes, also granite and shale." Bryce relieved her of the camera as he answered. Since she was occupied with writing, he snapped pictures for her while expounding on the theme. "The Colorado began to form the canyon about six million years ago. Some of the rocks found in the deepest part of the canyon date back two billion years."

Dawn's pen paused on the paper as she glanced at him in surprise. "Two billion!" she repeated in astonishment.

"Umm," Bryce murmured, snapping a purple-shaded mesa in the distance before lowering the camera and smiling at her. "Fossils found in the canyon indicate that animals and plants thrived here millions of years ago."

"Incredible." Dawn's pen flew across the paper.

She came to another abrupt halt when she thought she discerned movement as they drew near to the river. "Are there animals now living in the canyon?" she asked.

"Of course." Amusement laced Bryce's tone as Dawn brought up the notepad, preparing to record his every word. "There are approximately 275 species of birds and about 120 other kinds of animals."

Dawn's pen paused and she frowned. "Name some, please," she said without looking up.

"You're really an information bug, aren't you?" Bryce observed in a teasing voice. She nodded and shot him a grin that gained her a ripple of the laughter she was becoming addicted to. "Okay," he laughed. "There are bighorn sheep, elk, mule deer, pronghorn antelopes, mountain lions, beavers, squirrels and snakes."

"Snakes?" Dawn wasn't quite successful in repressing the shudder that shivered through her.

"Yes." Bryce wasn't quite successful at hiding a smile. "The white-tailed Kaibab squirrel and pink Grand Canyon rattlesnake live only here, in the Grand Canyon." His smile widened. "Thought you might find that tidbit of information interesting."

In truth, Dawn found the tidbit fascinating, almost as fascinating as the man who had imparted it. Though she readily admitted to the former, she kept the latter to herself.

At the junction where the murmuring creek waters flowed into the rushing Colorado, Dawn turned in a slow circle, staring in mute wonder at the spectacular panorama of nature. As her wide-eyed gaze drank in the beauty surrounding her, Dawn's imagination kicked into high gear. Her long, jeans-clad legs folding, she dropped to the ground.

Yes, yes, she could see it, Dawn mused, her pen moving on the notebook with gathering speed. Inspired by the canyon and the facts Bryce had given her, the segment of Dawn's story concerning a young woman lost in the canyon was unfolding in her mind faster than her pen could transcribe it onto paper.

"There are numerous places where a person could get lost in the Grand." Unaware that she had spoken her thoughts aloud, Dawn started when Bryce responded in a dry tone.

"Permanently lost."

Dawn's head jerked up. "But I don't want her permanently lost!" she exclaimed, speaking about her imaginary character as if she were real, as, to Dawn, she was. Briefly, succinctly, she outlined her plot for him, finishing with, "I'll use the pink rattlesnake in some way, but I won't kill her off." She frowned, so into her own thoughts that she didn't notice the understanding smile pulling at the corners of Bryce's mouth. "She must be found," Dawn continued. "But I need an angle, a twist—not the usual rescue by an organized search party." Toying with ideas, she stared into space and absently tapped the end of the pen against her teeth.

"May I offer a suggestion?"

Though Bryce's voice was soft, his question broke her concentration. The pen paused its tapping motion. "Yes, of course." Dawn smiled encouragingly, delighted that he'd taken an interest in her story. "What is it?"

"Sam."

"What?" Dawn shook her head, as if certain she hadn't heard him correctly. "What does Sam have to do with my story?"

"He's Havasupai," Bryce said, as if that explained everything, which, of course, it didn't. Dawn frowned.

"I know that, but..." Dawn lifted her shoulders and shook her head.

"The Havasupai live on a reservation in Havasu Canyon, a side canyon of the Grand that is outside the park's boundaries."

Dawn began to feel the inner excitement she always experienced when the creative juices were flowing. "Could she somehow stumble into this canyon?" she asked, once again referring to her character as if she were an actual person.

Bryce gave her a slow, wry smile. "Is there such a thing as literary license?" he answered, without really answering.

It was all the answer Dawn needed; she didn't have to know if reaching the reservation was impossible or merely extremely difficult; all she needed to know was that it was there. Her mind was racing along with her plot, as was the pen she sent flying across the paper. Then the pen stopped again; Dawn did require some background. She tore her gaze from her notebook to the dark eyes watching her with fascination.

"Can you give me some information about Sam's people?" The way Dawn bent over her poised pen revealed her confidence in his ability to fulfill her request.

Bryce laughed softly, not in amusement but appreciation. "The Havasupai are known as the 'people of the Blue-green Water.' They are superb horsemen, bred to the saddle. The approach to the canyon is from Havasu Hill Top and down the Topocoba Trail, which is a corkscrew trail on slippery rock of gray and bluff limestone, with twenty-nine switchbacks descending one thousand feet."

Dawn was writing down his every word. "You've been there?" she asked, glancing at him. "You've made that trip on horseback?"

"Yes."

Suddenly, Dawn could almost see the dangerous trail. Fear clutched at her throat and she shuddered. "Go on."

"After reaching the floor," Bryce continued, "you follow a red-walled, narrow ravine for some twelve miles. The ravine widens into a gorge and suddenly there are groves of cottonwood and willow trees and fields of crops, nourished by Havasu Creek, which was born of cold welling springs. Though there are still hogan-style domiciles, the Havasupai have built small cottages to live in." He smiled with memory. "I spent a summer there with Sam's people. The village has a New England look."

Dawn's imagination was rolling, spinning out the tale. She didn't hesitate in explaining her story to Bryce. "I've got it!" she exclaimed. "After roaming lost for some time, I'll have her stumble upon the ravine, where she is discovered, more dead than alive, by a young stalwart of the tribe. After nursing her back to health, the man takes her to her own people by way of the terrifying trail." Her smile betrayed her excitement. "How does that sound?"

"Sounds good to me," Bryce said in a tone of genuine interest.

"But that's not all," Dawn continued, voicing her ideas as they came tumbling into her mind. "While in the canyon, she falls in love with her handsome rescuer and, as he is equally attracted to her, they become lovers." Her lips curved into a contemplative smile. "Of course, her love for the Havasupai will cause my character all sorts of problems after he returns her to her family but—" she grinned at Bryce "—that's another part of the story and I'll work that out later." Dawn made a few more notes, then snapped her notebook shut. "I have what I need. Thank you."

Bryce smiled. "I should be thanking you. I enjoyed every minute of it."

They sat quietly for a while, gazing at the river, then Dawn said, musingly, "I wonder how an Indian makes love."

His laughter flowing over her like a caress, Bryce jackknifed to his feet and pulled her up beside him. "I told you I spent an entire summer with the Havasupai." His laughter faded into a sensuous smile. "Come back to the camp with me and I'll show you how they make love."

Later, Dawn lay smiling in Bryce's arms, not at all disappointed at having discovered that his interpretation of the way the Havasupai made love was exactly the same as how Bryce made love...which was hot and fast and thoroughly satisfying.

Replete and content, Dawn snuggled close to Bryce's strength and concluded drowsily that some forms of research were a whole lot more exciting than others.

Chapter Ten

It was time to leave. Dawn stood beside the raft and sent a long, lingering look over the campsite and narrow canyon. Bryce had meticulously restored the area. From her position on the shore of the creek, the cave looked as it must have looked for thousands of years. It looked as if it had never witnessed the passage of man.

And yet, Dawn mused, it had witnessed the blossoming love of a woman. It seemed proper to Dawn that she should come to know love in such a place. She had no idea what the future held. The word *love* had not passed between her and Bryce. Dawn was glad it had not. The circumstances of their time together in the canyon were the stuff of dreams and illusion, not the normal interaction of everyday life. She needed time, Bryce needed time, to sort out the emotions neither one of them had put a name to. Dawn drew her gaze away. It was beautiful, but it was not real life.

"Ready?" Bryce asked softly, as if not wanting to intrude on her thoughts if she wasn't.

Dawn hid her feeling of sadness behind a smile. "Ready. And this time, remind me to take pictures."

Bryce could have reminded Dawn about the rolls of snapshots they'd taken in the little canyon; she was relieved when he didn't mention them. The photos she'd snapped of the canyon and the cave would be used to refresh her memory when she recreated them in her story. The pictures she had taken of Bryce were for her.

The trip back was arduous, as they had to lug the raft overland around the sections of rapids. And, though she worked up a healthy sweat, Dawn consoled herself with thoughts of the pictures she'd taken of the swirling white water from the safety of the shore. The sun was directly overhead when they arrived at the rest house. It was hot and Dawn was tired. As she sank gratefully into a seat in the shaded structure, she frowned at Bryce.

"Is it always this hot in this part of Arizona in September?" she asked as she accepted the ham sandwich and can of fruit juice he handed to her.

Bryce took a long swallow of his own drink before replying. "It's very mild up on the rim this time of year in the afternoon and the nights can get downright cold. Here on the canyon floor, the afternoon temperature is usually twenty degrees higher than on the rim."

The mere mention of the rim filled Dawn with trepidation. The very last thing she wanted to do was climb onto the back of a mule and ride up that narrow trail to the rim. To delay the inevitable, she ate and drank very slowly.

Aware of her ploy and her fears, Bryce indulged her as long as was safely possible, then he walked determinedly to the door. "It's got to be faced, Dawn," he said compassionately but decisively. "And it's got to be now."

"I know." Dawn sighed and stood up. "I'm ready." She wasn't; she knew she never would be.

Bryce held out his hand to her. "I'll be with you. I won't let anything happen to you. Remember that."

Dawn placed her hand in his and felt his fingers tighten around hers, as if he were trying to give her some of his own strength. "I'll remember." She dredged up a smile for him. "Let's do it ... before I chicken out."

Since their supplies had been decreased by the food and water they'd consumed, Bryce loaded the mule quickly and efficiently. While he worked, Dawn took pictures and made notes describing the terrain. She walked over to him reluctantly when he called to her. With soul-wrenching tenderness he drew her into his arms. His kiss was sweet, and yet Dawn imagined she tasted the bittersweetness of goodbye. Bryce stood looking at her for a moment after she was mounted on the mule. Then he smiled.

"You're the most courageous woman I've ever known. You hang in there, no matter how scared you may be, whatever the cost. You'll be fine." Flashing a grin and thumbs-up sign, he walked to his mule and swung into the saddle.

The ride was a nightmare in broad daylight for Dawn. Even with her gaze riveted to Bryce's back, she caught glimpses of the yawning canyon. At first she tried to block it out by closing her eyes, but that proved even worse. With her mind's eye she could see the edge of the path, see the sturdy mule misstep and tumble over it, feel herself falling, falling. Dawn kept her eyes wide open and on the swaying back in front of her after that.

Dawn was as stiff as a board and as white as a sheet by the time the mule crested the rim. Turning in the saddle, Bryce took one look at her, then kept the animals moving until they were at the corral and well back from the rim of the canyon.

Sam was leaning against the corral fence waiting for them. Bryce didn't take the time to reply to his cheery "Yo."

Leaping from the mule, Bryce ran to Dawn to lift her from her animal and into a reassuringly crushing embrace. "You were again magnificent," he murmured. "Magnificent."

Dawn didn't break down this time; she didn't sob or even weep. But she clung to him until the shudders subsided...and because she was afraid she'd never get the opportunity to cling to him again. When he released his hold she stepped back and smiled. "All things considered," she paraphrased shakily, "I'd rather be up here."

"Is something wrong?" Sam asked anxiously as he approached them. "Is Ms. Kingsley sick?"

"Ms. Kingsley's fine." Bryce turned to his friend. "All she needs is a hot bath, a hot meal and a good night's sleep, all of which we're going to see to right now." Turning to a pack mule, he removed Dawn's bag, then, grasping her hand, he started walking toward the lot where he'd parked the truck. "See to the animals for me, Sam, and say good-night to Ms. Kingsley."

"Will do," Sam laughed. "Good night, Ms. Kingsley."

"Good night, Sam," Dawn called over her shoulder.

It wasn't until the word "night" was mentioned that Dawn noticed that the daylight was quickly fading. With a shudder she realized how perfect Bryce's timing was. Had they started for the rim half an hour later, it would have been dark by the time they crested the top, and she would have been a blithering basket case.

As it was, Dawn was close to blithering when Bryce pulled the truck up in front of the El Tovar hotel. Determined not to apply pressure of any kind, she clutched her bag and tried to keep her composure. When he shifted in the seat to smile gently at her, she wanted to weep the tears she'd held back at the corral.

"No regrets?" Bryce asked softly.

Not trusting herself to speak, Dawn shook her head.

"Good," he said, reaching out to brush his knuckles over her cheek as he had the night before their trip. "I have none, either." Hope began to run like quicksilver through her, but chilled when he let his hand drop to the seat. "But I think we both need time," he

went on decisively. "Time to regain a normal perspective. What happened between us was beautiful.
But I feel we should allow ourselves time to think and
decide if what we found together there in the canyon
was real, or a beautiful illusion."

Telling herself that Bryce was right, that she really
did need time to reach an intelligent, clearheaded decision, Dawn agreed with him.

"If you'll give me your keys, I'll arrange to have
your car brought to the hotel."

Fighting with everything in her to keep the threat-
ening tears at bay, Dawn rummaged through her bag
for the small change purse containing her car keys and
wallet. She thanked him as she dropped the keys into
his palm.

"I'll call you," he promised, closing his fingers
around the keys.

"I'll be there." Dawn clutched the bag and lifted her
chin.

Bryce smiled. He didn't kiss her; she didn't expect
him to. Dawn forced herself to get out of the truck and
walk up the steps to the hotel entrance doors. She
didn't look back when she heard the truck drive away.
It would have been blurry if she had.

El Tovar was lovely. Built soon after the turn of the
century, its rooms were spacious and decorated for
comfort. The quiet elegance and the friendly attitude
of the employees gave the establishment a unique,
special ambience. There was no elevator. Without
complaint, Dawn accepted her room key and carried

her bag up three flights of stairs. The climb was worth the effort. The windows in her room looked out over the canyon. From a distance and with four solid walls surrounding her, the canyon had no power to terrify her.

Bryce had the power to terrify her. Refusing herself the luxury of brooding about the man and the power he possessed, Dawn ordered a meal from room service, had a hot bath while waiting for it, and fell into bed immediately after consuming the food.

Dawn slept around the clock. Not in the mood for socializing with happy vacationers, she ordered coffee and toast from room service. She ate her toast and sipped her coffee while standing at a window admiring the magnificence of the canyon.

Magnificent. Thinking the word brought a smile to her lips. The man she loved thought she was magnificent. *The man she loved.* Dawn's chin lifted. She didn't need time. Time would not change the way she felt, the way she knew she would always feel. Forgetting the cup she held in her hand, Dawn stared at one of the seven natural wonders of the world. Though there had been many who disagreed, she believed it was well named.

It was truly Grand; not an illusion, but real. Wide and deep, it had been a part of the landscape for thousands of years and would be a part of it for thousands of years to come.

Real.

Like the very real love she felt for Bryce. Dawn knew her love for Bryce was as solid and honest as the man himself. The knowledge gave her peace.

He was waiting for her.

Lounging on the bench seat, one long, denim-clad leg thrust through the open door, Bryce swung a booted foot impatiently and waited for Dawn.

He had spent the night pacing and thinking. Bryce was tired, mostly of thinking. After examining the situation seven ways from yesterday, he had decided to hang the thinking and go on instinct. His instincts told him he'd be a damned fool if he let Dawn get away from him.

How many times in a man's life was he offered the gift of holding the beauty of a Dawn in his arms? Bryce asked himself, shifting on the hard seat. Not too damn often—he supplied his own answer. And what kind of idiot would refuse such a gift? He spoke the answer aloud: "Not Bryce Stone."

To pass the time and control his impatience, Bryce savored the memories he would always cherish of Dawn: memories of her show of defiance the night he had tried to scare her into getting another guide; memories of her determination and courage in the face of petrifying fear on the trips into and out of the canyon; memories of her scribbling notes to later be transcribed into a story of adventure and love, and memories of the sweetly satisfying love they had made an adventure of together.

The booted foot swung impatiently. He would not let her go; he could not. Bryce knew he would have to convince Dawn that they belonged together because without her, his life would be fruitless.

Dawn saw the truck the minute she drove into the motel parking lot. Her heart began pounding with a mixture of hope and fear and she had to grip the steering wheel to prevent the car from going out of control. When she was safely parked, she stepped out of the car and waited for him. Her hungry gaze skimmed his body in an attempt to see all of him at once. It had been less than twenty-four hours, and yet she felt she hadn't seen him for weeks.

Is this the way it will be if he has decided to walk away? she thought, feeling the sickness of longing already coiling in her stomach. Standing in the warm, fall sunshine, Dawn felt suddenly cold with dread. Then Bryce smiled and she began to run. His arms caught her and held her close, so close, as if he'd never again let her go. In broad daylight, in front of anybody who cared enough to look, he carried her to her motel room.

Words weren't necessary but they used them just the same.

"I don't want to go back to New Jersey," Dawn blurted out as the door slammed behind them. "I don't need to think, I don't need to get things into perspective. I know the difference between reality and illusion. I love you. That's my reality; it will always be my reality." Making herself stand still, Dawn looked at him with all her love shining from her eyes.

Bryce's warm laughter flowed over her like a healing balm. "I'm delighted to hear it because I love you, too." Reaching out, he pulled her into his arms. "Oh, God, do I love you." His lips were hungry, his mouth was hot, his hands were everywhere, moving restlessly, discarding clothing as they roamed.

The precious words were repeated at regular intervals over the minutes that followed, repeated in murmurs and groans and, finally, gloriously exultant gasps.

"I love you."

"I love you."

Daylight had surrendered to darkness when Bryce stirred himself to ask a few pertinent questions.

"Are you sure you won't mind leaving the East Coast to live in the desert?"

Dawn moved sinuously against him. "I can write anywhere."

Bryce stroked her thigh in appreciation of her exciting body language. "What about your friends, your family?"

Loving the feel of his hands on her, Dawn shrugged again. "There's only my father, and he and I don't exactly see eye-to-eye. And my friends will be my friends no matter where I choose to live."

"And you feel certain about your feelings?"

Dawn lifted her head to stare at him. "Yes, I'm certain. Aren't you?"

His smile was slow, and sexy as hell. "Oh, yes, I'm sure. Want me to prove it?"

Dawn's smile mirrored his. "Is the canyon deep?"

Bryce answered her with soft laughter that reached the core of her soul.

Joan Hohl

I am a writer of romances.

Well, that's obvious, you might think—especially since you're reading this in the *Silhouette Summer Sizzlers*.

But it's not so obvious, and, with your patience and indulgence, I'll explain.

As memory serves—and with the stretch of years, it doesn't serve too well—I was around eight or nine years old when I decided I wanted to be a writer. At such a tender age, needless to say, I did not harbor ambitions of becoming a romance writer! No, I merely longed to emulate my idols, the authors who could instantly transport me to exciting new worlds.

And here, reader, is where my explanation gets down to the nitty-gritty.

I was born into what today is referred to as a lower-income family, the middle child of three. I knew we were poor; when you live every day on the cutting edge of poverty, you can't avoid knowing that you're poor. Fortunately, since practically everyone I knew resided on that same edge, it really didn't matter all that much. We had shelter; we had warmth; we had food—and we had the local lending library.

Of all the family members, I was the dreamer, the child my mother called the one with her head in the clouds. I did not simply enjoy reading—I was passionately addicted to the printed word.

I secretly longed to write. But, with only a high school education, I considered my dream of joining ranks with my idols exactly that: an audacious dream.

Yet the dream persisted, kept alive, I confess, by the stories I plotted in my mind for my own amusement.

Sadly—heartfelt sigh—I never committed a single one of those plots to paper. Through my formative years, then through years of marriage and motherhood, as I worked outside the home at various jobs, the dream persevered.

Perhaps I'm the living example of what is called a late bloomer, because the ongoing dream began to exert control after I passed my fortieth birthday. So, besides reading literally thousands of books, and the fact that I was still basically uneducated, I thought, so what? My daughters, Lori and Amy, were past the age of needing my undivided attention, and, as I figured it, my life was very likely a bit beyond half over. What did I have to lose? Not a damned thing but time, and it was my time, after all.

But what to write about? Is there such a thing as fate? I feel sure there must be, for it was around this crucial point that I discovered the category romance novel, and the rest, as the saying goes, is history. I endured several years and many rejection letters before my first work was published.

I am a writer of romances simply because I love a good, mature love story.

THE IMAGE OF A GIRL

Billie Green

My Most Memorable Vacation

My husband and I both needed a break. We had been buried alive under the combined pressure of business, church, school and parenting. We were sure that a few days away would strengthen us so that we could come back and handle the pressure.

It would be just the two of us, somewhere on a riverbank in a tent-trailer that boasted all the modern conveniences. There would be no children, no neighbors, no bosses—just a man and a woman and nature. The theory was appealing; the reality stank. After two days of short-tempered wrangling over who was supposed to handle what, and what was and wasn't a necessity, we were off. More squabbling on the road: Yes, it is absolutely necessary that we stop for sunscreen. No, I didn't pack your yellow hat. I hate that hat, and if you really wanted to bring it, you should have packed it yourself. No, I don't want to wait until we find a cafeteria to eat lunch. I'm hungry *now*.

So far, our vacation was a bundle of laughs. Was it really necessary to leave home to insult each other?

Eventually we arrived at our secluded bank on the Brazos. Actually, it wasn't that secluded: the bank was lined with tents and trailers, but they were hidden from us by the trees. The next two hours were spent in getting organized and establishing blame for things forgotten and things that worked last time but didn't now. After a quick meal—yes, it's supposed to taste like that—we finally interrupted the tension with sleep. As we lay side by side, very careful not to touch each other, I felt the dampness from the river putting kinks in my hair while the thin mattress put kinks in my back. Minutes earlier I had been too tired to hold my eyes open; now they wouldn't close.

Suddenly a long, penetrating sound tore a hole in the stillness. I felt my husband shift beside me. Then he crawled out and looked through the plastic screen that separated us from the great darkness outside.

When he returned, I whispered, "What was that?"

"A wolf," he answered calmly.

"No," I denied. "Not here."

"Okay," he said agreeably. "It wasn't a wolf. It was a possum . . . probably stubbed its toe."

A giggle took me by surprise, and I huddled closer to him. "Was it really a wolf?"

"Yes, but don't worry. They've opened the floodgates on the lake, and the river is rising. Within an hour we'll probably be floating...wolves don't like to swim."

As we held on to each other and shook with laughter, I asked myself, "Why is this funny?" Then I realized that the laughter was from relief. Because I'd found him again.

We turned to each other in the darkness, and I hurt a little when I saw the loneliness leave his eyes. I hurt because I hadn't known it was there until it wasn't there anymore.

The deep peace of being back where we belonged overwhelmed us, and I made a silent promise to this wonderful but almost forgotten thing that was known as "us."

Never again would we become so busy living that we forgot to be in love.

Chapter One

Mike Nicholson crouched down beside the small spring, gently pushing back the ferns that grew around the edges. He knew the crystal-clear liquid rising up between the rocks was just ordinary water, but some-how—maybe because he knew this had once been a sacred place—it seemed different.

It was a small spring, trapezoidal in shape, and his reflection in the water was framed by the green plants that grew lushly in the cracks between the rocks. Briefly his reflected features were replaced by a smaller, more feminine image.

Shaking his head to dispel the vision, he rose to his feet and tilted his head back slightly, letting his gaze roam slowly over the area. The air was clear here, so clear it had a silver sheen to it that startled the eye and dazzled the mind. The open space in which he stood was haphazardly decorated with chest-high boulders, as if they had been discarded by a careless giant. Be-yond the clearing, to his right, the Andes soared to-ward heaven. Behind him was the forest, but just a little higher up the trees disappeared and only grass grew. Beyond that there was nothing but rock and snow.

Human emotions are so illogical, he thought, shoving one hand in the back pocket of his khaki slacks. He could look at this land and, on one level, view it with the detached eye of a scientist. On another level he was awed by the grandeur of the terrain and the equal grandeur of its history. But on the deepest level, one he didn't allow to surface very often, Mike felt a strong sense of possession. These were his mountains; the Andes belonged to him as surely as they had once belonged to the Inca.

Why was he standing around philosophizing this morning? he asked himself in disgust; then he frowned. Philosophizing? Whom was he trying to kid? He was daydreaming. He was daydreaming like an acne-faced, hyperhormoned teenager. And it was all because of that damned jar.

Mike had had a dream last night, and had woken only reluctantly from it, wanting to go back and recapture it. And so, instead of acting like the rational human being he had always considered himself to be, instead of putting it out of his mind and going to the site to work, Mike had come to the place that had once been sacred to the Incan people. Maybe to her.

He shifted restlessly, uncomfortable with his own thoughts. He had to stop this nonsense and get things back to normal. Even though it was still early, he was usually hard at work by this time. And it was damned hard work. Armchair archaeologists who limited their digging to the pages of the *National Geographic* and old adventure movies were accustomed to imagining pith-helmeted eccentrics canoeing up the Orinoco, zealously guarding jewel-encrusted idols from the last surviving cannibals as fleets of piranhas playfully nipped at their paddles.

Reality was light-years away from that scenario. Reality was detailed organization, massive paperwork and hour upon hour of governmental red tape. It was endless days of backbreaking physical labor with a few potsherds the usual reward. At the present time, reality was digging fifteen acres inch by inch, aided only by a trowel and whisk broom.

Mike had been intrigued by this particular Incan site since first reading about it five years ago. Then, when he discovered he would have a month free for the first time in years, he had known instantly how he would use his unexpected freedom.

Given the skimpy findings turned up by past expeditions to the site, Mike had assumed he would be here on his own, but he had been mistaken. A small Wisconsin university had sent an expedition to the site for the dry season. They were a small group—an archaeologist, a botanist, three students and one Indian worker. Although it was officially their site, Mike's reputation had, as usual, smoothed the way for him. Rob Unger, the archaeologist and man in charge, seemed genuinely pleased to have Mike at the site. Occasionally at night Mike joined the others for a drink and some talk. But only at night. During the day he stayed on his own and worked a different part of the fifteen-acre site. Which was why no one had been around when he uncovered the jar.

That morning, the morning when he found it, he had awakened, as he usually did on a field expedition, at dawn. For a few minutes he had lain in his tent, staring up at the canvas above him. He had watched it gradually turn from solid black to green as the sun rose. And as he lay there, he had had a feeling. Like many scientists, Mike worked on instinct. So much of the time, success depended on chance. Most archaeologists, the unlucky ones, went through their lifetime without a single important find. But Mike had already recovered several genuinely important artifacts. As a result, he had learned to trust his instincts.

That morning he had had a hunch that something might happen; he had felt it was one of the days when a man should press his luck, and his hunch had paid off. Two hours after beginning work, he had uncovered the bulging side of a jar. Even though his movements were careful and unhurried, his blood had raced. It was always that way. He had never settled into complacency regarding his work. Even the smallest fragment of the past excited him.

Discovering that it was a ceramic jar was a bonus he hadn't hoped for. Most archaeologists sooner or later began to settle into a particular corner of their business. Mike's corner was pottery. He had done his doctoral dissertation on the ceramic works of the Inca. The shapes, the textures, the variations and specifications of the geometric designs, the chemical breakdown of the paint, the manufacturing procedures, the uses of the finished pottery—anything anyone ever wanted to know about Incan ceramics, Mike could tell them.

Although there were many fine examples of Incan pottery in existence, this particular jar was different from anything Mike had ever seen. Like their woven cloth, the Incas' pottery was characterized by the colorful, precise geometric designs that were used for decoration. The occasional human figure was usually a one-dimensional portrayal of a warrior or prisoner of war.

One side of the jar Mike had found showed stylized corn beneath the symbol of the sun god. On the other side, in a style as graceful and elegant as a Lascaux cave drawing, was the image of a girl.

Mike flexed his shoulder muscles, feeling impatient with himself. Just the thought of the girl made his blood sing, as it had when he first cleaned the jar. His behavior was out of character; he knew it, and it irritated the hell out of him, but he couldn't seem to do anything to stop it. From the moment he found the jar, his actions had been inexplicable. He hadn't told anyone about the find. He had carefully charted its location on the map, then taken the jar to his tent. Even after cleaning it and watching the beauty of it unfold, he had kept the news to himself, telling himself that he simply wanted to study it for a little while before sharing it.

Study it? he thought ruefully. He had become obsessed by it. Or by her.

She wasn't a goddess. He was sure of that. Reproductions of Incan gods and goddesses were squat semihuman things. The figure on the jar had once been a living, breathing woman.

She wore a flowing sleeveless dress, white, with yellow geometric figures at the hem. On her long black hair was a white covering that was reminiscent of a veil. It fell from the crown of her head down her back, but didn't cover her hair or her face. It was the face that held his attention for hours on end. There was a compelling mixture of joy and sadness in the dark eyes, of vulnerability and strength in the delicate chin.

Mike closed his eyes, leaning back against a boulder that still held the chill of night. Eventually, he knew, he would have to give the jar up. He would have to report the find to Rob and then to the Peruvian authorities, and make arrangements for his university to study it before returning it to the Peruvian government sometime in the future. Negotiations for the removal of artifacts were always tricky and should have been started days ago.

But he wouldn't do it now, he told himself with a self-mocking smile. Not yet. Not until he had his head on straight. Because, on top of everything else, he now had the stupid dream to contend with. He couldn't recall ever having had so vivid a dream. In it, Mike had been in a forest, surrounded by dark green. Sunlight filtered down through the trees, settling on a fine mist. Then suddenly the girl from the jar was there, walking toward him. Her fragile beauty took his breath away. He felt a supernatural energy pulling him forward. But when he reached out to touch her, the dream had dissolved and, against his will, Mike had come awake.

When the mists of sleep cleared completely, Mike had been hit by the same feeling as the day he had found the jar, the strong feeling that something was going to happen. He wasn't a romantic, and he damn sure wasn't the type to mope around with a head full of daydreams. But the mood of this particular morning and this particular place had been impossible for him to resist.

He frowned slightly as he stared at the woods to his left. Why hadn't he noticed before how much this place resembled the landscape of his dream? The morning mist still filled the spaces between the trees, giving the area an ethereal, Brigadoon-like appearance.

A slight rustling of leaves caused him to shift his gaze farther to the left, where the trees grew more densely. The sun streamed through the thick canopy of dark green, hitting the mist and turning it silver.

With a startled movement, Mike pulled away from the rock behind him. Someone was there, walking toward him. His heartbeat picked up slightly as he strained to see. Taking a step forward, he blinked, fighting the sun in his eyes.

Then he saw her. She stepped out of the mist and walked toward him, one hand raised to push her long black hair away from her face.

It was the girl from the jar.

Mike felt numb. His heart was pounding painfully. Then, just as in his dream, his hand lifted of its own accord, reaching out to her.

As he stared, mesmerized, the image said, "Hot damn! I did it—I actually found another human being in this godforsaken wilderness."

Chapter Two

Relief brought a surge of adrenaline as Faith walked eagerly toward the tall, lean man standing in front of the scattering of boulders.

"I can't believe I actually found someone," she said again, her tone lighthearted. "I figured I would wander around for years and turn into a local legend—the idiot American who roams the Andes, babbling, 'It's around here somewhere...I know it's around here somewhere.'"

Lifting the hair from her perspiring neck as she talked, she watched the man regain his original position against the boulder, his movements unnaturally slow and careful. He watched her with a dazed, almost avid stare that caused her toes to curl up in her tennis shoes.

She waved a restless hand toward the woods behind her. "That place was like the stage set for some splatter movie. Enough to give even a brave person—which I've never claimed to be—the creeps. They should put up those little maps that they have at malls. You know, the ones that say You Are Here in big red letters."

He didn't even blink. He simply kept his pale blue eyes trained on her face.

"Are you all right?" she asked with a slight nervous catch in her voice. "I'm afraid I don't speak Spanish—or anything else, for that matter, except English."

She examined his blond-streaked hair and lean, cavernous face, unnaturally pale beneath the tan. She was certain he wasn't Spanish or Indian. If she had had to classify him, she would have said Scandinavian, but even that didn't fit completely. Whatever his nationality, he didn't seem terrifically thrilled to see her.

"It's probably the altitude," she suggested sympathetically. "I haven't had time to adjust to it either...or to the temperature. It was steaming in Wichita Falls. This is heaven after that." She laughed. "I guess when you get up this high, heaven's not all that far away. When I was—"

"You must be one of the archaeology students."

The strange huskiness of his deep voice stunned her into silence. But only for a moment. When she was on a roll, it took more than shock to stop Faith.

"Must I be?" she asked quizzically. "Actually, I'm the manager of a dry cleaning establishment—'Give me your bedraggled, your besmirched, your huddled, gravy-smeared tablecloths yearning to be clean, the wretched refuse of your pizza party. Send these, the yellowed, tempura-tossed to me.' That's the Zip Cleaners motto. I can do the song, too—it's to the tune of the 'William Tell Overture'—but only after I've had at least three glasses of wine, and only for people who love me too much to throw rotten vegetables.''

The bewildered expression on his lean face made her laugh. "I know, it's corny. But Mr. Solley—he's the owner—is a doll, a little corny himself, in a totally sweet way. He's the reason I'm here. The company doesn't offer a paid vacation, but he gave me one as a bonus. And since I haven't had one in three years, I wasn't going to argue."

She drew in a breath of the crisp air and smiled. "I can't believe I'm actually here. You see, for as long as I can remember, I've had a thing about the Aztecs. Ellen—she's a travel agent and a dear friend—tried to talk me into going to Cozumel instead, but—''

"This isn't an Aztec site," he interrupted, his gaze oblique and slightly wary. "It's Incan."

Apparently the huskiness of his voice was a natural condition. It was different and, to Faith, strangely compelling.

"I know, but this was cheap. I couldn't afford the Aztec dig." She paused, wrinkling her nose in concentration. "Actually, with Buster along, it's costing me almost as much as the Aztec dig." She met his gaze. "Buster's nine—did I tell you he's my son? He was supposed to be with C.C. for the two weeks that I was here. That rat," she said, her voice indignant. "My first vacation in three years. I had it all planned. Buster would go with C.C.—"

She broke off, and her brown eyes reflected the concern that sometimes kept her awake at night. "A boy needs to know that he has a father. A functional father, not just a call now and then from someone with an unfamiliar, masculine voice. He needs to know that somewhere there is a man who was not only responsible for his birth but who is made different by the fact that he has a son. That's important, isn't it?"

Without waiting for a response from the man beside her, she continued. "C.C. promised that he wouldn't shove him off on a sitter. He promised he would spend time with Buster. I don't know why I believed him. When has he ever lived up to his responsibilities? C.C.'s my ex-husband—very much ex. Buster was only six months old when C.C. took off for parts unknown. Anyway, when C.C.'s girlfriend called last week and canceled for him, there was nothing I could do but bring him with me—Buster, not C.C. I had planned this for too long, I couldn't just give it up. And I wasn't about to let that pig ruin this for me, too—C.C., not Buster."

She smiled. "I like Buster. That may sound like an obvious statement, but believe me, it's not. Most parents love their children, but they don't always like them. Do you have kids? Being a parent can take away from your individuality, your *you-ness*. I was looking forward to being just a person—not a mother—for a little while."

She laughed, remembering Buster's machinations on the plane trip from Dallas. "But I really do like him, and if he can't do the male bonding thing with his father and I can't look for my lost me-ness, I'm glad we're together.'' She frowned. "At least, I was until he disappeared.''

She leaned against the rock beside him. "We got into camp about two hours ago—isn't Rob Unger a doll? He was very understanding about Buster being with me. He took me to see the tent Buster and I will use, and when I turned around he was gone—Buster, not Mr. Unger.''

She leaned toward him earnestly. "You know, after I had time to think about it—when you're lost in the woods, there's a lot of time to think—I decided Buster was probably with the cook. He always manages to find food. And secrets. That's probably where he is right now, blackmailing the cook out of something to eat. That boy can smell a stale doughnut a mile away and find a skeleton in the closet before it even realizes it's bony.'' She shrugged in resignation. "But by the time I thought of that, it was too late. I was already lost.''

Bending down to scratch the back of her knee, she glanced up at him. "So do you know the way back, or are you lost, too?''

He didn't reply immediately. First he passed a hand across the right side of his face; then he gave his head a hard shake. After a moment he said hoarsely, "Do you always talk this much?''

"Only when I'm nervous or worried. Or embarrassed. Or tired. Or angry. Or—'' She broke off, then said thoughtfully, "Son of a gun, I guess I do. C.C. used to say I talked to keep from thinking. But then,

C.C. rarely said anything complimentary about me. He said he left to get some peace and quiet. But that was an outright lie. He left to follow a pink, French-cut bikini. I think C.C. decided early in life that it was more convenient, not to mention more fun, to keep his conscience below the belt.''

The man beside her laughed, and for the first time since she had stumbled across him, he looked relaxed. "I'm sorry I asked," he said, shaking his head.

"Most people are," she admitted with a grin. She liked the way the smile softened the harsh lines of his face. "By the way, I'm Faith Bowen." She wiped her hand on her white denim jeans and extended it to him.

"I'm Mike Nicholson," he said as he shook her hand.

"You're with the dig?"

"I'm here on my own." Then, as though he realized the words had been unnecessarily curt, he added, "Sort of a working vacation."

"Like mine? But you probably planned on an Incan site all along." She ran her gaze over his rugged but neat khaki slacks and shirt. "You look like that kind of person. The orderly type. The kind who builds computer programs or sells term life insurance."

When he laughed again, Faith decided he had the sort of face that grew on one, the sort of face that becomes more and more attractive as the personality behind it comes through.

"I'm organized enough to show you the way back to camp," he assured her.

When he pushed himself away from the boulder to walk toward the forest, Faith fell in step behind him.

"Did you bring a map of Aztec sites with you?" he asked over his shoulder.

She chuckled. "No, I brought one book on Peru and one on the Incas, but I haven't had time to read either of them yet. All I know is that we're not far from Cuzco. Do you know much about Peru?"

"Enough to know where not to wander," he said, and she heard the smile in his voice. "Peru is divided into four geographical regions. To the west, on the coast, is a desert area that's dryer than the Sahara. Most of Peru's large cities are there. Next are the highlands—the Andes and the western foothills. There aren't many trees in the highlands, but the valleys have a thick cover of grass that the Indians use for grazing their llamas and sheep."

"On this side of the mountains—the east side—is a region known as the Selva. The Low Selva is made up of flat plains covered with thick rain forests and jungles. The Amazon starts there. Between the mountains and the jungles is the High Selva. The eastern foothills of the Andes."

"And that's where we are," she said, as she tripped over a hidden root and had to grab his arm to keep her balance.

"That's where we are," he confirmed. "The High Selva is covered with thick forests. It's here that the chief headstreams of the Amazon rise."

She whistled in admiration, then tripped again. "You must have those travel brochures memorized. What about the site? Have you been here long enough to find out about it?"

He slowed their pace slightly. Probably out of self-preservation, Faith thought wryly. If she kept grabbing wildly at him every time she tripped, eventually they would both end up on their backs in the undergrowth.

"The site was discovered about thirty years ago." As he spoke, he sounded more like he was standing behind a lectern than wading through the tangled vines of this semijungle. "The amateur archaeologist who found it ran out of money and enthusiasm and abandoned it almost immediately. Since then archaeologists and anthropologists have brought field expeditions here off and on, but since it isn't an important site, project funding is difficult to come by."

"Not an important site?" She shrugged in resignation. "I guess I kind of expected that. You don't usually get cut-rate Important."

For a few minutes only the sound of their passage through the heavy growth broke the silence. But that was only because Faith was too busy with her thoughts to talk. She had built fantasies around this trip, fantasies that featured Faith discovering unidentified but magnificent relics from the past. Fame and glory would naturally follow; archaeologists would flock to hear her lecture; the most important TV shows would plead with her for an interview.

But Faith was nothing if not adaptable. Since magnificent artifacts were out of the question, maybe on this trip she would find Truth. She could see herself standing on a lonely but majestic peak, surrounded by the Great Nothingness that was life. Then a serene presence would seek her out, and it would say—

"Are you meditating, or simply having a seizure?"

Faith shook her head to clear it. That wasn't the voice of a serene presence, she told herself. Glancing around, she found that they had left the forest behind and were standing in a rocky clearing. A green tent stood several feet away, and Mike was staring at her in frustration. It was a look she was familiar with.

She laughed softly. "Okay, not Important . . . but I still might find something," she said stubbornly. "I paid a lot of money to be here. At least, it was a lot for me. So if there's any justice in life, I'll find something. I'm not asking for something superspectacular, like a golden necklace or a frog with emerald eyes, just *something*. A hunk of hieroglyphics, maybe."

"You mean something trivial like the Rosetta Stone?" There was a hint of laughter in his voice. "The Inca didn't have a written language. I'm afraid the most you'll uncover will be a few potsherds—if you're very lucky."

"Maybe," she said. "But they could be Important potsherds."

Suddenly the amusement faded from his eyes and was immediately replaced by the nerve-tautening intensity that had been there at the beginning of their encounter.

"The camp is a hundred yards that way... behind that outcropping of rock," he said, gesturing with a concise wave of his hand.

She smiled. "Thanks."

He didn't take his eyes from her face, and Faith had the distinct notion that he was trying to make up his mind about something, that he was trying to reach a decision as he studied her features.

After a moment, he broke the strained silence. "Do you want to see something?"

The words were low and soft, and there was a disturbing quality in his raspy voice that caused her mouth to suddenly go dry.

"Is it on your person?" she asked, watching him warily.

He gave a startled laugh, shaking his head as though he were trying to decide whether or not to be annoyed. "It's in my tent. It's an artifact. I haven't shown it to anyone yet. Since you're so eager to find something, I thought you might like to see it." He paused, frowning slightly. "But I'd appreciate it if you didn't tell anyone about it yet. I need more time to study it."

"Well... sure," she said doubtfully. "But I'd better go check on Buster first." She began to move slowly away from him, walking backward. "You just hold on to your... um... artifact, and I'll be back in a little while to see it."

What a weird man, she thought as she turned and hurried away from him. He was attractive in a gaunt, distracted way... but strange.

Mike watched until she was out of sight, then turned and entered his tent.

Why in hell had he done that? he wondered as he sat on the army cot that rested against one wall. He didn't want to show the jar to anyone, especially to someone who wouldn't have even a vague idea of its importance.

Making a sound rich in disgust, he knew he had asked himself a stupid question. It was all because of the girl on the jar. And the dream.

When Faith was still, when she wasn't talking or tripping over vines, her face became confused in his mind with the girl on the jar. The long, black hair. The large, dark eyes. The shape of her jaw. The unconscious grace in her movements. All these things were replicas of the girl on the jar. But there was more. There was something intangible that he couldn't put his finger on. Maybe it was the way he felt when he looked at her. He felt the same pulling attraction he had felt in the dream.

It was crazy, he told himself. He was letting himself be carried away by a fantasy, and it was going to have to stop. Faith Bowen was not a vision from a dream. She was an ordinary woman from Wichita Falls, Texas.

Ordinary? No, never ordinary, he decided, laughing softly when he thought of the way her features had changed to reflect a running range of emotions as she talked . . . and talked.

Faith Bowen was animated, intelligent and attractive . . . but just a little strange.

Chapter Three

Although the walk back to the campsite was downhill, the terrain was rough and rocky, and Faith was breathing hard by the time she stumbled back into civilization.

In this case, civilization consisted of four small tents, barely big enough for sleeping, and a large communal tent arranged around an open space. A table holding an aluminum tub sat off to one side, and in the center was a small camp fire pit surrounded by several canvas stools.

Primitive but functional, she thought with a smile. And for the next two weeks it would be home for her and Buster.

When she saw her son step out of the large tent, relief and anger—those ever-faithful parental companions—swept through her. She would kill him, she decided. But first she would comb his hair.

The red hair Buster had inherited from his father would never lie flat. A million cowlicks had chosen her son's head for their final resting place. When he laughed—which was frequently—the tooth he had chipped in a skateboard skirmish was visible. The hair and the tooth matched the rest of him. Buster was all angles and had the thin, hungry look of a famine victim, but he exuded hyperkinetic energy. The color of his skin was usually a combination of whatever color the local dirt was and the sickly green of healing bruises. Although Buster was not a pretty child, everyone who met him was—sooner or later, willingly or unwillingly—captivated.

Today he wore a T-shirt and his favorite denim shorts, the shorts Faith was constantly throwing out and he was constantly retrieving from the trash.

"Hey, Mom! Where've you been?" he yelled as he ran toward her. "You should have been here. Marcos—he's old, but he's a student and the cook—Marcos showed me a genuine Peru bug. It was a scavenger beetle. You know what that is? It's a bug that eats the rotten meat of dead animals. It was really gross," he said with enthusiasm.

"Well, that makes the whole trip worthwhile," she said. "We paid all that money and came halfway across the world to see a bug that eats decomposing flesh."

"Yeah," he agreed. "And you missed it. Where've you been?"

"Oh, I just thought I'd take a little stroll." She reached out to smooth down his hair and watched it spring back up the moment her fingers withdrew. "It's years since I've been lost in desolate mountains. I decided I shouldn't wait another second."

"You got lost?" His young voice was indignant. "And you didn't take me with you?"

"I promise—Buster, where are we going?" she asked as he began to pull her in the direction of the communal tent.

"I want you to meet Marcos. *Marcos*," he yelled as they moved toward the canvas structure. When they entered, a heavy, bald man turned toward them. "Marcos, this is my mother—but she's all right."

"For a mother," Faith said, laughing as she shook the older man's hand. "I hope Buster hasn't been bothering you."

"No, ma'am, not at all," he said, smiling shyly. "I enjoyed having him around. Your Buster has a genuine hunger for knowledge."

"When you've known Buster a little longer you won't sound so pleased about that," she said ruefully. "Give him a few hours and he'll know everything about everyone in camp, even the stuff the FBI couldn't dig up." She smiled. "And please call me Faith—even if I am a mother."

"Glad to have you along, Faith. After lunch I'm going to show Buster where we're digging. You can come along if you like." He glanced down at Buster. "You want to run to my tent and get that green bag for me? I've got some spices in it."

As her son left at his usual breakneck pace, Faith turned to study the man working over a butane camp stove. Beneath the sleeveless shirt he had powerful shoulders, and the lines in his face were not gentle—they looked as if they had been etched with a blow torch. It was difficult to think of him as a student. He looked more like a longshoreman.

"You're thinking I'm a little old to be a college student?" he said without looking up from his preparations. "I am, but there's no help for it. It's just the way things worked out. You see, six years ago when my wife died, I sank into this funk—I guess you could call it a depression—that I couldn't seem to pull out of. Then one day...it's funny, but I still can't remember exactly what it was that lit a fire under me, but I just up and told the foreman at the factory to shove it—like in the song, you know. I shook the dust off my life savings and enrolled in college."

"I think that's wonderful," Faith said softly with genuine admiration in her voice. "I'm doing something like that myself. Since I don't have any life savings, I can't quit my job, but I manage to get in one or two classes each semester. Someday—" She laughed. "What would we do if we didn't have someday?" She glanced around, taking in two long tables. "Didn't someone overstock the tables? I thought there were only eight, counting me and Buster. Are you people antisocial, or just sloppy eaters?"

When he laughed, the massive stomach that overhung his belt bounced alarmingly. "The tables aren't just for eating. We use them for sorting and cleaning and classifying, and there's always paperwork. We usually do all that just before dinner. The battery-operated lamps aren't bright enough for delicate work, so we roll up the sides of the tent and pick up the afternoon sunlight.''

"Delicate work?" She sighed and hopped up on the table beside the stove. "I don't have a clue, Marcos. I probably know more about brain surgery than I know about archaeology—and I know nothing about brain surgery, so you can guess how much I know about all this. Maybe I made a mistake in coming here, but heaven knows when I'll get another vacation, and I simply couldn't waste it in one of those Fun in the Sun places Ellen was pushing. I went to Acapulco years ago, and the flirting among the mating set was so...so *urgent*. It was the saddest thing I've ever seen. I love learning about new things—you wouldn't believe the questions that pop into my head at the oddest times—but I would rather not have learned about that kind of thing." She shook her head vehemently. "No, I'm glad I came here, but, Marcos, there's no tour guide." She met his bewildered eyes. "So, what do you think?"

He drew in a slow breath. "I think you've got the eyes of an angel and a smile that could end a war, but I don't know what in hell you're talking about." The last was said with almost comical frustration.

Faith pulled up one knee, wrapping her arms around it. "I mean that you all know what you're doing, but I've got 'dumb' written all over me. Won't the others resent having a nonprofessional getting in their way?"

He snorted loudly. "The only thing that's dumb is your thinking anyone in their right mind could resent you. It won't take you long to catch on. Just listen and watch."

"Marcos," she said hopefully. "I'm listening now. What kind of delicate work do you do? I thought you just got a shovel and dug until you uncovered something."

"Not exactly," he said, chuckling. "Even the digging is more delicate than that, but what I was talking about was the work we do in here. Most of the artifacts that archaeologists find are from trash heaps." He paused as though gathering his thoughts. "Say you're an Incan housewife and your water jar springs a leak. You get a new one from the potter, and you take the old one to the dump. The jar is useless, so you don't lay it gently on the pile, you just chuck it on top. And if you're mad at your husband, you take out your frustrations on the jar and make sure you chuck it extra hard so it'll break, pretending it's his head maybe. After a while your jar is covered by a lot of other trash, and maybe these other wives have been there taking out their frustrations on jars and furniture and tools. After a while the weight of the trash pile breaks the jar a little more. Then, when your people move to a new site or are wiped out by the Spanish, nature goes to work and starts piling up five hundred years of dirt on top of that trash heap."

He glanced at her. "What do you suppose that jar looks like when we finally get here to dig it up?"

"Like my everyday china the day after my husband walked out?"

"You got it," he said, grinning in appreciation. "Little bitty pieces of a jigsaw puzzle. Only the pieces have been mixed up with a lot of other jigsaw pieces. We've got to make all those pieces fit together again."

Faith was fascinated. She had had no idea what was involved. But now that she did, she was itching to get started. Without conceit, she knew that she was quick. If someone could take the time to show her what to do, she was positive she could make a go of this.

"And you really don't think the others will mind my being here?" she asked, smiling hopefully.

"Not these people." He grinned. "Especially if you smile at them like that. We've got a great group of people here. Rob is my professor back in Wisconsin, but out here he treats us all like equals. Let's see, there's Janice Mahan—she's a botanist, and she's studying the plants around here. Then there's Sissy and Tip—students like me, only a little younger," he added with a grin. "Oh yeah, I forgot Pacha. He's our Indian worker. He looks like old sobersides, but once you get him laughing, he can't stop. They're a great bunch of people. I've been on some digs where some of 'em just want to have a good time and let everyone else do the work. But not this one. There's not a free-loader in the bunch. Every one of them pulls his own weight."

At that moment Buster came skidding to a halt in front of them. "Is this it, Marcos? I didn't look inside in case it was adult stuff. Mom won't let me look at adult stuff this year. She's got a mark on the kitchen wall, and as soon as I'm tall enough to reach it I can.''

Faith gave a slightly helpless laugh. "You make it sound like I've got the hard-core pornography put up until you're tall enough to reach it. You could have told him you're talking about PG-13 movies."

Marcos's brown eyes sparkled with amusement. "I'm beginning to see a family resemblance between you two."

"Thanks a lot," Faith and Buster said at the same time and with the same degree of indignation.

As Marcos began digging in the canvas bag for the spices, Faith, keeping her voice casual, said, "You didn't mention Mike Nicholson. Do you see much of him?" At his questioning look, she added, "I ran into him up there." She waved a hand in what she thought was the direction of the woods.

"Dr. Nicholson keeps mostly to himself during the day. Sometimes he comes down to the camp at night. Along with everything else, he's got a great singing voice."

"Dr.?" she repeated weakly.

"You don't know who he is?" Marcos looked astonished. "I can't believe it. You've never heard of the man whose theories on dating have rearranged the thinking of most historical archaeologists?"

"Dating? What did he do—explain why blind dates aren't as bad as everyone's heard?" Grimacing at his blank look, she said, "Sorry, just a little joke. I know what you mean. But who *is* he?"

"He's a cultural anthropologist and archaeologist specializing in the Inca. He could have been the head of the cultural anthropology department at his university, but he turned it down because he was too busy. Why, the man's almost a legend." Marcos didn't try to keep the awe out of his voice. "Dr. Nicholson's made some major—I mean big-time—discoveries. He's got to be one of the most respected men in his field. The only reason he's not well-known to the general public is because he's not a publicity seeker."

Faith almost stopped breathing. And she had thought he was a nut. My God, she thought as she felt excitement shoot through her bloodstream, he had wanted to show her something. A genuine artifact.

"I—" she began hoarsely, then cleared her throat and began again. "My only excuse is that I'm part of the general public." She slid from the table, her eyes wide with dismay. "I need to talk to Dr. Nicholson. I really need to talk to him."

"Go ahead. You can leave Buster with me," Marcos said. "He said he wanted to help me with lunch."

She smiled in relief. "You're an angel, Marcos. Just promise you'll tie him to a rock or something if he gets in the way." She gave Buster The Look. "Behave yourself. I'll be back in half an hour."

But Buster had already forgotten her. He was busy exploring the nonadult stuff in the green bag. As she left the tent, he yelled, "Don't get lost again without me."

Retracing the path to Mike's tent, Faith had time to go over the information Marcos had given her. She had no trouble picturing the man she had met earlier as a college professor. She should have known he wasn't a vacationer like herself. He was knowledgeable. He was articulate. And he must have thought she was an unvarnished idiot.

She gave a little moan of embarrassment. What a predicament. Even if she hadn't acted so stupidly, people with letters after their names intimidated her; they made her feel inadequate. If it weren't for the promise of seeing a genuine Incan artifact, she would be terrified of approaching him. But she couldn't pass up this opportunity. He had said no one else knew about it. Which meant that Faith would be the second person in hundreds of years to look at it—whatever it was. The thought sent excitement bubbling through her system.

A few minutes later she swallowed heavily and slowly approached his tent. "Knock, knock?" she said, her voice only slightly squeaky. "Dr. Nicholson?"

He appeared immediately and, after a second, held back the flap, standing aside to let her enter. Faith glanced surreptitiously at him, and her heart sank. His face had a closed look, the look of a man who had changed his mind, she thought in dismay.

"I found Buster," she said, keeping her voice determinedly cheerful. "As usual, he landed on his feet. He made friends with Marcos—the maneuvering little monster."

He didn't say anything; he simply continued to look at her with that solemn, considering expression. If he was considering, Faith told herself, then she still had hope.

"Dr. Nicholson—"

"I don't use the Dr." He paused. "I had the idea you had never heard of me."

"Are you kidding?" she asked in wide-eyed surprise. "Not know you? Why, you're practically a legend. How could I not recognize the name of the man who's—who's made *major* discoveries and whose theories on dating have rearranged the thinking of most historical archaeologists?" Her laugh was slightly breathless. "How silly. Of course I knew who you were. So," she said in a gust, "what did you want to show me?"

After a moment he turned and pulled something wrapped in cheesecloth from a wooden box. She held her breath as he carefully unwrapped a vase and held it out to her.

Faith swallowed and wiped her perspiring hands on her jeans. She was afraid to touch it. The idea that it had been made and held and used by an almost mythical people was overwhelming.

After a long moment she accepted the vase, grasping it with both hands. The beauty of it, the perfection, made her catch her breath. It wasn't even chipped. The colors—brown, black, white and yellow—were as sharp as if they had been painted the day before instead of hundreds of years ago.

Reverently, she examined the painting on the side. The figure of the sun was like the one on the television commercials, the one that turned grapes into sweet, plump raisins especially to go into boxes of cereal. Only this sun wasn't smiling; it was angrily beaming down on stalks of corn.

"Turn it over," he said, his husky voice low and intense. "Look at the other side."

With gentle, painstakingly slow movements, she turned the vase over. On the other side was a slender young girl, her hands raised slightly, the palms upturned. Faith looked at her silently for a long time, studying her face and the hands.

Finally, still looking at the vase, she grimaced and said, "What a wimp."

When she heard him draw in a sharp breath, she glanced up. He was angry. No, she decided, he was downright furious. It was apparent in the narrowing of his deep-set eyes, the tightening of his strongly defined lips.

"Look at her," he ordered stiffly. "Can't you see the intelligence and sensitivity in her features?"

"She may be intelligent," Faith said, her chin lifting in a stubborn movement. "And she may be sensitive. But that doesn't keep her from being a wimp. That's in her features, too."

"You have no idea what you're talking about." He sounded frustrated, as though it were of vital importance that she understand. "I've studied the jar carefully. I believe that she's one of the Chosen Women—one of the Virgins of the Sun. The dress and veil are of finely woven cloth. Only those of noble blood and the Chosen Women were allowed to wear such cloth."

"Chosen Women? Chosen for what?"

"Women of great beauty and intelligence were selected by government officials to prepare the food used in religious ceremonies." He had put on his professor voice again. "They also wove the cloth for the royal family, for priests and for sacrificial victims."

"Well, I can see how that would take great intelligence and beauty, not to mention sensitivity," she said dryly.

His nostrils flared, and red spots appeared on both cheeks. "Chosen Women were the only people other than the sons of nobles who were given a formal education. They were greatly honored in a period of history notorious for the denigration of women." Each tightly spoken word jabbed at her. "The emperor sometimes gave one of them to a favored noble, or to a man who had performed a special service for him."

Faith had forgotten that he had letters after his name. She had forgotten that he was world-famous. He was simply a man who had succeeded in irritating her. "You mean like a bonus for a job well done?" she asked sweetly.

He swung away from her, then turned back and pinned her with a blazing stare. "You obviously have no understanding at all of the Inca."

"No... I'm an Aztec fan, remember? And I don't see why we're arguing. You can't be sure she was one of those silly women."

"They weren't silly. And I'm positive." He frowned. "Except for the sandals. The sandals are wrong. They're crudely woven things. Peasant gear. They don't match the rest of the costume."

"Maybe they were comfortable," she suggested. "You should see the things I wear around the house."

But he didn't hear her. He seemed to have blocked her out as he wrestled with a private problem. "Maybe it's some sort of symbolism that's been lost in time."

"Maybe she was too much of a wimp to ask for good ones."

When he met her gaze, she knew that he was seeing her again. And he didn't appear to like what he saw. "Don't tell me you can't see the resemblance to yourself?"

Faith gasped twice, like a fish out of water. "You're kidding." She looked again at the vase. "I admit the coloring is similar," she said reluctantly. "But that's all. For heaven's sake, the girl's a—"

He took the vase from her, then pulled the tent flap open. "You can go now."

She stood for a moment in awkward silence. She wanted to argue or apologize or *something*. But when he continued to stare over her head, she shrugged and left the tent.

On the way back to camp, Faith kicked out viciously at a tuft of tall grass. Way to go, Faith, she told herself. You had a chance to learn from a legend, and what did you do? Once again you let your mouth overrun your brain. Lady, you really messed up this time.

Chapter Four

On her hands and knees, Faith scraped at the soil with a small trowel, removing a teaspoon of dirt at a time. She was hot and sweaty and her knees hurt—and she was having the time of her life.

As Mike had predicted, she had found nothing, but she didn't mind. The dedication and professionalism of the team were rubbing off on her. She had come to realize that the Nothing she was finding was almost as useful as the Something she had wanted to find. The string-bordered four-foot-square area that was her territory was on a map along with all the other squares. Each bit of metal, each clay shard, was charted on the map. Eventually someone would look at the Nothing spots and the Something spots and have a good idea of how the people who once inhabited this village had gone about their daily lives.

When she heard Buster's high-pitched laughter she glanced toward where he was working with Marcos. In the week that they had been there, her son had fared better than she. He had already found a stone implement and part of a bronze knife. Now the whole team regarded him as a good luck charm, and everybody wanted him close by as they dug. She smiled. Buster always landed on his feet.

Rising to lean back on her knees, she saw that people were beginning to leave the site. Quitting time, she thought, shaking her head when she realized how quickly the day had passed. She hadn't been this absorbed by dirt since she was five years old.

She stood stiffly, leaning down to brush the dirt from her bare legs. Her **aching** back caused a low groan to escape her.

"A stiff back will be **a permanent** condition before you leave here."

Faith glanced around at the woman who fell into step beside her. Janice wasn't Faith's idea of what a scientist should look like. At five-one the other woman was a good six inches shorter than Faith, and every inch of her was curved. Her blond hair fell into elegant lines even when she was hot and sweaty, as she was now. And Janice's brain was as curvy as the rest of her. At first Faith had been intimidated by the other woman's intelligence—spectacular good looks and superior intelligence shouldn't come in one package—but she soon learned that the blonde was shy and easily intimidated.

Glancing toward the steep rock face to their left, Janice smiled. "When are you going to try scaling the Rock?"

Apparently climbing the Rock, as they called the cliff, was some kind of rite of passage. All the others in the group had climbed it.

"I know my limitations," Faith said. "Ask me to rise above humble beginnings, to ascend to new creative heights, to surmount all odds, to work my way up the ladder of success, to mount a horse or a campaign. If pressed, I just might be able to scale a fish. But don't ask me to climb a mountain. Even if I weren't terrified of heights, with my luck, I would get halfway up and an earthquake would hit."

Janice laughed. "Chicken. We've all done it—even Mike has climbed the Rock."

"Did I hear my beloved's name?"

They paused, allowing Sissy to catch up with them. Sissy looked like Faith's idea of a scientist. She had a prominent nose, brown plastic-rimmed glasses and no figure. But a quirk of nature had given Sissy flirting eyes and the mind of a practical joker. Sissy also had a giant crush on Mike.

"I think he's become everyone's beloved," Janice said quietly. "When I listen to him talk, my mind seems to open up. My range of possibilities multiply and—"

"—and my nipples get hard," Sissy finished for her. "He has the most compelling eyes. They're set so deep in his head he has shadows on his cheekbones. It gives me the shivers just to look at him. Svengali time. And his—"

"—his knowledge of botany surpasses that of people I've met who were trained in the field," Janice chimed in again.

The two women were too busy carrying on their joint monologue to notice that Faith was shaking with laughter.

In the week that she had been at the site, she had heard everyone but Pacha, the Indian worker, rave about Mike Nicholson. And since Faith didn't speak Spanish or Quechua—Pacha's only languages—she wouldn't know if he were raving about Mike or not. But it didn't take an interpreter to understand the respect that was in Pacha's expression when he was around Mike. The entire crew acted like respectful groupies crowding around a rock star.

Once or twice Faith had caught a glimpse of something unexpected in Mike's eyes. She didn't know quite how to explain it, but it was a distant look, as though he were separated from the rest of them by an invisible wall. And seeing it, she had felt lonely. Which was ridiculous, of course. As she watched him interact with the others, she knew she must have been mistaken about what was in his eyes. Mike couldn't be lonely. In the outside world, he was at the top of his profession, and in the smaller world of this particular site, he was idolized.

At least once a day Mike dropped by. Work always stopped the minute he appeared. He and Rob would move around the area, discussing the work in progress as Buster devotedly trailed in Mike's footsteps.

The first time he showed up, Faith was a nervous wreck, wondering if he would make his dislike of her known to the others. But from all appearances he had forgotten that their disagreement had even taken place. In fact, from all appearances, he had forgotten that he had ever met her. He treated Faith with the same distant courtesy with which he treated everyone else in the group.

In the past week a strange thing had happened to Faith. She—the world-class talker—was drying up. When Mike was around, her tongue seemed to be glued to the roof of her mouth. She hung around in the background and listened to him talk to the others. And the more he talked, the more fascinated Faith became.

Occasionally she would turn and catch him staring at her with that strange intensity that had been there at their first meeting. She didn't know if it was the resemblance he imagined she held to the figure on the jar, or if it was because he thought she was an idiot. Either way, it made her uncomfortable. Every time he turned those pale, electric eyes in her direction, she would feel an uncomfortable tightening of her stomach muscles, and her palms would start to itch.

Thinking about it now, she shivered. Svengali eyes, she thought, smiling. If she didn't watch it she would start drooling in tandem with Sissy, she told herself wryly.

Back at camp, Faith joined the others at the metal tub of water that Pacha always left on the table for them. The water came from a stream that ran a half mile away from the camp. They all sponged off the worst of the dirt out in the open, then went to their tents for more intimate cleaning. It was a little primitive, but after a week Faith was getting used to it.

"Buster!" she called to her son's disappearing back. When his back vanished along with the rest of him, she shrugged in resignation. She would tackle him at bedtime and try to remove some of the grit. Then, when they got home, she would have him steam-cleaned.

Faith bit her lip, her eyes distracted. Her son had always been independent, and lately he seemed even more so. That was good, she told herself. It was healthy for a child to be independent. But in the back of her mind was the niggling worry that Buster's independence was an act of survival. Because there was no adult male around, Buster had to take on that role.

At dinner she watched her son with Marcos and Pacha. Although he seemed to enjoy the company of the younger men in the group—Rob and Tip—he eventually gravitated toward the older men, the strong men. And everyone, including Faith herself, was quickly forgotten if Mike was around. Buster copied the way he walked and the way he sat. It would have been funny if it hadn't caused such an ache in Faith's heart for her fatherless son.

When the dinner dishes had been cleared, people began to gravitate toward the camp fire. Faith took her usual place, leaning forward to draw stick figures in the dirt, her thoughts still on her son.

Even if she could force C.C. to be a father to Buster, she thought moodily, was he the kind of role model she wanted for her son? If only her own father were still alive. He would have been a positive influence. Her father could have shown Buster what a man should be. Faith could only tell him, and words seemed a desperately poor substitute.

"Frowns are not allowed," Tip said, breaking into Faith's intense concentration as he sat down beside her.

Tip, at twenty-four, was two years younger than Faith. He was naturally pale, and his wiry brown hair was cut close to his head in a way that should have looked neat but instead made him look like an escapee from a mental institution.

As he began to strum his guitar, he glanced at her wistfully. "Sing for us, Faith. Sing that frog song."

"You run into some strange perversions in the scientific community," she said, glancing at him from the corners of her eyes. "A grown man with an unnatural fascination for a frog."

"Stay out of my sex life and sing."

"Oh, I don't—" Faith began, scraping her toe in the dirt shyly.

"Yes, sing," Janice broke in. "If you don't, Tip will, and it's too nice a night for heavy metal."

"Gee, guys, you're embarrassing me," she said, fluttering her eyelashes with surprised innocence. "You don't really want me to sing, do you?"

Marcos pulled up a canvas stool to the circle around the fire. "Aren't you gonna' sing for us tonight, Faith? Your voice matches your beautiful angel eyes."

This had become a nightly routine. They would beg, and Faith, with patently false modesty, would demur.

One of them usually settled things by knocking her off the stool, and with the ritual complete, they always laughed.

"Okay," Faith said, sighing as she gave in to pressure too great to bear. "But tell me one more time about my beautiful eyes."

"You have beautiful eyes!" they shouted together.

Laughing, she waited until Tip started the melody, then began to sing. Faith had gone through a lot of stages in her life—some good and some not so good. Through trial and error she believed she had reached a place where she was strong enough to face life on its own terms. She wasn't the lover or the dreamer described in the song she sang, but something about the words always touched a hidden part of her. It was as though she were waiting, knowing that something unknown but wonderful was just around the next corner.

As she sang the last words, her fingers curled around her itching palms, and she glanced up. Mike was standing just outside the circle of light cast by the camp fire. Svengali eyes, she thought, and shivered uncontrollably.

"Mike!" Sissy squealed and shifted her position to make room for him. "You haven't sung for us in ages—not since before Faith and Buster got here."

When Tim handed him the guitar, Mike spent several minutes tuning it to his satisfaction. Then without warning he began to sing. The deep, rough sound washed over her in warm waves. She didn't recognize the song, but it had a gentle sound reminiscent of a sixties folk song. Follow me, he sang. All things are possible if you'll simply follow me.

She watched his face and his long fingers on the strings and felt light-headed; she listened to the sensual sound of his husky voice and felt lighthearted. If he walked out right then, she thought in a daze, she *would* follow. She would follow on her hands and knees, if necessary.

Blinking, she sat up straighter. Where on earth had that come from? She was beginning to sound like Sissy.

When the song ended, more than one person sighed, and Faith knew she wasn't the only one under his spell. After several seconds people began to talk, and there was a nervous quality to their combined voices, as though they were embarrassed at having felt so much.

Moments later, when Marcos began "Blame It on the Bossa Nova," normalcy was restored with a jolt, and the group roared with laughter. Marcos's voice sounded a little like a rock breaking.

Faith laughed along with the rest of them, feeling almost weak with relief. Whatever it was, the strange mood that had gripped her while Mike sang had disappeared.

As Sissy began her imitation of Carmen Miranda, using the salt and pepper shakers for maracas, Mike rose from the stool and stepped back into the shadows. From there he could watch Faith unnoticed.

He had spent a lot of time in the past week watching her and watching how the others reacted to her. People were drawn to her. He saw it happening over and over. They were attracted to something rejuvenating in her personality, something that she didn't seem to be aware that she possessed.

The way she had them all in the palm of her hand irritated him. He resented the hell out of it, and he didn't know why. It was simply another unfathomable emotion in a long line of unfathomable emotions he had felt lately.

"Mike . . . hey, Mike!"

Mike reluctantly looked away from Faith and the circle. Buster came to a sliding halt in front of him, throwing dust a foot in the air.

"These are Peru lightning bugs," Buster said. He held up a jar filled with fireflies. "I could probably get a fortune for them from the kids in Wichita Falls, but Mom won't let me take them on the plane."

Squatting beside the boy, Mike took the jar. "Those are genuine Peru lightning bugs, all right."

"Why do they light up like that?"

"Five chemicals are bound together in their abdomen. Adenosine triphosphate, luciferin, oxygen—" He glanced at Buster's face and laughed. "They light up so they can find each other in the dark."

"That makes sense," Buster said, showing his approval of the simpler version.

"Are you having a good time here?" Mike asked. He remembered how Faith had been worried about the boy not spending enough time with his father. "It must have been disappointing for you when you couldn't stay with your father for your vacation."

"Yeah, we were going to go to the water slides." He shrugged in unconcern, still watching the bugs. "We can go some other time."

"Do you get to see your father much?"

"No, but I talk to him on the phone sometimes."

"That must make it hard when you want to ask his advice about man things."

Buster laughed, his eyes sparkling with humor. "Advice from Dad? He's pretty nice, but he doesn't know a thing about kids. I wouldn't ask him—it would make him feel funny when he didn't know the answer." His voice grew confidential. "You see, he doesn't have experience at this stuff. It wouldn't be fair to expect him to know things about kids when all my life he's been somewheres else."

He didn't seem to be pining for a father figure, Mike thought dryly as he watched Buster walk away. In fact, the boy seemed to have a singularly pragmatic view of adults in general.

Straightening, he glanced back at the camp fire and frowned. Faith was no longer in the circle of people around the fire. Suddenly Mike felt tired. It was time for him to call it a night.

Walking away from the camp, he picked his way carefully up the rock-strewn path. He had gone about fifty yards when he saw her.

Tonight Faith wore a camisole top and loose cotton slacks. Mike had seen them by the camp fire and knew they were pale blue, but in the moonlight, they had become silver. Her dark hair was pulled up on the back of her head in a knot. As she leaned against a large boulder, the moonlight turned her to a statue of silver and ebony. Tonight she was the very image of the girl on the jar.

She didn't see him immediately as she stood staring up at the star-filled sky. But when the rocks shifted beneath his feet, she turned her head slightly in his direction.

Every practical thought left Mike's head, and he moved toward her like a man in a trance. When she raised her head and met his eyes, neither of them said a word, but, just as in the dream, he reached out to touch her, and this time the dream didn't end; this time she didn't dissolve into nothing.

Without any conscious thought, he cupped her cheek in one hand and leaned forward slowly, bringing his lips to hers.

It startled him and made him catch his breath when he found that her lips were warm and vital. They parted slightly as he gently brushed his mouth across hers, then again, and again. Pulling back slowly, he stared down into the deep darkness of her eyes.

"Hello," she whispered softly.

He smiled. "Hello."

Reluctantly, he let his hand drop away from her face and leaned against the rock beside her. The soft, opalescent evening closed around them, sealing them away from the ordinary world. They stood together without speaking for a long time. Mike felt the tension in the back of his neck, tension he hadn't been aware of, gradually ease.

Why didn't he feel the resentment toward her that he had felt earlier? he wondered, then lazily shoved the thought aside. It didn't matter. The night was too soft and warm, too druggingly beautiful, to allow negative emotions to intrude. He was too comfortable to wonder why he felt peace, like a warm quilt, slide over and around him.

Too soon, she turned to look up at him in regret. "I guess I'd better go back and make sure Buster's in bed," she said softly.

He raised a hand to her shoulder, intending to simply tell her good night. But as he felt the smooth flesh beneath his fingers, the words slipped completely out of his mind. Did the rest of her feel like satin? If it felt this good to touch her bare shoulders, what would it feel like to have her naked thighs pressed against his? How would her breasts feel against his chest?

He stared at his dark fingers resting on her pale flesh, and erotic visions rose up, shocking him with the suddenness of their appearance.

As he stared at her, he saw her eyes grow wide, as if she were startled by something in his face, but when he leaned his head toward her, she made no effort to stop him. She moved into the kiss as though she needed it as badly as he did.

The instant their lips met, the smoldering fire blazed out of control. There was no leisurely exploration. Between them, it was instant need. His hand shook slightly as he grasped the back of her head and plunged his tongue deep within her mouth, into the hidden sweetness.

She tasted so good. So damned good. He couldn't think. He only knew that suddenly he was hungry for her; without warning, he was starving for her. Sliding one hand to her rounded buttocks, he pulled her closer. But it wasn't enough. He couldn't get close enough to ease the ache that had begun to grow in his body.

Hours or minutes later—he could never be sure which—Mike began to gentle the kiss, bringing them both back to earth gradually. He didn't want to stop; he wanted to take her to his tent and spend the rest of the night feeding the hunger she had built in him.

But he knew he had to fight what was happening. Faith had obligations. And Mike needed time to think.

Drawing back, he stroked her cheek, letting his hand rest there for just a moment. "Good night, Faith," he whispered.

For a moment she simply stared at him. Then she smiled nervously and moistened her lips. The simple action caused his muscles to contract in reaction.

"Good night, Mike."

When Mike walked away, he was unaware that he was whistling softly. And he was equally unaware that the image on the jar had been completely wiped from his mind.

"Oh criminy," Faith whispered, her eyes wide in shock as Mike disappeared into the night. Then she slid bonelessly to the ground, sitting with her head slumped against her knees, her heart pounding wildly.

The first kiss had been the kiss of a fairy-tale prince. It had been a soft, slightly unreal caress, part of the moonlight and Elysian landscape.

It was the second kiss that had rocked her right off course. The fairy-tale prince hadn't been around for the second kiss. It had been a sensual demand from a living, breathing man. And it had started her atrophied hormones pumping like mad.

Why was she so frightened? she wondered frantically. She couldn't remember ever being this scared, not even when C.C. walked out on her. Anger had held her together then, but there was no anger to lean on now. All she had was this overwhelming, almost suffocating, rebellion of the senses.

It was desire or lust or whatever other label sounded good, she assured herself. That was all. Desire, plain and simple.

But it wasn't plain, and it definitely wasn't simple. She had been so sure she was immune to that particular complication. In the past eight years Faith had met a lot of attractive men, a lot of downright sexy men. And not once had she been more than slightly tempted. She had been so proud of the control she had over her own body. But tonight that control had been shot to bits.

Placing her two fingers over her right wrist, she checked her pulse. No, she wasn't imagining it. Her blood was really running for the roses tonight.

She didn't blame Mike for what had happened. In fact, she almost forgot him as she sat and silently fought a war with herself.

In her mind, Faith went back eight years earlier in time, back to the days immediately after C.C. had left. She had been furious at her husband's desertion. But one night, as she lay awake cursing him for what he had done to her and Buster, she realized that there was no pain. There was anger and frustration and violent indignation. But no pain. It hadn't hurt her when he left.

To Faith, the only reasonable explanation was that she had never loved C.C. She had let her emotions run away with her, and because of her mistake in judgment, her son was left without a father. How could she ever trust herself again?

Come on, she urged herself silently. Get a grip on yourself. She was simply caught in a hysterical reaction. This wasn't at all like the situation she had been in with C.C.

What was the worst that could happen? she asked herself, pulling up every ounce of reason she possessed. She might be falling for Mike a little—okay, maybe she was falling a lot. But so what? In a week she would be gone from this place, and she would never see him again. The situation couldn't possibly hurt her *or* Buster.

Gradually she began to realize what was wrong with her. She wasn't afraid she would make the same mistake she had made with her ex-husband. She was disappointed in herself for once again losing control of her emotions.

"Big deal," she said, rising to her feet. "So you found out you're still human enough to feel desire for a man. That's not exactly trauma material."

It sounded good, said aloud like that. And she was positive it made sense. So why did she feel a little like a child banging uselessly on a pan to keep the goblins away?

Chapter Five

After picking up a gray knapsack and slinging it over one shoulder, Mike stood and looked at the walls of what had once been a fairly large home. It was situated on a large terrace overlooking the town proper—the section the university group was working. Between his territory and theirs was a sheer wall of white stone known as the Rock. Fallen earth and rock to the right of the cliff had partially covered the Incan steps that led from the town to the terrace where Mike stood. Farther to the right and below the town were terrace after narrow terrace, held in place by low stone walls, where the Inca had once grown corn and potatoes.

For a long time he stood perfectly still and simply stared at the surrounding terrain. Mike was an observer. And although most people believed his detached manner was a product of his choice of career, it was the other way around. Because he was an observer, he had chosen science as his life's work.

He viewed the present world with the same objectivity he gave to his work. It was a comfortable place to be. He didn't rip himself apart over man's inhumanity to man. He was separate from it. He could regret the suffering without letting the cruelty diminish him. He simply didn't feel enough a part of the world to take its flaws on his shoulders. He had the ability to file them away as a symptom of the human condition.

When he was in his early twenties Mike had done the soul-searching bit, wondering if perhaps the reason he felt no universal guilt was because he considered himself superior to the rest of mankind. Eventually he'd realized that he felt as he did not because he was more, but because he was less. There was an ingredient missing in his makeup. An essential ingredient. Whether it was called fellowship or brotherhood, it was the indefinable thing that tied a single man to the rest of mankind. And it was absent in Mike.

The realization had been traumatic for him. It had frightened him badly, badly enough to make him rush into a marriage in the effort to prove he was "normal." Predictably, the marriage had been a disaster. He had never been able to connect with Carla, not even in the beginning. He had loved her, in his own way, but his way wasn't what Carla had needed. Even when they made love, a part of Mike had been separate; a part of him had been observing, rather than feeling.

One of the symptoms—or one of the punishments—of being an observer was that nothing was instinctive or automatic. Mike could never remember a time in his life, not even when he was a child, when he hadn't been in complete control of his physical and mental responses. Every action, every reaction, was weighed carefully before being carried out. Even his much touted instinct was simply a combination of knowledge and experience, he was sure. The deep recesses of his brain would automatically compute the possibilities. So his famous "hunches" were nothing more than logical guesses.

There were a lot of pluses in his type of existence. He would never be subject to mass hysteria. Although he occasionally felt anger, he was never ruled by it. He didn't say or do things that he later regretted. Logical rather than emotional thinking had built him a solid reputation in the scientific world.

There was only one minus on his type of existence, but there were times, late at night when the darkness began closing in around him, when Mike felt that the one minus wiped out all the pluses. The minus was that Mike was alone.

Until last night he had believed, and almost been resigned to, the fact that he would always be separated from the rest of the world by the missing ingredient in his soul. Then, for one moment, for the briefest instant, Mike had felt the warmth of belonging. Last night, when he had found Faith in the moonlight, he had acted instinctively and reacted emotionally.

A kiss in the moonlight. It seemed such a small thing, something that probably happened to men all over the planet on a regular basis. But to Mike it was a revelation. For a flash of time, it had felt like salvation.

He shifted his stance in an abrupt, restless movement. He hadn't done much work today. That wasn't like him, but he couldn't stop thinking about that kiss and wondering why it had happened. Why now? And why with this particular woman?

Gradually, as the day passed, he had felt himself withdrawing again. He could remember his reactions, but he couldn't reproduce the precise emotions he had felt. He had become alone once again.

Now, as he walked away from the site, he poked around in his brain to gauge his reaction to his return to isolation. Relief, he thought with a frown. It was an enormous sense of relief that he felt now.

How strange, he thought as he climbed over a pile of rocks. He almost began to analyze the peculiar reaction. Almost. With a small shake of his head, he decided it didn't matter. It was enough to know that his separate but familiar world had righted itself and all was in order.

As he slid down the rocky incline that led to his tent, he began making plans for his trip to Cuzco. It was time he started making arrangements with the authorities for the removal of the jar.

He swung around an outcropping of rock and paused for a moment. Faith's son sat on the ground in front of his tent, obviously waiting for Mike's return.

When he saw Mike, the boy scrambled to his feet and gave the seat of his shorts a halfhearted pat to remove the dust. "All finished?" he asked.

"The five o'clock whistle blew a little early today," Mike confirmed. When Buster squinted one eye in bewilderment, Mike smiled and added, "Yes, I'm through for today." Stepping into the tent, he held the flap so Buster could follow him, then dropped his knapsack to the floor. "Did you get lucky again today at the site?"

"Not me," Buster said. "But Sissy found a piece of metal right after she rubbed my head, so I figure that scam is good for a few more days."

Mike laughed. Apparently Buster didn't believe in luck, either. "Are they all paying you?"

"Yep. It's dumb, but like I told Mom, I'm not twisting anybody's arm. Can I help it if they want to give me money?" he asked, shrugging with the expression of a grubby angel.

"Don't give me that innocent look," Mike said, grinning. "I recognize a con man when I see one."

Mike watched the boy as he wandered around the tent, picking up one item after another, then setting them down again. Mike decided Buster's nonchalance was just a little overdone.

"Why don't you sit down, Buster?"

As the youngster settled on the cot, he studied Mike with a look that was frankly assessing. "So," Buster said at last, "tell me about your work, Mike. What kind of money does an archaeologist make?"

Mike choked off surprised laughter. What was in the boy's devious little brain? he wondered. Inhaling slowly, he kept his expression serious as he sat on the cot beside the boy.

"That depends on the archaeologist," Mike said. "Digs like this one are usually funded by universities and other institutions. I teach at a university in Austin, and they pay me for that, as well as giving me money for my work." He rubbed his chin thoughtfully. "Let's see . . . I also write books and articles, so I can tell students and other archaeologists what I've learned. Occasionally, I lecture. I think that just about covers my income."

Buster nodded judiciously, then gave Mike an inquiring look. "Books? Are they best-sellers? I saw a guy who writes mystery books on television, and he's like a millionaire or something."

"I'm afraid none of my stuff compares with his, but I guess a couple of the textbooks could qualify as best-sellers."

"I see." Buster rested his right foot on his left knee in imitation of Mike's casual pose. "So I guess you're not hurting for money."

"No, I guess not," Mike agreed.

The boy was silent, his features twisted in concentration, as though he were digesting the information he'd received before going to the next item on the agenda. After a couple of minutes, he glanced up again. "Sissy thinks you're cute. She told Janice that you make her—"

"I don't think you should tell me about other people's private conversations," Mike said sternly.

"Sure," he said, accepting the criticism without rancor. "But she likes you, and so does Janice. Do most women like you?"

For the life of him, Mike couldn't see where the boy was headed. Giving a mental shrug, he decided he would just have to go along for the ride. "I hope they do."

Buster met his eyes. "Do you kiss all of them the way you kissed Mom?"

Mike glanced quickly away from Buster's inquiring eyes. He felt heat surge into his face. What in hell was he supposed to do now? he wondered in dismay. Buster must have seen them the night before, and heaven only knew how it had affected him. Kids had been traumatized by less. A vivid memory from the distant past rose up before Mike could shut it off. The memory of his own mother.

Keep it casual, he told himself. He had to let Buster set the tone. Clearing his throat noisily, Mike forced himself to meet the boy's small dark eyes. "I take it you saw your mother and me last night. Did it bother you?"

"Sure," he said, not sounding traumatized in the least. "At first I wanted to punch you in the stomach. But I couldn't be sure you wouldn't punch back. I wasn't scared," he assured Mike quickly. "But Mom didn't look like she needed rescuing. I've never seen her kissing anyone. I mean, not like they do in the movies, anyway. But then I got to thinking that Mom's only twenty-six—my friend Jason's mother is thirty-eight and some of those movie stars are older than that." Then he sighed and continued. "Anyway, the thing is, if Dad had hung around, I would probably be seeing stuff like that all the time and I would be used to it. Right?"

"Right," Mike said weakly. He didn't know whether to laugh or to run. He should have known Faith's son would be intelligent but convoluted.

"So—do you?" Buster asked.

Mike blinked twice in confusion. "Do I what?"

"Do you kiss all women the way you kissed Mom?"

"No...not all of them."

"How many?"

"I don't know how many," Mike said irritably, feeling the same frustration he always felt when talking to Faith. "I don't keep a score sheet on—"

"If you were married, would you kiss other women?" Buster interrupted. "Jason's mother said Dad ran around on Mom. I don't think she would like it if you were the sort of man who did that. If you were married, could you go without kissing other women?"

"I think I could manage that," he said dryly. "But since I'm not married, the question hasn't come up." He frowned. "Is that what you're worried about? Did you think I had a wife somewhere and was being unfaithful to her by kissing your mother?"

Buster shook his head. "Naw, I know you're not married. I asked Marcos."

"Then why—"

"Do you have to go away from home very much? I mean, on digs and things?"

Mike inhaled slowly, pulling up his reserves of patience. "I'm usually away several months of the year."

"I see," Buster said. Mike knew a psychiatrist who said those two words in exactly the same tone. "Is that why you're not married? Because you couldn't take your wife and kids with you?"

"I could take a family—if I had one—anywhere I go."

"So why aren't you married? Don't you like kids?"

"Okay, that's enough," Mike said, rising to his feet. "It's not that I don't enjoy being grilled, but I think it's time you told me what's on your mind."

"You sound just like a father," Buster said, looking inordinately pleased with Mike's stern tone. "That's good. The thing is, Mom needs someone to take care of her. I do my best, but I'm nine. When she can't balance the checkbook, I can't help her. I just barely got a C in arithmetic." His voice grew confidential, his eyes earnest. "One time they shut off the lights, and then she found the check for the electric company under the seat in the car. And once she tried to fix the toaster and nearly blew up the kitchen. She worries all the time about how much money is in my college account and whether I'm going to turn into a gangster because she's not there when I get home from school. If she had a husband, the right kind of husband, he would settle her down. He could take care of her." He shrugged his thin shoulders. "I figured you must like her a lot or you wouldn't have been kissing her like that."

He looked away from Mike, glancing down as he picked at a scab on his knee. "It's not for me, you know," he said, his voice too casual. "I mean, I do all right without a father. Mom is always talking about me needing a role model, but I get by okay. I worry about her, though."

Mike couldn't explain the sharp jab in his chest as he heard Buster earnestly denying his need for a father. It had the same ring of loneliness that he heard in his own voice when he said he didn't really want to be a part of the world.

But Mike couldn't think about that. He needed all his objectivity to get out of this predicament. Apparently Buster worried about his mother as much as she worried about him. And while Mike agreed that Faith's naive, slightly cockeyed way of thinking must make it tough for her to confront the real world, he couldn't become involved in either of their lives.

"I'm not going to talk about the kiss, Buster," he said gently. "Because that's my business and your mother's. And I think she would be a little upset if she knew you were trying to arrange things for her." Upset? he thought, hiding a grin at the understatement. She would be mad as hell. "Your mother's an adult, and adults like to work out their own problems. You can't do it for her, and neither can I." He laid a casual arm across the boy's shoulders. "Do you understand?"

"I guess—" Buster broke off when they heard Faith's voice, calling his name. He met Mike's eyes warily. "Oh criminy. You won't tell her? She'd scalp me for sure."

"Me?" Mike raised one brow. "I don't squeal on my friends."

A slow grin spread across Buster's face; then he ran out of the tent to meet his mother.

Faith's heart did a strange little sideways skitter when she saw Mike step out of the tent behind Buster. Since he hadn't shown up at the site today, this was the first time she had seen him since last night.

She had spent most of the day thinking about the way she had felt the night before when he kissed her, and now she knew she owed Mike a debt of gratitude. Until last night she had been positive that C.C.'s desertion had had no lingering effects on her. Now she knew she was wrong. Because of her ex-husband, she had been living for eight years in an emotional desert. Because of him, she had switched off her emotions. She had become a partial woman, a fragment of a human being. She had allowed an immature jerk like C.C. to deprive her of the fullness that life had to offer.

Her reactions to Mike the night before—she didn't know whether her required healing time had been reached, or whether it had been a reaction to this particular man—but whatever the cause, last night Faith had been set free. And, in a typical overreaction, her senses had gone into overdrive. They had come to life with an acuteness that was almost painful. She had always enjoyed the sights and sounds and feel of the world, but now she knew that for most of her adult life she had been trapped in a state of seminumbness. The world around her had suddenly taken on a sharply defined clarity. It shouted at her. It reached out to her. It grabbed her by the shoulders and gave her a hard shake. The very air she breathed was laughing.

If she wasn't careful, she would make a fool of herself. So, after hours of deliberation, Faith had decided that the only way to handle the situation was to pretend that the incident had never happened.

Now, looking at Mike, she realized that the only problem was that she had forgotten to let her body in on the decision.

"Marcos said you were up here bothering Mike," she said to Buster as she reached the tent; then she glanced at Mike. "Hello, Mike. I thought maybe Buster had skipped the country. I was looking in my bag for hand cream—dirt isn't wonderful for the skin—and the passports were missing. Panic time. I'm not cut out to be a citizen of Peru." Oh, wonderful, she thought in disgust. The lock on her tongue had been removed with a vengeance. "I was making plans to have us smuggled out of the country when I found them both tangled up in Buster's underwear. But you know, I never did find the hand cream."

Please God, she prayed silently, rip out my tongue. Rip it out now before I start reciting the Declaration of Independence.

"So," she said, avoiding Mike's eyes as she paused to catch her breath, "what have you two been up to?"

"Man stuff," Buster said, trying to look mysterious.

Faith tilted her head, glancing up at Mike in inquiry. "Have you been teaching him to spit? I told him he wasn't allowed to spit until he's a teenager."

"Will you, Mike?" Buster asked hopefully. "I'll bet—"

"No," Mike interrupted firmly. "I won't. Not even if you were a teenager." He raised one brow as he looked at Faith. "Is spitting your idea of 'man stuff'?"

"No, but it's Buster's. Spitting, picking his teeth and scratching his behind in public—he likes to hang around the stockyards," she explained apologetically. Glancing at her son, she said, "We'd better go, or we'll miss dinner."

"Why don't you both have dinner with me?"

Jerking her head up, she met Mike's eyes. He looked as though the invitation had surprised him almost as much as it had her.

"Well . . ." she began hesitantly.

"Yeah, that's great!" Buster said enthusiastically. "We'd love to, wouldn't we, Mom? I'll go tell Marcos we won't be there for dinner."

Before she could stop him, Buster was tearing off down the trail to the camp. She turned back to Mike, smiling ruefully. "I guess we're staying for dinner."

"That's fine," he said quietly, his features now composed and distantly polite. "Why don't you grab a chair and make yourself comfortable while I clean up?"

She sat on a green folding chair, crossing her legs casually, pretending to relax as she watched him from the corners of her eyes. It was a strange situation, she thought, as he reached for a bucket and began to pour water into a metal washbasin. Last night she had been physically closer to him than she had been to a man in nine years. And yet she didn't know Mike. She didn't know him, and she couldn't be comfortable around him. She had felt perfectly at home in his arms, but she couldn't think of what to say to him in a casual conversation.

At that moment Mike reached down and pulled the navy-blue sweatshirt over his head, and every thought flew out of her brain. Her hands tightened on the arms of the chair, and she almost moaned aloud. She hadn't expected this, but now that it was happening, she couldn't look away. The lean muscles of his body gleamed bronze in the sun. It wasn't a soft body; there wasn't an ounce of spare flesh. He was all muscle, giving the impression of economical but enormous strength. There was a small scar low on the right side of his back. She wanted to touch it. She wanted to feel the texture of it beneath her fingertips.

He turned slightly, giving her a view of his chest, smooth and hard and brown. As she stared in breathless fascination, a trickle of water ran down his chest and was caught by the waistband of his jeans. A shaft of desire such as she had never felt in her life shot through her body.

Stop it, she told herself silently. She was simply feeling the lingering effects of the night before. The encounter had knocked her off her feet, and she was still reeling. She was going to have to walk a careful line until she had adjusted to her newly awakened awareness.

She only hoped, now that she was alive again, that she didn't react to every attractive man the way she was reacting to Mike. That would make life a little too interesting, she thought with a soft, shaky laugh.

For the rest of the evening she managed to keep her tongue from running away with her. She sat back and listened to the two males. After a while she began to envy her son. Mike was more relaxed around Buster than she had ever seen him. As she watched them prepare dinner—canned stew and crackers—Mike talked and joked, completely at ease. The blatant hero worship on Buster's small face caused a tightness in her chest until she realized that her expression probably matched her son's. When this unusual man really opened up, he was impossible to resist.

During dinner she was included in the warm, comfortable circle established by the other two. And later, as the three of them cleaned up after the meal, Mike joined comfortably in the word games Faith and Buster usually played while they worked.

"Defense," Buster said, glancing at his mother to warn her not to give away the answer.

Mike rubbed his chin thoughtfully. After a moment, he shrugged. "I give up. What is it?"

"It keeps de cows in," Buster said, folding over with laughter at Mike's pained expression. "Now it's Mom's turn."

They both looked at her expectantly. "Okay..." Faith said slowly. "Okay, I've got it. Fantasize is the size Fanta wears."

"Boo," Mike and Buster said in unison.

"You're both just jealous," she said haughtily. "That's the best one tonight. It's your turn, Mike. Let's see if you can come up with a better one."

"Without even straining my brain," he drawled lazily. "Substandard...the level of quality set by an underwater vessel."

Buster's admiring "Wow!" didn't quite cover Faith's muttered, "Big deal."

Mike laughed. "Okay, Buster, your turn again."

"Okay," Buster said, drawing in a deep breath. "You just watch my smoke. Remit is to put your glove on again. Relief is what the trees do in spring. Rehearse means to buy a new car for the funeral. Refuse is putting more string on the dynamite. Recoup means—"

"Enough already! You win," Faith said, shaking her head.

"Where does he get them?" Mike asked, still laughing.

"He spends hours and hours with his head buried in the dictionary, the competitive little monster," she said, watching Buster run off to chase moths. "I usually allow him only two re-words a night, because he can go on forever with those. Since I make him learn the real definitions of each word, I figure it's building his vocabulary." She glanced up to find Mike studying her face.

"You're a good mother," he said softly.

She snorted inelegantly. "I'm a mother who's hanging on by her fingernails. But we make do," she added. "Right now this mother had better get her child to bed. Buster! Time to go. Come be polite."

"Thanks for dinner, Mike," Buster said as he reached them. "It was good. Will you come by the site tomorrow?"

"I'm afraid not. I'm going to Cuzco on business, but I'll be back the day after tomorrow." He paused, glancing away briefly before meeting Faith's eyes. "Why don't you both come with me?"

"That's a terrific idea!" Buster said enthusiastically. "Mike could take you to see all those ruined things you were talking about, Mom."

"Oh, Buster, I don't know..." she began awkwardly.

"My business shouldn't take too long," Mike said. She felt a spreading warmth when he smiled at her. "I would enjoy showing you around. We could even stop at Machu Picchu on the way.''

"That's dirty pool,'' she said, laughing. "I would give an arm and a leg to see that. But I'm afraid—''

"No, wait, Mom. Listen,'' Buster said urgently. "We wouldn't even take up much room in Mike's car—because I can't go. Tip paid me in advance to stand next to him tomorrow, and Marcos always needs my help at lunch.''

"Buster, I can't leave you here alone,'' she said.

"Marcos will watch me. And so will Sissy. They really like having me around. Honest, Mom.''

"I know they do, but—'' She broke off to give him a suspicious look. "Why are you trying to get rid of me? Have you got something planned that you know I'll disapprove of?''

"Aw, Mom,'' he said, in a tone of injured innocence.

Mike reached out and took her hand. "If you really want to go, I could use the company on the drive. You wouldn't even have to pay for a hotel room. Some friends of mine live just outside the city, and they have plenty of room for you, too.''

This was crazy, she thought, moistening her lips. Just the touch of his hand made it impossible for her to think. She couldn't remember a single one of the excellent reasons she had for not going.

"Well, you did it," she said, laughing breathlessly. "You hit my cheap spot. If Marcos will watch Buster, I'd love to go with you."

It was hours before Faith settled down enough to wonder what on earth she had gotten herself into.

Chapter Six

It was a miracle. Ordinary Faith Antoinette Bowen was standing on a ledge in the back of beyond and gazed down upon a miracle—Machu Picchu.

In the distance, massive snow-clad summits rose in rugged splendor. Far below, the Urubamba River echoed from the deep gorge carved on three sides of the mountain shoulder. On the fourth side a pinnacle stood guarding the mysterious, mist-shrouded city that lay shelf upon shelf and almost seemed to melt into the shaggy blue-gray mountains.

"I can't catch my breath," she whispered.

Mike smiled. "It's the altitude."

"No." She shook her head vehemently. "And it's not even my sincere cowardice regarding heights. It's...*this*. I've never seen anything like it. It seems to be a part of the mountain."

He nodded. "They carved an entire city of two hundred buildings and a mile-long aqueduct out of solid granite. But the architect didn't destroy the topography," he said softly. "He merely caressed it."

She turned to face him. "Who lived here? And why here, for heaven's sake? That abyss—" She felt dizzy just remembering it. "It's the only thing I've ever seen that truly deserves that name. Why here?'' she repeated.

"You've partly answered your own question," he said, smiling slightly. "The abyss, the river, the mountains—what enemy could get past that? This was the last stronghold of a dying empire...maybe."

"Maybe?"

"All we can do is speculate. After Atahualpa's execution in 1533—"

"Atahualpa? No, don't tell me," she said, wrinkling her nose in concentration. "He's the one the Spanish ransomed for a roomful of gold—then, as soon as it was paid, they garrotted him. Am I right?"

"You've been reading your books," he said, chuckling. "Yes, he's the one. After Atahualpa's death, Pizarro appointed Manco II to be ruler of the Inca. But when Manco realized he was only a puppet, he rebelled and left Cuzco, taking a group of his loyal followers with him down the Urubamba. The story has it that he set up a mountain community in a region sealed off from the rest of the world—Vilcapampa. Some say this is it, that he came here to the city of the Virgins of the Sun and ruled with his three sons, free of Spanish domination."

"Virgins of the Sun? Aren't they—"

"The Chosen Women," he said, giving her an oblique, amused glance.

"Them again. This was their city."

"Maybe," he said, shrugging. "Out of 173 skeletons found here, 150 were women."

She shivered. "So what happened to our man Manco?"

"He ruled for thirty-nine years before he was finally captured and beheaded." Mike moved back a few feet to sit on a large, flat stone. "The last Inca," he continued quietly. "But he was captured while he was away from here. This place never saw a conquistador."

Moving to sit beside him, Faith let the mood of the place sweep her away. Was it only a few hours ago that she was being a nagging mother as she left Buster in Marcos's care at the site? The reality of that ordinary life seemed far removed from what she was feeling now. She had landed smack in the middle of a world long dead, a world inhabited by sun-worshiping maidens and doomed warriors.

Sitting on a boulder that seemed to be perched at the edge of the universe, Faith made a picture as vivid as the one in her imagination. She wore a scarlet sundress, the only dress she had brought with her, that was a startling contrast to the pale flesh of her shoulders and made her hair seem blacker than ever. From a wooden deck behind and above her, more than one admiring tourist used her as focal point for souvenir snapshots of the ruins.

As the wind gusted around them, Faith wrapped her arms around herself, lusting secretly after Mike's brown corduroy jacket, and raised her gaze to his face, studying his expression as he stared at the ruins with complete absorption.

"You really love this, don't you?" she asked quietly. "Your work, I mean."

He nodded. Without glancing at her, he removed his jacket and settled it around her shoulders. "I love it. I've loved it since I was ten, and I don't suppose I'll change after all this time."

"You've studied the Inca since you were ten? When I was ten my one burning ambition was to be able to do splits without causing permanent damage."

He laughed. "I wasn't studying the Inca then. Back then I was listening to stories from the history teacher who lived next door. That's when I decided I wanted to be an archaeologist. My parents humored me until I got into high school, then they decided they had let it go on too long. They wanted me to come back to earth and start thinking about what I really wanted to do with my life. Even Mr. Converse—the history teacher next door—tried to discourage me." Mike grinned. "He said I would starve to death. According to him, the only way to make a living as an archaeologist was to teach, and even that was shaky. He thought I should take over my father's newspaper. He said it was a fact of life that there would always be bad news and there would always be people who wanted to read about it, and I should cash in on that fact."

"But you stuck to your guns and showed them all," she said, becoming involved in the story.

"No, I studied journalism," he said, smiling apologetically. "At least, I did for six months. Six months of being a square peg in a round hole. Then I switched to anthropology. I've never regretted the decision."

Faith looked out over the ruins. "Not even when you consider the fact that you're studying people who weren't allowed to survive?" She met his eyes. "Doesn't it bother you? Knowing that an entire people who once lived in these mountains were systematically and deliberately wiped out."

"You don't have to study history to run into that. It's happening right now, all over the world. Would I sound cynical if I said it's the nature of the beast?"

"You sound very philosophical." She was silent for a moment. "Can you accept that excuse? Can you accept it and just go on about your business?"

"It's what we all have to do. Today we have a tragedy, but tomorrow there are still vegetables to be planted and ditches to be dug. In my private moments I can hurt because I'm a piece of mankind, and mankind is not a nice animal. But I can't let that hurt take over my life. It wouldn't accomplish anything."

For a long time she stared at his face, tracing with her gaze the harsh angles, the craggy features. If all of mankind were like this man, she thought, it would be a gentler animal.

"You're a very caring person, aren't you?" she said, her voice quiet.

He gave her a surprised, almost shocked look. "You must not have been listening. I said I don't take on the world's problems."

"But you care," she said earnestly. "Don't you know how many people—even the people who work to fix the problems—don't really care? They argue and complain and get angry, but they never have that private moment of pain on behalf of their fellow man. The fact that you do makes you a caring person."

There was an almost undetectable trace of bitterness in his eyes. "I'm not, you know. As a matter of fact, I'm a cold son of a bitch."

There was something in his voice and his blue eyes that brought a soft, lurching ache to her heart, then a swift rush of anger. "Who told you that?" she asked, her voice harsh. "Who dared to tell you that?"

His smile was a cynical caricature. "Lots of people. I think my mother was the first." He stood abruptly. "Why don't we go get a hot drink?"

As they sat on the terrace of the inn overlooking the ruins, Faith felt him pulling away from her. He was almost visibly withdrawing into the distant politeness that was beginning to set her teeth on edge with frustration. Now that he had given her a glimpse of the man behind the forbidding facade, she wanted more. She wanted to grab him by the shoulders and shake him, shouting, "Let me back in! It's cold out here."

But she didn't. All she could do was follow his lead. After lunching at the inn above the site, they began the drive up the mountains. The road to Cuzco was set with breathtaking, precipitous zigzag turns, each sharper than the last, and in every direction was the profile of the formidable mountains. Faith had never before had reason to be grateful for her cowardly attitude toward heights, but when she sank down in the seat beside Mike, closing her eyes tightly, she heard him laugh. And as he laughed, the wall that had risen between them grew less impenetrable. When he pulled her next to him, their thighs and shoulders touching, joy eased gently through her body, making her forget everything except Mike. Faith could have stood on the edge of the abyss and laughed.

As they climbed, the temperature dropped steadily. They had left Machu Picchu at eight thousand feet and were traveling to a place that reached two miles into the atmosphere.

It was late afternoon when they arrived in Cuzco. Indian women, their beautifully woven goods spread out on the sloping sides of the highway, were beginning to close up shop for the day. Even viewed in semidarkness, it was an exciting city. To Faith, it was even more. It was an exotic, fairy-tale place. She made careful mental notes on everything. The tile-roofed buildings, the cars on the street, the dark-skinned people, even the menu at the elegant restaurant where they dined went on her list.

"Llama tartar?" she said as Mike stopped in front of a house on the outskirts of Cuzco. "Do you believe it? Llama tartar."

"Why didn't you order it?"

"No, thank you," she said, laughing. "Just knowing it exists is enough."

Stepping from the car, she gazed at the house. It wasn't what she had expected. Totally modern, it could have been picked up and set down in Omaha, Nebraska—or Wichita Falls—without causing a stir. Frowning slightly, she took in the darkened windows.

His friends must be out for the evening, she decided, glancing at the man beside her. "Do you have a key?"

He smiled. "It would be a little difficult to get inside without one."

Faith studied his face as they walked up the sidewalk to the front door. Something about his smile worried her. "When will your friends be back?" she asked, keeping her voice casual.

Unlocking the door, he walked into the house and switched on the light. "August, I think Frank said," he said over his shoulder. "Yes, I'm almost sure he said they would be back in August."

Faith swallowed heavily. "Not tonight."

"No, tonight we have the house to ourselves." He met her gaze. Curiosity—and something she couldn't identify—gleamed in his pale eyes. "Does that bother you?"

"Of course not," she said. Her voice sounded too confident, as it always did when she was lying.

"Good." He walked down the hall, with Faith trailing helplessly behind. "You can use this room." He set her overnight bag on the floor just inside the door. "The bathroom's through there. There should be fresh towels if you want to freshen up. I'll be in the den.''

She watched him walk out, slumped weakly to the bed, then muttered slowly, "Okeydokey."

She glanced at the door, then at the bed, then at the floor. "There's nothing to be nervous about. Of course there isn't, silly. Don't be such a child. And for heaven's sake, stop *talking*."

She clamped her hand over her mouth and rocked back and forth, feeling as confused and scared as she had the night he kissed her. She and Mike were friends, she told herself. Just friends. One might even call them colleagues. Yes, that was it, she told herself firmly. They were colleagues and companions. Historical companions. There was certainly nothing for her to be worried about. A companion was a companion. It didn't matter if said companion was male or female.

Several minutes later, after washing up and freshening her makeup, she walked into the den, feeling much more confident after her silent pep talk with herself. She felt confident for two seconds; then she took in the soft, flickering light from the fireplace— the only light in the room—and the bottle of wine, accompanied by two glasses, on a low table.

Mike turned as she walked into the room. "Come sit down." He patted the love seat beside him. "It's been a long day."

Faith moved forward slowly, staring at the narrow space beside him. "I think...I think I'll sit here on the floor. It's closer to the fire."

She sank down, leaning forward as she wrapped her arms around knees that were strangely weak. When she heard him pour the wine, she turned, murmuring, "Thank you," but didn't meet his eyes as she accepted the filled glass from him.

She took a sip of the wine, smoothed the fabric of her dress over her knees, then cleared her throat. "Your friends, Frank and..."

"Frank and Marcie."

"Frank and Marcie. They have a lovely home." She glanced quickly around the room, anywhere but at Mike. "The color scheme is unusual. It must be nice, being able to afford a color scheme. You should see my house—not that I don't like it, you understand. It's comfortable and—"

"Faith." He slid to the floor beside her. Lifting her hand, he brought the wineglass to her lips. "Drink."

Startled, she swallowed half the glass before she knew what she was doing.

"Now, take a deep breath." He watched her inhale slowly, then smiled and said, "How do you feel?"

She grinned, meeting his eyes. "Better. Just a faint, lingering urge to chatter."

He laughed. "It's not that I don't enjoy hearing you talk, but there's really no need for you to be nervous."

"No, there isn't, is there?" she said, leaning back against the love seat with a sigh. "Have you known Frank and Marcie long?"

"I've known Marcie since she married Frank ten years ago." He settled comfortably beside her, extending his long legs toward the fire. "I've known Frank for more than thirty years—since I was seven. The day after he moved onto my street, he swiped my water pistol and I pushed him into a mud puddle."

"True friendship is a beautiful thing," she said, her voice sincere, her eyes sparkling.

He grinned. "It seems to work for us."

"You're not still pushing him into mud puddles?" She turned to examine his face, his gentle, smiling eyes. "I bet you were a hell-raiser back then."

He took a sip of the red wine. "No, I was probably the moodiest kid you ever set eyes on. I don't know why Frank stuck by me. I spent more time at his house than I did at my own."

The distant look, the lonely look, touched him briefly before he visibly shrugged it away and refilled her glass from the bottle beside him on the floor.

"You were an only child?" she asked softly.

"Yes, thank God." Catching the look of inquiry on her face, he grimaced. "Ours was not your average American family. My parents were constantly at each other's throats, and I just tried to stay out of the way." He leaned his head back and stared at the ceiling. "That's the way they both wanted it. You see, my mother walked out when I was six. It was my fault."

The flat, cold statement made her gasp in protest. "No," she said, moving closer to him.

"Oh yes, it was. I walked in on her and one of my father's employees—he couldn't have been more than eighteen." His face lost all expression as he continued. "I won't tell you what I saw, but it wasn't the kind of scene a boy wants to imagine his mother in. She must have told my father about it, because a couple of days later, I heard them arguing. She said she wasn't going to stay around 'that little bastard with those damned hurt eyes.' When she left, I remember spending half the day in front of the mirror, trying to see what she saw. Trying to make it go away." He exhaled slowly. "I did...and she came back. But we were never a family again."

He lowered his gaze to Faith. "Don't cry," he said softly.

She hadn't known she was. She couldn't feel the tears on her face; she couldn't feel anything for herself. She could only feel for him. Faith wasn't a violent person, but she knew that if she'd had his mother in the room at that moment, she would have done the woman a bodily injury.

"I hate her," she whispered hoarsely, burying her face in his shoulder. "I really, really hate her."

He laughed. "There's no need for that. It hasn't hurt in a long time. This is the first time I've ever talked about it. I don't even think about it anymore. I don't know why I told you. Here, drink your wine."

He watched her take a drink, then refilled the glass. "Tell me about your parents."

"I'm almost ashamed," she said slowly. "They were wonderful."

"Silly. Just because I had terrible parents doesn't mean you should have, too. I'm glad yours were nice."

"They were terrific." Lazily, she snuggled closer into the comfortable niche of his arm. "Pops was almost bald, but I thought he was the most handsome man I had ever seen. So did Mama." She laughed softly. "I remember once..."

Her voice faded away, and she stared at the fire for a moment, then glanced back at Mike. "What was I saying?"

"You were talking about how handsome your father was," he said. His expression was serious, but there was a mysterious twinkle in his blue eyes.

Faith stared at him for a long time in silence, then shook her head slowly. "You think you're so clever," she said, chuckling. "Refilling my glass every time I turn my head. But you're not so clever. I know exactly what you're trying to do."

"Oh?" He raised one brow. "What am I trying to do?"

She let her head slide back to his shoulder and smiled beatifically. "You're trying to get me mellow, so I'll sing the Zip Cleaners anthem for you."

His husky laugh seemed to float around her and settle gently on her flesh. Raising his hand, he ran a single finger down the length of her nose. "You're close. But, as a matter of fact, I'm trying to get you mellow so you'll relax enough to let me make love to you."

As the words sank in, Faith's dark eyes grew big and round. "Oh," she said weakly.

Chapter Seven

Faith stared at Mike in blank surprise, and the relaxing effects of the wine abandoned her completely.

"Oh," she said again. "I didn't know...at least, I thought for a second—when I saw that your friends weren't home, and then when you said August—but then I decided we were...well, colleagues..." She shook her head. "Not exactly colleagues, because of all those letters behind your name, but maybe *friends* or companions, you know, who share a common interest. So I put it out of my mind. Then, of course, there was no light except the fire—and two wineglasses somehow look so *intimate*. But when you..."

Shaking with laughter, Mike grasped her shoulders and kissed her hard. "Shut up, Faith," he whispered against her lips.

She stared into his sparkling eyes for a moment, then nervously moistened her lips. But the feel of him and the taste of him were still on her mouth, and the action weakened her. Drawing a shaky breath, she said, "Yes, I will. At least, I can't very well talk when you're kissing me."

He smiled down at her. "Does that mean you want me to do it again?"

"Yes—I mean no." Pulling away from him, she leaned against the love seat and raked her fingers through her dark hair. "To tell you the truth, I don't know what I mean."

"That makes two of us." He raised her chin with one finger, his expression sober as he examined the confusion in her face. "I seem to have taken you by surprise. Maybe it was a mistake, but I thought you were the kind of person who likes everything up front and out in the open."

"I do. I mean, I am that kind of person. It's just—you see, I don't have any guidelines for this kind of thing. New situations always throw me. But I'm very adaptable," she added quickly. "If you'll tell me the rules, I'll try to stick to them."

"As far as I know, there are no rules for 'this kind of thing.'"

His voice was gentle, but Faith knew he was amused. She didn't mind. In fact, she wouldn't have minded if he had wanted her to wear a jester's cap, as long as it kept the distant look from his eyes.

"Just be honest with me, Faith," he said quietly. "Tell me what you're feeling right now."

"I feel like hiding under the bed," she admitted ruefully. "Is that normal?"

"For you? Most likely." He laughed, then picked up her hand, running his thumb gently over the knuckles. "What else? What do you feel about me?"

"You don't ask the easy questions, do you?" she murmured. "I'm attracted to you. So what else is new? Every woman who comes within lusting distance is attracted to you.''

His fingers tightened briefly but fiercely on hers. "You're attracted to me, I'm attracted to you. I think we're making progress.''

"We are?" she said doubtfully. She gave a soft whistle, a helpless confused sound, and shook her head. "This is really something. I purposely stay away from the fleshpots and go to the back of beyond to play in the dirt, and this happens.'' She laughed. "It makes me wonder what would have happened if I'd gone to Cozumel.''

He put his arm around her shoulder and pulled her back against him. To her surprise, the action was more comforting than sensual. "You would have been propositioned by a muscle-bound, pearly-toothed certified public accountant instead of an ugly archaeologist.''

"A world-famous, incomparably sexy archaeologist.'' She raised her head, meeting his eyes. "You know, things like this don't happen. Not to me. Not to a mother-slash-homemaker-slash-dry cleaners manager.''

According to Marcos, Mike had been at the site for two weeks before Faith arrived. She supposed that when a man was in the habit of making love—and a man as attractive as Mike was surely in that habit—three weeks was an uncomfortable length of time to do without.

She glanced at him. "Why didn't you ask Sissy or Janice? Or would that have caused too many complications, since they're both members of the academic world, too?"

"I wonder where that wonderful mind of yours is taking you now?" he murmured, almost to himself. "Janice and Sissy are both intelligent, thoroughly nice women, but I have absolutely no desire to..." He paused thoughtfully. "I guess that about says it. I have no desire. For either of them." His voice was dry but emphatic.

"No chemistry?" she said, nodding in understanding. "I know what you mean. Rob is perfectly gorgeous... but no chemistry."

"That's a relief."

She studied his harsh features, searching diligently for a clue. "But with me, chemistry?"

"The whole damn laboratory—from the minute I laid eyes on you."

The intensity in his deep, rough voice sent a shiver of excitement running through her. "It just doesn't make sense," she said weakly. "I can see that if we spent months and months together you might eventually be won over by my top-notch niceness. But I'm not the kind of person who floors people. I'm the rule."

Laughing helplessly, he gave her a quick hug. "You are the most fascinating, and the most frustrating, woman I've ever met. And you've lost me again. You're what rule?"

"You know how they say that something unique is the exception to the rule? I'm the rule, the ordinary thing that the unique is the exception to."

He stared at her for a moment in silence, then turned his head to look into the fire and said quietly, "I've known you for a week, and I can tell you with absolute certainty that you've never seen an ordinary day in your entire life. You think you're ordinary because you live inside you. You're used to you. But believe me, darling, you would never get lost in a crowd."

He was sincere, she told herself in amazement. He had called her fascinating and darling...and he'd meant it.

At least, he sounded as if he did, she thought, letting doubt creep in. Faith hadn't had much experience with compliments, not the male-female kind. Maybe this was the way all men talked when they wanted to sleep with a woman. For all she knew, singles bars overflowed with this kind of thing.

He shifted his position restlessly, his expression wry. "You know, this is not going exactly the way I had planned it." He glanced down at her, frowning slightly. "Maybe I shouldn't have brought it out in the open like that. I'm not the smooth-talking, romantic type—but I guess you've noticed that. Would it have been better if we had stumbled onto each other in the middle of the night and gotten carried away by spur-of-the-moment passion?"

She rubbed her chin thoughtfully. "I don't know. Maybe. Passion is a sort of spontaneous thing, don't you think? At least, I've always supposed it was. Calculated passion somehow doesn't have the same ring."

Chuckling, he regained his comfortable position beside her. "This is probably the strangest conversation I've ever had with anyone." He paused, and when he spoke again, his voice was incredibly gentle. "Haven't you been with anyone since your husband left?"

She shook her head in a slightly distracted negative motion. Mike was right. It was a strange conversation, and the strangest part was that she wasn't embarrassed by the intimate quality of it. With Mike, it felt right.

"There was never the time," she explained. "And I suppose part of it was that I never met anyone I had any chemistry with." She frowned. "I guess I should have. It was practically my duty, emotionally speaking. If I were used to affairs, your—" She paused. "'Proposition' isn't the right word. 'Suggestion' is better. If I were used to affairs, your suggestion wouldn't have sent me into neurotic fits."

He was silent for a moment. "I can't be sure, but I don't think anyone has had quite that reaction to the idea of sleeping with me in the past." When she laughed at the chagrin in his voice, he stood and pulled her to her feet. "Bedtime. No, don't look like that. Me to my bed. You to yours."

He stroked her cheek with a feather-light touch. "I'm not going to pressure you, Faith," he said, his voice matter-of-fact. "I want you very much. One of my major failings is that when I feel most deeply, that's when I can't seem to form the right words. When it's important, I'm inarticulate. But don't ever doubt that I want you . . . very much. I want to learn the texture of you. I want to feel the softness of your skin beneath your clothes. I want to inhale the scent of you. I want to taste the essence of you." His hand tightened on her neck, and he drew a rough breath. "As a matter of fact, I would very much like to absorb you into my bloodstream." His lips twisted in a wry smile. "But I want you to want that as much as I do. That's necessary, Faith. It can't be any other way."

Then, as though they had been discussing nothing more urgent than the weather, he walked her to her bedroom and politely said good-night.

Two hours later Faith lay in the unfamiliar bed, her eyes wide open as she stared at the dark ceiling. She wished he hadn't said that last bit. The part about touching her and tasting her. He had started a fire in her that just wouldn't go out.

For more than nine years, since before Buster was born, Faith had dampened her natural need for sexual fulfillment. Somewhere in those first few months of marriage to C.C., when she began to see what kind of man she had married, she had lost her desire for him. All these years she had assumed that she had lost her desire, period. The night Mike had kissed her in

the moonlight, he had shown her that her thinking had
been wrong. Then tonight, with just a few words spoken in his raspy voice, he had redefined sexuality for
her.

She shifted restlessly, remembering the hunger in his
voice and in his eyes. It was real. No man was that
good at pretending.

On the other hand, she couldn't help thinking about
the jar he had shown her. Did that have anything to do
with the way Mike felt about her? Did he want Faith,
or was it the girl on the vase he wanted to make love
to?

She wished she had never seen the damn thing. He
said he had wanted her the minute he saw her, but she
remembered the stunned look that had been on his
face when she walked out of the woods. He had been
stunned because she looked like the image of a girl
from the past. Because she resembled that stupid
Chosen Woman.

It was all so confusing, she thought in frustration.
Then suddenly, she became still. She had forgotten
something.

She had forgotten the look on his face as he told her
that appalling story about his mother. She remembered the way she had felt when she saw the loneliness in his eyes. At that moment she had felt she would
give her life to make it go away.

The same look had been in his eyes when he told her
that he wanted her.

Groaning, Faith rolled over in the bed. This sounds serious, she thought warily. Oh yes, it definitely sounds serious.

What happened to not getting involved? she asked herself silently. What happened to not trusting her judgment, or her emotions? What happened to not making any more mistakes with men?

But she knew the answer. Mike had happened.

She was in love with him, she thought with a sigh. It was almost a relief to admit it. She loved him, and, even if it were only for a little while, he needed her warmth.

She rose from the bed and was moving toward the door when she heard a loud crash, then a muffled curse. She jerked open the door and ran down the hall.

"Mike?" She opened the door to his bedroom. "Mike, are you—"

The words were cut off as she stepped squarely into his waiting arms. He buried his face against her warm throat, his hands molding her hips. "Is this spontaneous enough for you?" he whispered against her flesh.

She gave a breathless laugh, loving the feel of his hands on her. "I decided it didn't matter if it was spontaneous. From you, I'll take my passion any way I can get it."

His arms tightened around her. For a long time, he didn't say anything; he merely held her. Then he whispered, "Thank you, love."

Lifting her in his arms, he carried her to the bed. "I didn't tell you how beautiful you are," he said as he laid her on the bed. "But you are." He slid the loose cotton gown from her shoulders. "You are."

She could see him in the faint moonlight. He wore the bottom half of cotton pajamas. Reaching out, she ran her fingers down his bare chest. "I've been aching—" She swallowed painfully. "*Aching* to touch you."

He met her eyes. "Have you? Have you really? I didn't know. Since the first day, I've been watching you ... watching how you move and how you laugh. But I was always watching you with the others. You didn't seem to want to get close to me." He gave a rough laugh. "I didn't think you liked me much. But then, when I kissed you ..." He exhaled a shaky breath. "You were so damn responsive, I didn't know what to think. I couldn't stop thinking about it. Thinking about what it would be like to ..."

He lay down beside her, the full length of his body against hers, her naked breasts pressed to his hard chest. It should have felt strange to her after nine years of being alone. But it didn't. It felt so natural, so right.

She had missed this, she thought in wonder. Not sex. She had missed Mike. All her life, without knowing it, she had been missing Mike.

Working slowly, with carefully gentle movements, Mike removed her gown, then slid away from her, only to return moments later. Now there was nothing between them, not even rational thought.

As he touched her, as he kissed her shoulders and her breasts, he spoke in a husky whisper. "I want to tell you what this means. I want to tell you how it feels, but I don't have the words. There aren't any words, Faith. I don't think they've been invented."

"You are telling me," she said, her eyes loving. "You tell me every time you touch me."

Kneeling between her thighs, he slid his hands beneath her buttocks and raised her slightly as he buried his face in the smooth flesh of her stomach. His breath was becoming harsh and labored, and the sound of it was more sensual than all the love words ever written.

"I can't get enough," he said with deep frustration.

Moving quickly, he placed his hands on either side of her head, staring down at her. He held himself above her, and even though their bodies were not quite touching, she could feel the heat. And she could see the question in his eyes.

"You said—you said I had to want it the way you do," she said. Her voice didn't sound right. She sounded hoarse and slightly drugged. "I want you as I've never wanted anything in my life. I feel as if I'll die if I don't have you. Will that do?"

Closing his eyes, he inhaled deeply. "Oh, yes. That will do just fine."

Lowering his body, he gripped her hips, joining them with one smooth thrust. Faith bit her lip to keep from crying out at the pleasure that rocked through her. How could she have lived so long without this? Without him?

It was the last thought she had before giving herself up to the tide of sensation that swept over her. Almost immediately she was shaken by uncontrollable, unbelievably intense spasms of release. Before she could return to earth, it happened again. And again. The husky laughter she heard in her ear had the sound of pure joy, of loving triumph. And when she thought there could be no more, she felt the incredible aching tension build in her again. This time, when she reached that unknown place, he was there with her.

He held her tightly, rocking her, gently easing her back to sanity, whispering loving words in her ears until her eyes closed in satisfied exhaustion.

With his head next to hers on the pillow, Mike watched Faith as she slept. He didn't touch her; he simply watched her. He wanted to memorize every feature. He wanted to be able to close his eyes and conjure up every bit of her.

God, she was beautiful, he thought in wonder. So beautiful. So loving.

For the rest of his life, he would hold the picture of how she looked when he touched her, as though he had brought all the joy in the world and laid it at her feet.

Then another, less welcome memory intruded. Uneasily, he recalled the way she had looked when he told her that he wanted to make love to her. She had been scared; that much had been painfully obvious. Was it just him, or was she wary of all men? She had been let down by Buster's father. It was logical that she should be afraid of being hurt again.

Mike didn't like to think of her ex-husband. It hurt to think that she had cared enough for a man to marry him. What hurt most was that the past might close doors for them in the present. If she was that frightened by the idea of making love, how was she going to react when Mike told her that he loved her? When he told her that he wanted to marry her?

Her son had been right—Faith needed someone to take care of her. And Mike desperately wanted to be that someone.

He reached out to touch her face, feeling an almost overwhelming surge of emotion. By some miracle, he had found the woman with whom he wanted to spend the rest of his life. He had finally found someone who was more important to him than his work, more important to him than life itself.

He couldn't believe that he had backed away from this feeling. Like a scared kid, he had hidden his emotions in the depths of his heart.

He was still scared, he admitted silently. Now that he had found her, it would kill him to have to go back to what he was, back to the loneliness that had ruled his life before Faith walked into it.

Please God, he prayed silently, if You'll just let her feel a fraction of what I feel, I won't ask for another thing in this life.

Chapter Eight

Faith was dreaming. She was dreaming that she stood on the mountain peak she had once seen in her imagination, the majestic place that would open the door to Truth. The sun shone around her with dazzling force, and as she lifted her face to it, the wind came up from nowhere, whipping around her. It was harsh but caressing as it stroked her flesh. With determined but gentle force, it entered her mind, then her heart. And suddenly Faith knew.

Opening her eyes with slow, lazy movements, she stared into the crystal-blue eyes of the man lying close beside her on the pillow. "Mike," she murmured, smiling as the memories of the night before became entangled with her dream. "It was you. You were the wind."

He halted the process of kissing her elbow to look at her reflectively, his eyebrows drawn together, almost meeting. "Too insubstantial. Couldn't I be a tree instead?"

Laughter bubbled up inside her. Grasping his face with both hands, she planted a brief, satisfying noisy kiss on his lips, then scrambled from the bed. Wrapping her arms tightly around her naked body, she glanced back at his lazily reclining figure, her pulse leaping at the sight of him.

"Do you suppose it's the altitude? Is that why my heart's dizzy?" Feeling electric energy grip her, she returned to the bed and grasped his shoulders in slender, urgent fingers. "Do you feel it, too? Mike, I can *feel* the blood moving through my veins. I can *feel* the thoughts in my head."

With swift, economical movements, he flipped her over, throwing one long leg across hers as his fingers threaded through her hair. "Yes," he said, and his raspy voice sent a rush of desire surging through her. "Yes, I feel it. But it's not the altitude." He kissed the slender V at the base of her throat. "It's you. And it's me." He kissed the valley between her warm breasts. "It's us. It's the magic of us."

As she ran her hands down the hard length of his back, she wondered how she would be able to do without touching him for the rest of her life. Closing her eyes tightly, she whispered, "Help me make the magic now, Mike."

"Oh, yes," he groaned and covered her mouth with his.

It was almost noon before they managed to leave his friends' house. Faith didn't want to leave even then, but there was Mike's business to take care of, and the city of Cuzco to explore. While his business didn't take more than half an hour to complete, Faith felt there would never be enough time to see all of Cuzco.

Spanish architecture dominated the area, but the legacy of the Inca could be seen at every turn. This— the oldest inhabited city in the western hemisphere— had once been the center of the Incan universe.

As they toured the city, Faith couldn't believe that the man walking beside her was the same man she had met only a week earlier. The stern professor was gone. He was her best friend. He was her first love. He was her childhood sweetheart.

He indulgently gave in to any whim that happened to pass through her mind, and, as though he had never been to Cuzco, shared her frantic excitement. At Kenko, an amphitheater whose immense blocks were so tightly joined that a knife couldn't be inserted between them, he echoed her oohs and aahs with angelic innocence until she threatened to throw a genuine Incan rock at him.

They didn't pause in their frenetic round of sightseeing, each of them feeling the need to crowd as much into the magic morning as possible. They saw Tambomachay, a bathhouse in an imperial reserve, its fountain still giving forth water as it had done for centuries. Remnants of Incan walls were everywhere, maintaining continuity with the city's rich past.

It was when they visited the Indian market that history came to life. The purring-clicking sibilance of a strange language rose into the thin, cold air around Faith. Then she realized she had heard it before. It was Quechua, Pacha's native tongue, and the ancient language of the Inca.

Llamas, the regal cousins of the camel, walked the street beside shoppers, the animals' tall, pointed ears decorated with streamers of colored wool or little bells of copper or silver.

"Mike," she whispered, grabbing his arm as he walked beside her. "I swear that animal is sneering at me."

He glanced at the llama that stood a few feet away. "Don't get any closer. If you annoy them, they'll spit at you."

"Thank goodness Buster's not here. He would try to get it to teach him how." She glanced around. "Speaking of my son, I'd better get a souvenir. It's a tradition with us. If I stay away overnight, I have to bring a gift or he doesn't let me back in the house."

He laughed. "That sounds like Buster," he said, moving with her toward a row of booths.

The Indians, mostly women, were pursuing a leisurely trade as they had for time out of mind. The babies that some of the women carried on their backs seemed to be a part of their brightly colored costumes. Faith saw mass-produced, dime-store trinkets next to intricate, handwoven rugs. The old and the new resting comfortably side by side. A few steps away a woman was offering a haunch of llama meat to another woman, who was reluctantly adding a potato at a time to the pile on the ground.

From the confusing collection, Faith chose a brown-and-cream handwoven poncho for Buster and laughingly accepted a silver llama on a chain from Mike.

"Okay, souvenirs taken care of," Mike said. "How about a drink?"

Faith studied his face. It was too innocent. Behind the aloof features she had once thought so cold, there was an evil sparkle that she was beginning to know and distrust. "A drink of what?" she asked suspiciously.

"Well...I suppose we could have *chicha*," he said, his tone offhand. "It's the native beer."

"Beer? That sounds harmless. Too harmless," she added, her eyes narrowed. "There's a catch somewhere. What do they make it out of—those genuine Peru bugs Buster's always talking about?"

He raised one brow, looking as haughty as the llama. "So young and so suspicious," he said in regret. "*Chicha*'s made of corn."

"Corn. Sounds interesting...and nontoxic." She moved closer to the booth selling the beer. "I like to try new things. It's just corn, right?"

"Would I lie to you?" His lips twitched, and laughter gleamed in his eyes. "The formula has been around for centuries."

He spoke to the woman at the booth, slipping money into her hand as she gave him a filled mug. Turning, he held the mug out to Faith. "You take corn, chew it to a pulp, spit it into a crock of brackish water and let it ferment. Guaranteed to put hair on your chest."

As her expression changed, Mike set the mug down, then leaned against the booth for support as both he and the Indian woman roared with laughter.

"You would have let me drink that stuff, wouldn't you?" she accused, as they walked away from the booth.

"Me? Of course not. Well, maybe a sip."

Blocking the punch she threw, he grabbed her up and swung her around. Revenge forgotten, Faith couldn't look away from his face. As overwhelming as the sights had been, it was Mike who made the day special. During the day, hundreds of minor triumphs had to be celebrated by a kiss, by a touch, by a special look. And as each minute passed, Faith became more and more certain that no one had ever loved anyone the way she loved this man. Never in the history of this city, in the history of the world, had anyone felt love as deeply and as richly as she did for Mike.

All morning he had watched her. He watched, and then he smiled. Just as he was smiling now.

Setting her back on her feet, Mike kept his hands at her waist and stared down at her. He would never get tired of looking at her. Each time seemed new and different and more wonderful than life allowed.

"Did I ever tell you that you're crazy-slash-adorable-slash-too sexy for words?" he asked, inhaling the perfume that was distinctly Faith.

How had he survived for so long without her? he wondered. Without this wonderful craziness she brought? Kissing her was like breathing in mountain air after a year in a smog-filled city. It revitalized. It invigorated. He could feel years of tension easing out of him.

For Mike, Faith held all the beauty of life in her hands. And even more astonishing, she was willingly sharing it with him. A lifetime of loneliness melted into nothing. She seemed to be saying, It's all here— life, happiness, excitement—it's all here for you. All you have to do is reach out and take it.

As she gazed up at his smiling face, Faith felt a sharp pain in her chest. The day was slipping away from her. There hadn't been enough time. She wanted to go back to his friends' house and hold him one more time. Just one more time.

But she knew it couldn't happen. Buster was waiting for her. Real life was waiting for her. And, as much as she loved her son, she couldn't help but feel a poignant sense of loss when they had to leave Cuzco behind.

Hiding her emotions, she did her best to keep Mike amused on the drive down the mountains. She told stories about her hometown folk and about her life with Buster. She told him about the classes she took each semester as she slowly made her way toward a degree in education. And when the stories ran out, they sang—everything from the Everly Brothers to Cole Porter. Only a music lover like herself could understand the pure joy of finding a voice that blended perfectly with one's own.

Hours later, but still too quickly, they came to the end of the rough dirt road that ran to the east of his tent. Faith closed her eyes briefly in a silent goodbye, inhaling slowly to ease the ache in her chest.

It was over. It had been only thirty-six hours, but those hours had changed her life forever. She would never be the same. One day, she told herself silently, sometime in the distant future when the pain faded, she would thank him for giving her these memories.

She smiled up at him. "I guess this is where I tell you what a wonderful time I had. And I did, Mike," she said earnestly. "I can't tell you how wonderful it's been."

Resting his arms on the steering wheel of the Rover, he didn't meet her eyes but stared straight ahead. "Has it?" he said quietly.

"Of course," she said, bewildered by his tone.

He shifted slightly. "Then why shouldn't we have more wonderful days together? Can you think of a reason?"

"I don't know what you mean." She laughed hesitantly. "Unless you own a plane, Austin to Wichita Falls is a little far to go for a date."

When he turned and met her gaze, she caught her breath at the intensity burning in his pale blue eyes.

"Marry me, Faith," he said in the same flat voice. "Marry me and let me take care of you and Buster."

Faith's mouth went dry. Never in her wildest dreams had she imagined anything like this. It made her dizzy; she couldn't think straight.

"Wait," she gasped. "I didn't—you're going too fast for me."

"Yes, I know. It's happened faster than I could have thought possible, too." He started to reach out, then dropped his hand. "Think about last night."

She felt heat come into her face as a fire raced through her bloodstream. With just a few words he had brought it all back, all the stunning pleasure, all the aching beauty.

"We have something special together," he said as he examined her features. "You haven't had all that much experience, but I have. And believe me, what happened between us last night was not ordinary. It was a once-in-a-lifetime thing, Faith. Why should we let that go? It was meant to be. I found the vase, and I found you. That means something." He drew in a slow, labored breath, then repeated harshly, "That means something."

The jar. She bit her lip to keep from crying out. For a moment she had thought—she had truly thought—that he felt something for her. But it was all because of the girl on the jar.

She couldn't respond. She wanted to. She tried to form words and thoughts, but she couldn't get past the hurt. It felt like a betrayal. Desertion by the man she had married hadn't brought a minute's pain, but the absence of just one small word from this man hurt like nothing she had ever felt. One small word, she thought. Love. Mike hadn't said anything about love. She was only now realizing just how desperately she wanted to hear that word from him.

"If you're worried about how Buster will take it, don't." He shifted his position restlessly, as though her silence made him uncomfortable. "Your son wasn't shy about letting me know he wanted me to marry you. He says you need someone to take the burdens off your shoulders. You told me that he needs a father, and your ex-husband can't be depended on for that. I would be a good father to him. We're already friends. So you—"

Faith's head jerked up abruptly, stopping the flow of words. "Buster came to you and told you—" She was too angry to finish the question. Too angry and too embarrassed. It was almost a relief to feel those emotions. Those were feelings she could handle.

Exhaling shakily, she said stiffly, "I'm sorry he put you through that. It must have been awkward for you."

"Didn't you hear what I said?" he asked in frustration. "I want to marry you."

"You're not proposing to me," she said through tight lips. "You're not even seeing me. You're seeing that girl on the vase. Her, and Buster's protective misconception of me."

He had a stunned expression on his face as he reached out, too late to take her in his arms. "Faith—"

"No," she said, moving away from him to press herself against the door. "Let me finish." She ran a trembling hand through her hair. "I'm not that wimp on the vase, and I'm not the helpless person Buster has told you about. Yes, I'm inadequate here. You've seen that for yourself. I've never even been camping before this trip. I'm out of my environment. Why shouldn't I be inadequate? I would be inadequate on a trip to the moon, too. But so would you.''

She clinched her fists tightly, feeling her nails dig into the palms of her hands. "Let me tell you about myself, Mike. My parents died when I was eleven. For five years I was passed around from one relative to another. That's enough to mess up a kid, but I survived. And I got good at surviving. I was sixteen when I married C.C. *Sixteen*, Mike. I was just a baby. Too young to know that his promises were lies. But I learned quickly enough. When he walked out on me, I was eighteen and had a six-month-old baby." She met his eyes firmly. "He never sent a penny. Not a penny. I had no training of any kind. I was just a dumb, frightened kid. But I survived. I carried Buster on my back like those women in the market today, and I scrubbed office floors at night. I could have gone on welfare, but I didn't. I survived. On my own. I fed Buster and clothed him and housed him. On my own. And in between all that, I raised a pretty damn good kid."

She released a shaky breath. "I'm strong, Mike. I had to be. Yes, I've made mistakes and I have weaknesses, but who doesn't?"

Opening the door, she stepped out of the car. Her eyes burned with the need to cry, but she refused to give in to it.

"Go find your vase and take care of it, Mike," she whispered, her eyes tired and filled with sadness. "That girl needs you. I don't."

Chapter Nine

Without moving, Mike watched Faith until she was out of sight. Then he opened the door and stepped out of the car. As he walked toward the tent, his movements were stiff and awkward, the movements of an old man. He felt old. He felt as though his blood were slowly being drained from his body.

Inside the tent, he looked around, examining the place. It felt unfamiliar, as though he were looking at someone else's possessions. Although he sat on the cot and stared for a long time, he couldn't seem to take in the colors. The world was suddenly composed of various shades of gray.

Lying back on the cot, he didn't try to relax his tense muscles. He knew it was impossible. He simply lay stiff and straight and listened to his jerky pulse ticking the minutes, then the hours, away as the light faded and the long night began.

His slow, steady breathing seemed to echo around him in the emptiness. Emptiness.

He hadn't shifted his position when the new day began to lighten the enclosed world around him, hurting his eyes. Moving slowly, he got up from the cot and moved to the chest on the other side of the tent.

After removing the cheesecloth from the jar, he returned to the cot and sat down. Holding the jar between his knees with both hands, he turned it slowly, over and over, as he stared not at it but at the recent past, at the night before. He tried desperately to remember the way she had looked when he made love to her, but he couldn't. All he could see was the way she had looked when she said she didn't need him.

Swallowing a dry lump in his throat, he glanced down at the jar, then away from it. Then, slowly, his expression changing, he looked at it again. Standing abruptly, he walked out of the tent and examined the jar in the sunlight, his heart beating loudly in his ears.

After a moment he closed his eyes tightly and let out a slow breath.

The night had been a long one for Faith. She had managed to get through the evening, answering Buster's excited questions and even laughing at the good-natured envy of the rest of the group. She would have liked nothing better than to crawl into the woods and hide, but this was a part of life. And as she had told Mike, she was a survivor.

Today, with only a couple of hours of restless sleep behind her, she didn't feel equipped to face the others, but she made herself go to the site. Although she went through the motions of working, she couldn't stop thinking about Mike and what had happened between them.

Life was so strange, she thought, giving an ironic laugh as she scraped at the dirt. Life had hidden Mike from her for all these years, then had given her a glimpse of real happiness, only to snatch it away again. It would have been better, easier, if he had never proposed. She almost hated him for that. He had forced her into an intolerable position. Knowing that he didn't love her, she had—by her own words— broken all links between them.

Why hadn't she let Ellen talk her into going to Cozumel? she thought in despair. If she hadn't come to the dig, she wouldn't have met Mike; she wouldn't have fallen in love, and she wouldn't be ripping her heart out for him now.

If only they had met under ordinary circumstances. Mike would have seen her as she really was, without the taint of the image on the vase between them. He could have seen that she was very able to take care of herself in her own world.

But then, he most likely wouldn't have looked at her twice. If he hadn't found the jar and fallen for the Incan girl, he most likely wouldn't have noticed Faith at all. Why on earth should he? she asked in disgust. She had told him more than once how ordinary she was. In her own world, he would have seen that for himself.

By wanting him to love *her*, the real Faith, exclusively, was she asking for too much? she wondered. People fell in love for all kinds of reasons, sometimes for all the wrong ones, and still managed to have a good life together. Maybe at times Mike got her mixed up with his Chosen Woman, but surely there were times when he was also seeing just Faith. Maybe it was up to her to take this fragmented beginning and help piece it into something solid.

With all her heart, she wanted to believe that. But in the back of her mind was the fear that someday he would wake up and say, "You're not her."

The thought brought a pain so swift and so sharp that she had to place one hand on the ground to keep herself from falling. She couldn't take a chance on it ending like that. Not for herself, and not for Buster.

Drawing a deep breath, she glanced around and saw that the others were leaving for lunch. Faith wasn't hungry, but she needed to move. She needed to get away from her thoughts for a little while.

Buster caught up with her and began to chatter enthusiastically. She glanced down at his un-pretty face. The fact that her son had gone to Mike with his problems had surprised her. He had never before indicated that he felt the lack of a father. Buster must have seen something special in Mike. As she had.

Suddenly, as she looked down at Buster, it was not her son's face she saw, but Mike's. And, as though he were standing beside her, she heard him say, "When I feel most deeply, that's when I can't seem to form the right words."

Faith caught her breath painfully. She had been listening to his words yesterday. Why hadn't she been watching his face? Why hadn't she heard what was behind his words?

She felt an urgent, overwhelming need to see him, to talk to him. This time she would watch his face. That was all it would take. If she watched his eyes, she would know. She would...

She glanced down as Buster began pulling at her arm with visible impatience.

"I'm sorry, Buster," she said, her voice distracted. "What did you say?"

"I was telling you about the Rock, but that's all right. I'll tell you the rest when I get back. Okay?"

"What?" She tried to get her thoughts together, but her heart was beating so fast that she couldn't think. "That's fine, Buster. You tell me the rest when you get back."

As soon as Buster ran off, Faith leaned against a boulder that rested on the edge of the path. As soon as she stopped shaking, she told herself, she would go to him. Even if she saw in his eyes that he didn't love her, she owed it to him, and to herself, to tell him how she felt. If she didn't, she had a feeling she would regret it for the rest of her life.

"Tired, Faith?"

She glanced up and saw Marcos walking toward her, in the direction of the camp. Pulling up a smile, she fell into step beside him. "No...just a little shaky." She glanced at him. "Did you abdicate as chief cook and doughnut maker?"

He laughed. "No, Pacha took over for me today." He paused. "I wonder why Mike didn't come by the site today?"

She shrugged stiffly. "You know Mike. He likes to be by himself."

"I wonder," Marcos said quietly. When he caught her glance, he went on. "You're probably right. Everyone thinks the same thing, but I've spent more time with him than the rest of you, and I think—" He broke off, shaking his head.

"What?" she asked, grasping his arm. "What do you think?"

"I think he's the loneliest man I've ever seen," he said softly. "So lonely it hurts to look at him."

She ran a distracted hand through her hair. "But he doesn't have to be, Marcos. Everyone loves Mike. He could have a harem, if he wanted."

He nodded. "Do you think that would make him less lonely? Mike's the kind of man who doesn't fit in a crowd. He needs that one special person who can come into his life and fill up the emptiness. If he were willing to settle for less he wouldn't be alone...but he would still be lonely."

Glancing down at her, he reached out and gave her a hug. "You don't need to be worried about Mike, though. He's a big boy. That kid of yours is another thing altogether. I can't understand why your hair isn't gray."

"Did he give you a lot of trouble while I was gone?"

"Of course not. We both loved it. He makes me miss my grandkids." He glanced over his shoulder at the path behind them. "Did he forget something at the site?"

"No." She frowned. "Why do you ask?"

"I just wondered why he was going back when there was no one there."

She stopped walking abruptly. "There's no one left at the site? Then why...?"

"I don't know," Marcos said, looking worried suddenly. "When he ran past me, he said he would see me later and that you knew what he was doing."

Faith bit her lip. He must have been trying to tell her something earlier when they were walking together. What was it? He had been talking about...

"Oh my God!" she gasped. "The Rock! He was talking about the Rock!"

Swinging around, she began to run. Toward the site. Toward the cliff that rose behind it. She heard Marcos yell that he would get the others, but she didn't answer. Her heart was going crazy with fear.

Please God, she begged silently. Please let Buster be all right. Please don't let Buster get hurt.

As she rounded a curve in the path, she heard him yell, and she skidded to a halt. Raising her gaze, she saw him immediately. He was halfway up the fifty foot rock face, looking so incredibly small against the white cliff.

Then, as she watched, holding her breath, he lost his grip.

Chapter Ten

For an endless moment fear held Faith captive. The world dimmed as she felt herself sway. She wanted to give in to the blackness that was closing in.

Forcing herself to stay upright, she watched as her son slid five feet, his hand grabbing at the rock. A smothered whimpering noise caught in the back of her throat as he managed to stop his sliding fall by grasping a small, pointed protrusion.

She stood paralyzed as her son dangled in the air, twenty feet from the ground. Then, with blessed speed, her maternal instincts kicked into gear, freeing her. She ran across the site to the foot of the cliff. And, without hesitation, she began to climb.

She knew she wouldn't be able to approach him from below. There was nothing below him except a sheer drop, and to attempt that would only cause them both to fall. She would have to pass him and climb to the ledge above and slightly to the right of him, then pull him up.

"I'm coming, Buster—no, don't look down! Just hold on for a little while longer."

"My hands hurt." His voice sounded weak, and so scared. "I don't know if I can hold on."

"Sure you can." She had to struggle to keep her voice calm, but she knew she couldn't let him hear the fear. "You're the superkid, remember? Just hold on tight for a little while. I'm almost there."

With every word, she moved upward, uncaring that her hands and knees were being scraped raw. She knew only that she had to get to him.

"When we get down, I'll get the camera and take a picture of the Rock. When—" She paused as she lost her foothold and fell hard against a sharp point. Gripping a crack in the rock, she held on and felt around with her foot until she had found another support. "When we get home, you can show your friends the picture. That'll be better than Jason's pictures of Disneyland." She drew in a hot, dry breath. "I'm almost there, Buster. I'm almost there."

Mike walked into camp and glanced around. Frowning, he saw Marcos running toward the path carrying a rope. The other three men and both the women were just ahead of him.

As Janice ran past him, Mike caught her arm. "What's wrong? Where's everyone going?"

"It's Buster," Janice told him, her eyes worried. "They think he's trying to climb the Rock."

Mike stiffened. "Where's Faith?" he asked tightly.

"She's already there," Janice said. "When Marcos came back here to get the others, she went back to the Rock."

Dropping her arm, Mike began to run. He arrived at the site just behind the other men. Raising his eyes, he scanned the cliff, and then he saw them. Faith was a few feet to the right of Buster. And they were both almost twenty-five feet up the rock face.

"Don't try to grab him now," he whispered hoarsely. "Not now, love. You'll both fall."

As though she had heard him, she passed Buster and began to pull herself onto a narrow ledge. She had almost gained it when she suddenly wobbled and one knee slid off the ledge.

Mike clenched his fists so tightly they hurt. He had never felt so helpless in all his life. The tension in him eased slightly when she regained her balance, then quickly rose to her knees. She braced her lower back against the rock, then reached down and grasped Buster's wrists.

The next few minutes, as Faith slowly pulled Buster up, felt like a lifetime as Mike stood stiff and still, whispering encouragement to her, telling her over and over again how much he loved her, how much he needed her.

Then, finally, Buster had his knees on the ledge beside Faith. Letting go of the boy with one hand, she pulled him tightly to her.

As the others cheered, Mike felt relief shake through him. He leaned weakly against the stone wall of an Incan building and wiped cold sweat from his face.

He cleared his throat roughly, then shouted, "Faith, are you all right? Is Buster okay?"

For a moment there was only silence; then he heard her voice. It was weak and shaky. "We're fine. But, Mike?"

"Yes?"

"I'm afraid to look," she shouted breathlessly. "I don't think we can get down again."

He gave a harsh laugh. "That's all right," he shouted. "We'll get you down."

Tip, Rob and Pacha were already on their way up the half-covered steps that rose beside the cliff, taking the rope with them. Within minutes they began to slowly lower Buster to the ground.

Mike stood below the cliff and caught the boy tightly in his arms. But Buster didn't want to be held. Although he was a little pale, his natural exuberance had reasserted itself, and he stood beside Mike, yelling words of encouragement to his mother as she was lowered safely to the ground.

Mike stepped to catch her, but Marcos reached her first. Mike had to watch as the older man caught her in his arms and supported her.

Buster ran to his mother, hopping around with excitement as he talked about the adventure they had just had. Dropping behind, Mike watched as the three of them walked ahead of him along the trail.

Although she was still leaning on Marcos and smiling down at Buster, Faith's mind wasn't on them, or on the adventure she and her son had just had. It was on Mike. He hadn't said a word since he had told her they would help her down from the ledge. She could feel his gaze on her and knew he was behind them on the path, but he made no effort to catch up.

When they reached camp, everyone gathered around her and Buster, talking excitedly. Faith smiled ruefully as she watched Janice and Sissy making a fuss over Buster. The little monster, she thought, wanting to strangle him and hug him at the same time.

At that moment she felt a hand on her arm, and before she could even look up, she was being pulled into the tent she shared with her son.

Raising her gaze, she met Mike's eyes. Her lip trembled slightly; then suddenly she was in his arms. He held her tightly against him, so tightly that she couldn't catch her breath, but she didn't care. She only knew that his embrace was where she had always belonged.

"Don't—" he began harshly. She could feel him swallow; then he began again. "Don't ever scare me like that again."

When she felt a tremor shake through his body, she moved even closer to him in a protective movement. "No...no, I promise."

"I spent all morning writing," he said, with his face pressed to her hair. "I thought maybe if I wrote the words you would understand."

"Don't," she whispered roughly. "I was wrong, Mike. I was so wrong."

"So was I." He moved away from her slightly, but he didn't loosen his tight grip on her waist. "Out there at the cliff, when I realized that you could—" He broke off and drew a deep breath. "When I thought you could be hurt, I knew that if anything ever happened to you...I wouldn't want to live, Faith. I wouldn't want to be in the world if you weren't in it. That's why I've got to explain to you about the jar."

"You don't—"

"No." He shook his head jerkily. "I have to. I looked at the jar this morning. It's the first time I had seen it since I showed it to you." A self-mocking smile twisted his lips. "You were right—she doesn't look a thing like you. But the thing you don't understand is that I didn't have you mixed up with her. I had her mixed up with you. When I thought of the girl on the jar, it was your face I saw, not the other way around."

Dropping his hands from her waist, he turned away from her. "I admit I was initially intrigued by the likeness I thought I saw. But later, as I watched you, it wasn't a long-dead woman I was thinking of. It was you. I resented the way you drew people to you, and I couldn't figure out why I should feel that way. I understand now. I didn't want to share you with the others. I didn't want your warmth to be for anyone except me."

He turned to face her. "I changed my mind about the girl on the jar. She wasn't one of the Chosen Women. I don't know how I know, but I'm positive she was a sacrifice. And although she was a victim, she was a willing victim. You could never be a victim, Faith. You're strong and stubborn and loving. That was what you didn't understand. It wasn't the woman on the jar I fell in love with. It was you, Faith." He drew in a long, shaky breath. "I know that you don't need me, Faith, but I need you. I need you so badly I think I might die from it."

She shook her head frantically. "I didn't mean it—I didn't mean it, Mike. I was lying...to you and to myself. I was trying to convince myself that I could make it without you because—"

"I know," he said, pulling her roughly into his arms. "Because you were afraid. Like me. But neither of us will ever have to be afraid again."

"No," she whispered against his lips. "We won't ever be afraid or lonely again. You, me, and Buster—we're a family now."

The minute the words left her lips, they heard a whooping yell outside the tent. Pulling away from Mike, she walked to the opening and drew back the flap.

Buster had his hands thrown up as he jumped into the air in triumph. "Can I fix it or can I fix it?" he yelled in excitement. Glancing over Faith's shoulder at Mike, he said, "Didn't I tell you? You people should listen to me more often. Hey, Marcos! You want me to find you a wife? There's this lady that works in the lunchroom—"

Laughing helplessly, Faith leaned against Mike and looked up into his fiercely loving blue eyes. "Welcome aboard," she said.

Billie Green

I'm an observer. I'm more comfortable watching people than interacting with them. I've never seen a new place or met a new person that I've found dull. Everything piques my interest. Watching, listening and learning excite me.

There are two aspects to being an observer: the plus and the minus. On the plus side is tolerance. The character traits found in some human beings that are guaranteed to annoy or exasperate or anger a normal person don't get the same reaction from an observer. An observer merely finds these traits interesting symptoms of the human condition and will usually dig deeper to find the cause.

On the minus side is isolation. An observer is an individual separated from the rest of the world. The feeling of being different and separate results in the need to pretend. An observer, when it is necessary to venture into the territory outside her own head, must assume roles. Simply living in this world brings obligations. She has to pretend to be a mother. Or a friend. Or a writer. At the very least she must pretend to be normal and sane.

I'm fortunate in that I've found a partner who, while not understanding my nature, accepts it. He knows that I can make only quick trips into the outside world, then I have to run back to my home turf. When I can't cope with reality, he copes for me. He handles relatives and friends, pastors and teachers, and makes them believe that I'm an ordinary mother and wife. Although he doesn't enter my world, he's the valiant guardian at the gate. He's my trusted messenger. He's the tour guide who leads me through the foreign territory of the real world.

Sometimes I wish I were the kaffeeklatsch/PTO president/life of the party type person. But only for my family and my valiant guardian. For myself, I can't imagine living in a better place. On a daily basis, in any direction I look, wonders unfold for me. And because I'm a writer, I can share the wonders I discover with others.

Writing is my interaction with the outside world. It's the thing that ties me firmly to the rest of the human race and makes me not quite so separate after all.

Billie Green

FIESTA!

Barbara Faith

One Perfect Summer

There is a time in everyone's life for a change of season. That time came for me when I was in my late thirties. I'd been working at the same job for ten years. I'd lived in the same apartment in the same sunny city for twelve years. And I'd been dating the same men for what seemed like forever. If anyone needed a change of *something*, it was me.

The beginning of summer seemed a good time to make a change. I quit my job, put some of my things in storage and packed my clothes, my typewriter and my books into my not-too-dependable car. On the first day of June I began my journey to Mexico.

I had decided to go to a mountain town much like the one I wrote about in *Fiesta!* It's a small place, but there was, and is, a fine school for artists and writers there.

For the first few days I stayed in a homey-type hotel; then I rented a furnished apartment on the hotel grounds for fifty dollars a month. The wicker furniture wasn't comfortable, but there was a fireplace, a small room upstairs where I could write and a roof garden where I planted bright red geraniums.

I settled in to study Spanish, to write and to go to school. By strenuous penny-pinching I'd been able to buy myself a year. I had no time for fooling around or for dating.

Famous last words. Two weeks after I arrived, a woman friend I'd made at the hotel asked me to go out and listen to some music with her. We went to a place much like the one I described in my story. That's where I met Alfonso.

I knew right away, unbelievable as it may seem, that

he was the man I'd been waiting for. I felt such a sense of belonging with him, something I'd never felt with anyone before.

We fell in love that summer, and suddenly a whole new world opened up for me. I learned about an ancient culture, so different from my own. I began to speak pretty fair Spanish, and I started writing my first book. Alfonso took me to Mexico City to meet his family. They were warm and wonderful, and they gave this unsure-of-herself *gringa* a loving welcome.

Finally, just like all storybook romances, we were married—not once, but twice.

The first marriage was a civil one in the courthouse in Tampico, Mexico, on a sunny end-of-summer's day. The next took place thirteen summers later in a sixteenth-century church in the medieval village of Covarrubias, Spain. I carried wildflowers and held tight to Alfonso's hand as we repeated our wedding vows before a priest and afterward signed our names in a centuries-old wedding book.

Summer and love seem to go together. I'll never forget that special summer in Mexico, or all of the summers that have come after.

Chapter One

It was the coldest September anyone ever remembered in this part of Mexico It was especially cold in Santa Catarina, the colonial town high in the Sierra Madres where Annmarie Bannister had chosen to spend her vacation. Because the temperatures in Orlando were still in the high eighties when she'd left there, and because Mexico was—like in the song— south of the border, she'd expected it to be hot there, too. But it wasn't.

Annmarie shivered and buried her chin in the rolled collar of the heavy Indian sweater, wondering if she'd made a mistake in choosing Santa Catarina instead of one of the tropical resorts like Puerto Vallarta or Acapulco.

She'd been thinking about this Mexican trip for over a year, and had prepared for it by taking Spanish classes. But she'd been undecided about where to go until one of her classmates came to school with photos he'd taken there. Annmarie had looked at them with interest and when she'd come to a picture of Santa Catarina she'd known that was the place she wanted to go. A picturesque mountain town that had long ago been designated a national monument in order to preserve its Spanish colonial atmosphere, it seemed more Mexican to her than any of the beach-side resorts.

That had been almost seven months ago. She'd arranged to take her two-week vacation in September and for an extra two weeks without pay. By the end of August her Spanish had improved and she'd read everything she could about Mexico.

Last week she'd packed her clothes, closed up her apartment, and had a farewell dinner with both of her parents. They'd argued with each other and with her all through dinner and she'd felt a sharp sense of guilt, as well as relief, when she told them goodbye. At dawn the next morning she'd headed her eight-year-old car south. Four days later she reached Santa Catarina and found La Quinta, the small inn that her night school friend had suggested.

More homey than elegant, La Quinta had twenty rooms that opened onto an outside corridor, a dining room and a garden. The rooms were adequate and the garden was filled with red hibiscus and flowering bougainvillea, and the paths that crisscrossed to the center fountain were lined with calla lilies and blue-bells. In the middle of the day, when the sun was warm and the temperature rose into the sixties, hundreds of yellow butterflies darted among the flowers like golden rain.

But the mornings and the evenings were chillingly cold. This morning Annmarie had bundled herself into two sweaters when she'd gone into the dining room for breakfast. She'd just sat down at a table near the fireplace when a middle-aged woman with a pleasant face and a bad haircut stopped at her table and asked to join her.

When Annmarie nodded warmly the other woman pulled out a chair. "You're new here, aren't you? It's a great place. Did you come for the fiesta?"

"The fiesta?" Annmarie shook her head. "I didn't even know there was going to be one."

"There's always a fiesta in Mexico," the woman said with a grin. "But this one's special—it goes on for nine or ten days. There'll be Indian dancers, fireworks, parades, bullfights, you name it." She held her hand out. "I'm Rose Cameron."

"Annmarie Bannister. How long have you been in Santa Catarina?"

"Almost a year. I live in one of the apartments just in back of the hotel."

"But what do you do? It's such a small place. Don't you get bored?"

"Bored?" Rose laughed. "Not in Santa Catarina. There's too much to see and too much to do."

"Like what?" Annmarie asked curiously.

"Like the fiesta. Like the market on a Sunday morning when the Indians come in from the mountains. Like Saturday nights when the band plays in the kiosk in the park and all the local kids walk around and around the plaza and flirt." Rose looked up with a smile as the waitress approached. She ordered *café con leche* and turned back to Annmarie. "There are a couple of hundred other North Americans here. Some of them are retired. Some are artists or writers. Others are here to study art or archaeology or Spanish.

I've made a lot of friends. We get together for dinner once or twice a week. And I spend a lot of my time helping out in the local orphanage. I enjoy it, and I love the kids. I'll take you with me next time I go if you'd like to see it."

"Maybe," Annmarie said noncommittally.

"If you don't have other plans, why don't you come to dinner with me tonight, and afterward we'll go out and listen to some music?"

"I don't think—"

"The Posada Catarina is a great little place. Perfectly all right for a couple of women to go alone, if that's what's worrying you."

"No, that doesn't worry me." Which was a lie, of course. Annmarie was in a strange country, she didn't know the local customs, and she wasn't sure how she felt about going out alone at night. On the other hand, as long as she was in Santa Catarina she might as well get out and look around.

For years she'd been telling herself it was high time she left the security of the place where she'd grown up so she could see what the rest of the world was like. She knew she'd been overprotected as a child, and although she'd longed for adventure it had been hard to break away from the comforting, but sometimes smothering, attention of her parents.

Two years ago she'd moved into her own apartment. Both of her parents had taken it badly, despite her age. Her mother had cried, and telephoned her three times a day. Her father had constantly warned her about the risks for a single woman living alone.

They'd complained bitterly about this trip to Mexico but for the first time in her life Annmarie had stood firm. Now as long as she was here she was determined to enjoy herself. So she smiled at Rose and said, "Thanks for asking me, Rose. I'd love to have dinner with you and listen to some music."

"That's great. You'll like the place. The guitar music is wonderful and they've got a couple of really good singers—and a fireplace. That alone should tempt you."

Whatever it was that had tempted Annmarie, here she was, stumbling along the unfamiliar cobblestone streets with Rose Cameron.

The soft strumming of the guitars became audible as they rounded the corner. Beneath a sign that read La Posada Catarina there was a door. They entered and went down a few steps into a smoky, dimly lit room. Rose paused and looked around. "There's a table near the fireplace," she said, and began to thread her way through the crowded room.

Suddenly a rugged-looking man with a short red beard called out, "Hey, Rose, where're you going? Why don't you come and join us?"

Rose stopped and looked at Annmarie hesitantly then said, "Sure, Vince, thanks. This is Annmarie Bannister. She's new in town. Annmarie, I'd like you to meet Vince Stolarski and Diego Ortiz."

Annmarie nodded and said, "How do you do." She didn't want to sit with two men she'd never met, but the man whose name was Diego something stood up and pulled out the chair next to him.

"Please," he said in a slightly accented voice. "You have only just arrived in Santa Catarina? How do you like it?"

"It seems very...pleasant." She blew on her hands.

"But cold, yes? This is most unseasonable weather."

"That's what we say in Florida when the oranges freeze. The temperature was in the eighties when I left."

"So of course this cold bothers you. We must get you something hot to drink." Diego signaled for the waiter. *"Un ponche para las señoritas,"* he said. Turning to Rose he asked "Is that all right for you, Miss Cameron?"

"Yes, Diego. Thanks."

He turned back to Annmarie. *"Ponche* is like a mulled wine," he explained. "It will warm you."

She was very nice to look at, Diego thought, blond and blue-eyed, a typical *gringa*. Her cheeks were rosy from the cold and so was the tip of her rather pretty nose. It was impossible to see what her figure was like under the heavy sweater, and finally curiosity overcame his manners. "It's warm enough in here," he said, "Why don't you take your sweater off?" And he felt oddly pleased when she did, to see that beneath the bulky wool, she was wearing a long-sleeved blue dress and that her figure was as good as he'd hoped it would be.

When the woman with the guitarists began to sing, Diego asked Annmarie to dance.

Annmarie wasn't sure she wanted to dance with him, but before she could respond he was already standing, holding his hand out to her. She took it and let him lead her over to a small cleared space near the fireplace.

When Diego put his arms around her and Annmarie looked up at him, a peculiar thing happened. She suddenly felt at ease. That was the only way she could explain it. All of the strangeness of the past few days vanished the moment he took her in his arms.

He was taller than she was. His hair looked almost blue-black and his eyes were hazel with a warm flash of gold. There was a quiet elegance about him—in his carriage, in the way he moved, and in the cut of his clothes—which pleased her. She felt the warmth of his hand against her back, the strength of his shoulder under her hand. He cupped her hand in his and brought it up against his chest.

Annmarie closed her eyes and gave herself up to the music of the guitars, to the throaty voice of the singer and to the warmth of Diego Ortiz's arms.

"I'm glad you came here tonight, Ann Mary," he said.

"It's Annmarie. One word." She looked up at him and now she felt a mixture of emotions; the comfortable part was still there, but with it she felt a sense of growing excitement and just a touch of apprehension that wasn't altogether unpleasant.

He tightened his hand on hers. "I will call you Annamaria. Is that all right?"

Right now he could have called her anything, Sadie, Hildegarde, Mehetabel, it wouldn't have mattered.

"Where are you staying?"

In his arms she forgot the rules about never telling a stranger where you lived. "At La Quinta."

"Good!. So am I." He squeezed her hand. "I will walk you back there tonight, yes?"

"No. I . . . I mean, I came with Rose."

"Then I will walk the two of you back."

The music stopped but Diego didn't release her from his arms. Finally he brought her hand up to his lips and kissed it. "I'm very glad you came here tonight."

Annmarie looked at him. "Yes, so am I."

"That was a long dance," Rose commented when they went back to the table.

"The two of you looked pretty good together." Vince raised his glass. "How long are you going to be in Santa Catarina, Annmarie?"

"I'm not sure. Another two or three weeks at least."

"It's good luck that you came in time for the fiesta. It starts next week, you know."

"Yes, Rose told me."

"There'll be lots of things going on. Parties, Indian dancers, bullfights. You ever go to a bullfight?"

"No, and I never will. I think bullfighting's a vicious, murderous sport! I can't imagine anyone participating in it. I'm afraid if I went I'd root for the bull."

Rose frowned and glanced at Diego. "Be careful, Annmarie, Diego's a matador." She looked at him. "You're fighting in the first *corrida*, aren't you?"

He nodded, his expression suddenly closed. "Perhaps that will be the day the bull wins, Miss Bannister."

Annmarie looked at him. Hot color flushed her face. "I didn't mean... I...I'm sorry," she stammered. She saw Rose's embarrassed expression and Vince's angry look. She stood up, grabbing her sweater. "Please forgive me," she said to Diego.

Then, without a backward glance, she turned and fled the café.

The street outside the *posada* was quiet. A few lights swayed from their stanchions, patterning the cobbled streets. Couples stood in shadowed doorways, young body leaning against young body.

Annmarie was so furious with herself that tears stung her eyes. For the first time in a long while, she'd met someone she liked, someone she wanted to get to know better, and she'd ruined it with one stupid remark.

"Fool," she said aloud.

She heard footsteps behind her and quickened her pace. But when she heard her name she turned to see Diego coming down the street toward her.

"You shouldn't walk alone at night," he said when he reached her. "Especially in those heels. And you haven't put your sweater on. Here, let me help you."

He helped her on with it, then took her arm.

Because Annmarie didn't know what to say, she motioned toward the doorways and asked, "Why do they stand outside like that?"

"Perhaps they have nowhere else to go. Sometimes their families only have one or two rooms, and there are younger brothers and sisters, or of course there could be a father who doesn't approve of a young man calling on his daughter." Diego looked at her. "What about your father? Does he agree with your travelling to another country by yourself? Or are young American women so liberated they no longer care what their parents think?"

There was a strong hint of disapproval in his voice and Annmarie stiffened. "I care what my parents think," she said defensively. "But at the moment they're in the middle of an unpleasant divorce. I didn't want to take sides, so this seemed like a good time for a vacation."

Diego looked down at her. "A divorce? That must be difficult for you. I'm sorry."

"Don't be. They've been fighting for as long as I can remember. They should have been divorced years ago and if it weren't for me, they probably would have." She tried to pull away from him, but one of her heels slipped on a cobblestone and she would have fallen if he hadn't held her.

"Cuidado," Diego cautioned. "Careful." He tightened his arm around her. "You must wear walking shoes when you go out here. It is impossible to walk on these cobblestone streets with heels." When

she didn't answer he asked, "Do you have brothers and sisters?"

Annmarie shook her head.

"A *novio*, a boyfriend?"

"No." She looked up at him and stopped. "Diego, I'm so sorry about what I said earlier about bullfighting. I didn't mean it. I don't know anything about bulls or bullfights, but I hate violence and I can't imagine why a man would risk his life that way." She paused, and putting her hand on his arm said, "But I'd never want anything to happen to anybody...to you."

Diego looked at her face, illuminated by the pale light of a streetlamp. When he'd seen her enter the *posado* tonight he'd thought she was a pretty blond *gringa*, here for some fun on her vacation, and that he was going to be the one to make sure that her time in Santa Catarina was memorable. But when he had danced with her she'd seemed so fragile in his arms and a feeling he hadn't had in a long time came over him. He felt as though he wanted to protect her—because in some way he couldn't define, she was different from other women. Then he'd become infuriated when she'd made that remark about the bullfights.

Before he could stop himself Diego put his hand on the back of her neck, under her long blond hair, and drew her toward him.

"I'm sorry if I hurt you," she whispered.

"It's all right. It's because you don't know, you don't understand." The gentle pressure of his fingers drew her closer.

"Diego? Diego, I—"

But he stopped her words with a kiss so tender, so warm and caring that her lips softened under his and she sighed against him, content to be in the shelter of his arms.

When she stepped away from him a smile trembled on her lips. "We're like the couples who stand in the doorways," she said.

"Yes." Diego rested his hand against the side of her face and wondered what it was about this woman that touched him so.

The weather cleared and warmed. Annmarie didn't speak to Diego during the next few days, although she would have liked to. She saw him once in the street near the market, but he was talking to several men. He didn't see her and she hesitated to interrupt.

He looked different from the other night; he was wearing jeans, smooth Spanish boots and a blue-and-white checked shirt. His face appeared serious and she wondered if he was discussing the coming bullfight.

She'd seen posters advertising the *corrida* all over town, featuring Diego wearing his *traje de luces*, the traditional suit of lights. His body looked slender and graceful and there was an aesthetic, almost sensual expression on his face as he passed the bull close to the yellow and magenta cape.

Annmarie looked at the photograph for a long time. What kind of a man was this Diego Ortiz? she wondered. He was strong, he was sensitive. He was a killer of bulls. She shook her head, unable to reconcile the man who'd kissed her with such tenderness with the man in the poster.

She didn't know yet whether she would go to the first *corrida* of the fiesta. She didn't think she would.

Chapter Two

The bells started first, some of them ringing with a deep resonance that was pleasing to the ear, others clanging sharply with such staccato insistence that the pigeons nesting in the bell towers were routed from the church steeples. A chorus of bird songs mingled with the imperious crowing of roosters and the harsh yelping of street dogs.

The morning sounds seemed muted when the firecrackers started. At first there were only a few tentative pops, then a whole volley of explosive sounds burst into the air.

The first day of fiesta had begun.

The Indians began coming into town before sunup from the surrounding mountains and smaller villages—as they would for the next nine days. Their burros were loaded with wares to sell in the marketplace. Water jugs, serapes, huaraches, straw hats, mats, pottery and wicker chairs with painted seats. The ones who didn't have burros fastened wide bands to their heads and carried the weight of their wares on their backs. The women followed, most of them with babies wrapped tightly to their bodies in faded black-and-gray *rebozos*. Small children trotted behind.

Produce trucks, piled high with oranges, papayas and tangerines, bananas from Veracruz, strawberries from Irapuato, passed the Indians and rumbled ahead of them.

The bulls that would fight in the first *corrida* had arrived by truck the day before.

There was one last sharp explosion, followed by loud bursts and dwindling pops. Annmarie opened one eye and groaned; then with a sigh she sat up in bed and ran a hand through her tousled hair.

When she had dressed and went into the dining room for breakfast, Rose waved to her. "Vince is going to buy tickets for the *corrida* tomorrow," she said. "Shall I have him buy one for you?"

"I don't think so."

Rose cut into a thick slice of ham and said thoughtfully, "Look, Annmarie, it's none of my business, but it seems to me that as long as you're here in Mexico you ought to participate in things. I know that most of us North Americans think bullfighting is a vicious sport and we can't imagine why anyone would watch it. But actually, it isn't a sport, it's a fiesta, a spectacle that began hundreds of years before the birth of Christ on the island of Crete. It's been around for a lot of years and it's important to an awful lot of people—in Spain and Portugal, parts of France and South America, as well as here in Mexico.

"Boys in the States are brought up loving football and baseball; a Latin boy is brought up to love bullfighting and soccer. I just don't think we can summarily dismiss something that means so much to people in other countries just because it's not something we're familiar with."

Rose took a sip of her coffee. "End of lecture," she said. "Now, would you like to go to the *corrida* tomorrow with Vince and me?"

Annmarie really didn't have any choice, not after the speech she'd just been given. "Why, yes, of course I'd like to go," she said with a touch of irony. "How nice of you to ask."

"Good. We'll leave here about three-thirty and walk over to the bullring." She paused and looked toward the door. "Here comes Diego," she said, and with a wave of her hand, motioned him over.

"Buenos días," he greeted them. "May I sit down?"

"Buenos días, Diego." Rose motioned to a chair. "Yes, please join us."

"Gracias." He looked at Annmarie. "How are you getting along? Are you becoming more acquainted with our town?"

She nodded. "I've been to the market. I've poked in all the shops and I've seen most of the churches. I'm beginning to know my way around. Are you from Santa Catarina, Diego?"

"I was born in a small town near the coast, but I call Santa Catarina my home because I came here to live with my uncle when I was sixteen. He had a brave bull ranch outside of town and that's where I lived and began to train. My first *corrida* was here in Santa Catarina."

He thought that Annmarie looked very pretty and fresh this morning and he had an overwhelming urge to touch her. Because he did he forced himself to look at Rose. "Will you and Vince be at the plaza tomorrow?"

"Of course! I've even talked Annmarie into joining us."

"Are you sure you want to go?" he asked Annmarie.

"No." She laughed. Without thinking she touched the back of his hand and said, "But I'll go, and I promise you, I won't root for the bull."

"If you do I'll feed you to him." Diego rolled his hand over and captured her fingers.

Annmarie tried to look away, but she was held by the sheer magnetism of his eyes and by the warmth of his hand on hers.

"Well..." Rose cleared her throat. She pushed back her chair and stood up. "I've got to meet Vince," she said. "I'll see you two later."

"Fine." Diego let go of Annmarie's hand and stood up. When Rose left he said, "I like her."

"Yes, so do I."

"The nuns at the orphanage say that she's wonderful with the children. Did she tell you she helps out there?"

Annmarie nodded. "She asked me if I'd like to visit."

"Visit!" Diego laughed. "She's trying to recruit you." He took her hand again. "If you've finished your breakfast will you come out with me for a while?"

His eyes held her again and she murmured, "Yes."

He stood up, then pulled her chair back and led her out of the dining room. When they were in his car he said, "I thought you might enjoy getting out into the country. Did you visit anywhere else in Mexico before you came here?"

"I didn't really visit, I just passed through places. I crossed the border at Laredo. I spent the night in Monterrey and San Luis Potosi and—"

"You drove alone all the way from Florida?"

Annmarie nodded. "It was a long trip."

"You're too young to have made a trip like that alone. Your parents shouldn't have let you. A Mexican woman would never think of making such a trip."

"But I'm not a Mexican woman," Annmarie shot back. "Besides, I'm not a child. I'm twenty-four."

"As old as that?" Diego smiled at her. Her face was naturally fresh and her only makeup was a hint of color on her lips. She'd combed her shoulder-length blond hair back from her face and held it in place with a barrette. She was wearing a simple long-sleeved white shirt, a dark green skirt and sandals. She looked so infinitely desirable that it took every bit of Diego's willpower not to pull the car over to the side of the road so that he could kiss her.

He took the road that led up into the mountains. The air was cooler here, but the sun was warm and the day was bright with promise. They spoke little as Diego drove. He switched the radio on and found a station that played Mexican music.

Annmarie listened for a moment, and said, "That's lovely. I wish I understood the words."

"The name of it is 'Mañana.'" Diego began to sing, first in Spanish, then in English, words that told of a man far away from his love. "'When you are alone, remember me,'" he sang. "'When your lips yearn for my kisses and your eyes weep, remember me....'" He smiled at her. "We Mexicans are much too sentimental."

"No." Annmarie shook her head. "I like it. It's a beautiful song. I wish I understood more Spanish. I've been taking night classes back home, but I haven't learned nearly enough."

"There's a school for Spanish in Santa Catarina. You could study there."

Annmarie looked down at the hands folded in her lap. "But I won't be here very long," she said. "Not long enough to really learn."

"No, I don't suppose you will."

They didn't speak after that, not until Diego turned the car off the winding road onto a dirt trail that led through an overgrowth of shrubs and trees. When he stopped he said, "Come, I want to show you something."

They got out of the car and Diego took Annmarie's hand and led her through the trees. "We're going to climb a bit here. It's a little difficult but believe me, the view is worth it."

Diego held her hand to guide her over the rough spots, and when at last they reached the top he led her to an overhang of rock. "This is one of my very favorite views," he said.

It seemed to Annmarie that she could see forever. Valleys and rivers, small farms and fields stacked with sheaves of golden wheat—the landscape spread before them in a tapestry of muted colors. Lupine, field daisies and tall yellow sunflowers grew on the slope below. A spread of purple bougainvillea covered one half of a distant house.

"It's beautiful," she said.

"Yes, beautiful." But Diego wasn't looking at the scene before them; he was looking at Annmarie. She turned and saw the expression on his face, and her eyes, as blue and clear as the sky, widened with the awareness that he was going to kiss her. He thought for a minute she was going to step back. But she didn't; she only waited.

Diego put his hands on her shoulders. He gazed at her questioningly, then drew her against him and kissed her.

His lips were soft against hers, then the kiss grew and deepened. He put his arms around her, drawing her close to his tall, lean body. She trembled against him and because he didn't know if it was from the cold or because she was afraid, he opened his jacket and folded it around her.

"Annamaria," he said against her lips. "I've wanted to kiss you like this, to feel you against my body like this, from the first moment I saw you."

She tried to step away from him, but still he held her.

"Not yet, *querida*." He cupped her face with his hands and his eyes searched her face. Slowly, then, he kissed her eyelids closed, and her nose and the sweet indentation that led to her lips. He tried to hold himself back, but *por Dios*, he wanted to make love to her, here in this quiet place that he loved so much. He wanted to pull open her clean white shirt and kiss her sweetly rounded breasts. He wanted her to whisper his name and draw him close to her.

For one brief moment Diego kissed her with all the force and passion in his body. Then he gently put her away from him. "If we don't leave now, I don't think I will be able to let you go," he said softly. He touched the side of her face, smoothing the wind-blown hair back, and with a sigh he reached for her hand.

Annmarie looked up at him, not certain whether she was relieved or disappointed that he'd let her go.

It was dusk when they reached La Quinta. Diego stopped in front of her door. "I have to see my manager tonight. Tomorrow morning I will go to the *sorteo*, the drawing of the bulls. Will you have dinner with me tomorrow evening after the *corrida*?"

Annmarie nodded. "Yes, Diego, I'd like that."

"You don't have to go to the *corrida* if you don't want to," he said. "I'll understand."

"No, I want to go."

"You're sure?"

"No, but I'm going," she said softly.

He put his hand behind her head. "Do you know how lovely you are?" He drew her to him and very gently he kissed her.

Annmarie rested her head on his shoulder for a moment. Then she said, "I'll see you tomorrow, after the *corrida*." She hesitated. "When an actor in the States is in a show we say, 'Break a leg.' I don't suppose that's what you say to a bullfighter."

Diego shook his head and with a laugh said, "Not really."

"Then what?"

"*Suerte*, which means luck."

"Then *suerte*, Diego." She touched the side of his face. "*Suerte*."

Annmarie watched him drive away before she went into her room. She closed the door and sat on the bed and looked out through the lace curtains that faced the garden.

Something had happened today that went beyond a few kisses. She'd never felt with anyone what she'd experienced in Diego's arms. There'd been passion in his kisses and in her response, but the feeling went beyond passion. There'd been a sense of belonging when he held her, a sense of coming home. That frightened and bewildered her. She barely knew Diego Ortiz and she knew her time with him would be short.

He was a man foreign to anything Annmarie had ever known before. She didn't understand him. She knew very little about his country. She certainly didn't understand his profession. And yet . . .

The hour grew late. Darkness crept into the room, but still Annmarie sat there, staring out at the garden.

Tomorrow she would go to the bullring to watch Diego fight. The thought excited her, even as it repelled. What would it be like, she wondered, to watch him in his suit of lights as he called the bull to him?

At last she closed her eyes and leaned back against the pillows, thinking about tomorrow.

Chapter Three

The Plaza del Toros of Santa Catarina was almost filled when Annmarie, Rose, and Vince arrived. They made their way to three seats in the front row of the bullring, just below where the matadors would stand before they stepped into the ring. There was noise, laughter and jostling for seats, and an excitement in the air that was almost palpable.

Vince pointed to a wooden door just opposite where they sat. "The bulls will come through there," he told Annmarie. "Diego will fight first because he's the oldest in the profession, the one who took his *alternativa*, degree in bullfighting—first." He smiled at Annmarie. "I remember how I felt at my first bullfight. I imagine you're just a little nervous, aren't you?"

Annmarie tried to smile. "Nervous and excited."

"It won't be long now," Rose said as she glanced at her watch. "Bullfights are the one thing in Mexico that always start on time."

The sound of the clarion, clear and sharp and shrill, split through the murmur of hundreds of voices. The *pasosdoble* began and the people cheered. Through the door across the ring from them Annmarie could see a man mounted on a horse.

"That's the *alguacil*," Vince told Annmarie as the man, wearing a black velvet costume, rode into the ring. He approached the authority's box and doffed his plumed hat to ask permission for the spectacle to begin. When permission was granted he turned his mount and in a series of small, dancing, backward steps returned to the door from where he would lead the parade of *toreros*—the bullfighters—into the ring.

A shiver ran down Annmarie's back. She could feel the anticipation and the excitement all around her. Everyone in the plaza waited for the moment when the three matadors would step out of the shadows into the sun.

When they did she wasn't prepared for the sudden electricity of emotion she felt. She didn't see the other two men, she only saw Diego. His *traje de luces* was silver and black. The breeches that extended almost five inches below the knee were skintight. His short jacket was ornately embroidered in glittering metallic thread and encrusted with silver epaulets, and the sleeves and front were covered with silver sequins that glittered in the sun. Draped across his left shoulder was a *capote de paseo*, an ornately embroidered cape.

Behind the matadors came the *banderilleros*, the matadors' assistants whose job it was to place the brightly colored sticks and help to work the bull during the fight. Behind them came the *picadores*, who would pic the bull from horseback, and finally the *monosabios* who would help the *picadores*, handle the mules and smooth the surface of the sand.

The music, stirring and passionate, filled the plaza as they made their way across the sand to the opposite side of the ring. When they reached it they stopped. Diego looked up, searching for Annmarie, and when he saw her he took off his *capote de paseo* and went to stand directly below where she sat with Vince and Rose. When he handed the *capote* up, Vince stood and draped it in front of their *barrera*. "*Gracias, matador,*" he said.

"*Por nada.*" Diego looked up at her. A slight smile curved the corners of his mouth before he turned away.

There was a moment of expectant silence. The heavy door under the sign that read Toril opened, and the first bull exploded into the ring.

Diego watched for a moment before he stepped into the ring and furled his bright yellow and magenta cape. He called the bull to him, testing it in long, sweeping movements to take some of the uncontrolled wildness out of the animal's charge before he executed a series of *veronicas* that had the crowd jumping to their feet and cheering.

The *picadores* came to pic Diego's bull, then the *banderilleros*, and finally Diego stepped into the ring again. He held the *capote de torear*, the small red cape, and he called the bull to him in a strangely seductive voice.

"*¡Toro, ahaa, toro!*" The red cape swirled in the hot Mexican sun. He turned to face the bull, his body exposed, his stomach and groin on a level with the sharp white horns as he passed the animal close to his body.

All around Annmarie people shouted, *"¡Olé! Bravo, matador. ¡Olé, olé!"*

She couldn't breathe. Her stomach tightened with fear. She pressed her nails into her damp palms, unable to look away as Diego passed the bull closer and yet closer to his body.

She thought of the man who'd kissed her yesterday and knew that he had nothing in common with the man in the arena. She could see the beauty of movement and the great courage, but she couldn't understand it. With every pass Diego brought the bull closer, and when the bull stopped, confused, Diego turned his back and walked away.

At last it was time for the kill. Diego moved the *muleta* back and forth, fixing the animal's attention on the lure. When both man and bull were in position for the kill Diego brought the *muleta* down. The bull lowered its head and Diego moved, his body exposed and vulnerable between the sharp, gleaming horns. The sword went in and he leapt back before the horns could catch him. The bull staggered and the crowd exploded with cheers.

Rose put a hand on Annmarie's arm. "Annmarie? Are you all right?"

She had to wet her lips before she could speak. "Yes," she managed to say. "But I didn't expect . . . I didn't think it would be like this."

"He's awfully good," Vince said. "One of the best matadors Mexico's produced since Carlos Arruza. He's going to Spain to fight when the fiesta's over, and I hear he's got contracts in South America after that."

Annmarie barely heard what Vince was saying. She watched the other two matadors without speaking, and when it was time for Diego's second bull she tensed.

Just before the *faena*, the third and final act of the fight, Diego took his *montera*, the black bullfighter's hat, and came to stand below the *barrera* where the three of them were seated. He looked up at Annmarie.

"Stand up," Vince said.

When she did Diego said, "I dedicate the bull to you, Annamaria," turned and tossed the hat to her over his shoulder.

She caught it and held it against her breast.

It was as it had been before, only this time the bull was larger, the horns even sharper. Again and again Diego called the bull to him in a series of breathtakingly beautiful passes. Again and again he exposed his body to the razor-sharp horns. Each time he did, the crowd leaped to their feet to scream his name, to shout their *olé*s and their *bravo*s, to chant *"Torero, torero."*

Diego fell to his knees and called the bull to him. The giant beast passed, returned, paused. The big black body heaved with effort. Diego knelt before it. He touched each horn with his fingertips, then leaned an elbow on the animal's snout.

Annmarie couldn't breathe. Sweat broke out on her upper lip and unconsciously she clasped Rose's arm.

"God, I wish he wouldn't do that!" Rose murmured.

Diego stepped back, away from the bull, and the crowd went wild.

I can't stand this, Annmarie thought. I have to leave, I have to! But still she stayed, her gaze riveted on the man and the bull, hypnotized by a fear unlike anything she'd ever known.

She watched, spellbound, unable to look away when Diego called the bull to him again. The animal moved close to his body, stopped, then suddenly slashed up and out.

A horn caught Diego, lifting him, slammed him to the ground.

His helpers and the other two matadors rushed into the ring to distract the bull with their yellow and magenta capes. Diego got to his feet. Blood ran down his leg, but he waved the others away.

"He's all right," Vince said nervously. "He's going on with the fight."

Annmarie didn't know how she sat through the few remaining minutes. A bandage was quickly wrapped around Diego's leg to stanch the flow of blood. He picked up the cape and the sword and went back into the ring. He made more passes and when it was time for the kill he did it swiftly and cleanly.

The plaza erupted into cheers as he limped over to the *barrera* where she sat with Vince and Rose. She rose, her legs trembling so violently she didn't think she could stand. She hung on to the railing of the *barrera* and tossed the black hat back to him.

He looked up at her and frowned before he said, "Gracias," and turned back to receive the adulation of the crowd.

He made a tour of the ring while they threw flowers down to him, red carnations that were as bright as the blood that stained the bandage on his leg.

Vince and Rose asked Annmarie to go to dinner with them. She said that she couldn't, that she'd promised to have dinner with Diego.

"He may have had to go to the clinic," Rose said. Her face was kind and there was an expression of concern in her eyes.

"They won't keep him there," Vince said. "But it'll probably be late before he gets back to the hotel. Come with us, we'll make it an early night."

But Annmarie shook her head. "Thanks, Vince, but I'm really not hungry. I think I'll rest for a while."

But Annmarie didn't rest. She sat on the bench by the fountain in the garden. She listened to the birds that came to roost in the laurel trees, and tried not to think about Diego or the feelings she'd experienced when he'd been hurt.

She'd known Diego for only a few days, yet it had seemed to her today that when he'd been gored by the bull she'd felt the pain along with him. When his body had slammed to the earth she'd quivered from the impact.

And she was horrified when she remembered the callous words she'd spoken the night they'd met.

At last, when the hour grew late and the night grew cold, Annmarie left the garden. She'd just come up the stairs to the corridor when she saw Diego. He was limping, and by the dim light in the corridor she saw that his face was pale and drawn.

For a moment Annmarie hesitated, then she went to him and said only, "Diego?" and waited.

"We had a date for dinner," he said, looking at her.

"I'm sorry. Have you eaten?"

She shook her head. "No, but I'm not hungry."

"Neither am I."

"I saw the blood," she said, beginning to tremble, but Diego put his hand on the side of her face, then around to the back of her neck, caressing and soothing her skin.

"It's nothing," he said. "You mustn't look like that, *muchacha.*"

"I can't help it. When you fell . . ." She closed her eyes and let him draw her close.

"*Ya, ya,*" he whispered. "It's all right. These things happen."

"Not to anyone I know," she said against his shoulder.

"No, I don't suppose they do." He tightened his arms around her. "I'm sorry that happened today. It was your first bullfight—"

"And my last." She raised her face and looked at him. "How can you do that?" she asked. "How can you risk your life that way?"

"I don't risk my life. What happened today was a rare occurrence."

She stepped away and looked up at him. "I was so afraid," she said.

"My poor Annamaria." His face was thoughtful, sad. He cupped her face with his hands and drew her close for his kiss.

She was lost in the heaven of his arms and the warmth of his mouth, reluctant to move away when he let her go.

But when he did he put his hands on her shoulders. He looked at her and it seemed to Annmarie that all that he was, every warm and wonderful part of him, shone in his eyes. "Annamaria?" he whispered.

She looked up at him, unable to speak, then rested her head against his shoulder and slowly nodded.

Diego didn't turn the bedside light on in his room until he closed the drapes over the lace curtains. When he turned to her he drew her back into his arms and gently kissed her. "I want to see you when I undress you," he said.

Her heart beating fast against her rib cage, Annmarie put her hands flat against his chest. It wasn't too late to back out. But when she looked up at him she knew that she was wrong, it *was* too late.

Diego unfastened the buttons of the blue sweater. He saw the wisp of satin and lace that covered her small breasts and his mouth went dry. He reached for the snaps of her jeans and for a moment her hand closed over his, staying him. Then she sighed and took her hand away.

Diego led her to the bed and when she sat down he took her shoes off and drew the jeans down over her hips. The breath caught in his throat and he smiled with the sheer pleasure of looking at her. When she shivered in the chill of the room he said, "You're cold," and turned back the bed covers.

She got under them, still wearing the wisp of bra and her panties. There were spots of color on her cheeks and she worried her bottom lip with her teeth.

Quickly Diego pulled his shirt out of his pants. He took his boots off and carefully pulled his trousers down over his injured leg. When he was naked except for the bandage on his leg, he came to the bed and stood for a moment looking down at Annmarie.

Everything between them had happened so fast, but he knew in his heart that she was special. He hadn't intended to go beyond a casual friendship, with perhaps a little flirtation.

But Diego knew as he stood looking down at her that his feelings for her would never be casual. For a moment he hesitated, then Annmarie lifted the blanket and whispered, "Come in out of the cold, Diego."

He lay down beside her and gathered her into his arms. With one hand behind her head he cradled her close and kissed her. Her lips parted and softened under his, and when she lifted her arms to caress his shoulders, he was lost in her softness and womanly warmth.

She felt the whole man-length of Diego's body against hers and heard the harsh whisper of her name against her lips. She was lost, her mouth as hungry and as demanding as his. He touched her breasts and she sighed with pleasure.

"They're lovely," he whispered. "So small that I can cup them with my hands." He eased the bra away and gently caressed the firm roundness while he teased the sweet ripe buds with his thumbs.

Annmarie hid her face against the hollow of his shoulder to smother the moan that escaped her lips. "Oh, Diego."

He pulled her closer and with a smothered groan buried his face between her breasts. She threaded her fingers through the midnight thickness of his hair, then sighed when his lips closed on one rosy peak. Her hands tightened as his teeth tightened, caressed as his lips caressed. Her body was on fire now, too weak with longing to protest when he reached down to ease her panties off.

He returned to feast against her breasts, kissing, teasing and caressing with the moist warmth of his tongue until it was past bearing and she whispered his name with heart-stopping urgency.

Diego covered her with his body. He took her face between his hands and kissed her, demanding a surrender that she gladly gave.

"Be careful," she whispered against his lips. "Don't hurt your leg."

But Diego was beyond thought as he joined his body to hers. She cried out, smothering her passion against his shoulder, and lifted her body to his.

"Annamaria," Diego said against her lips. *Mi preciosa, mi alma, mi querida Annamaria.*"

Annmarie didn't understand all the words, she only knew that she'd never known anything like this before, had never felt like this before. Her body trembled under his as she wrapped her arms around him to draw him closer. She lifted her body to his and whispered his name as she met him thrust for thrust with small cries of pleasure.

He left her lips to take one nipple between his teeth, to lap and caress until she pleaded with him to stop. Her fingers tightened in his hair and she raised his face to hers, seeking his mouth.

Frantic, almost beyond thought, Diego kissed her. He was wild with passion now, trying to hold back, afraid of hurting her. But oh, the feel of her, the tightness of her holding him close.

Annmarie lifted her body to his. She whispered his name and it was too much, too long past bearing.

"Oh, Annamaria." Her name was a hoarse cry on his lips.

"Yes," she said. "Oh, yes, Diego. Please, yes. Oh . . .
Yes!"

He reached for her mouth, taking her cry, and mingled it with his as they climbed higher and higher into a whirling ecstasy that left them gasping for breath.

Annmarie's body shook with reaction. She was dizzy, disoriented, not even sure what had happened to her. She felt Diego's arms tighten around her and the thud of his heart against her breasts. They didn't speak, they only clung together, waiting for their hearts to still the frantic beating. At last Diego kissed her lips and smoothed the fair hair back from her face.

"Annamaria." The sound of her name hung like a gossamer thread in the quiet of the room.

She sighed against him. He stroked the long smooth length of her back. He spoke to her in Spanish, telling her how beautiful she was and how she pleased him. He told her that he'd never felt with any other woman what he'd felt with her. And he told her that he thought he was falling in love with her.

Annmarie loved the sound of the words, but she didn't understand them. At last, in English he said, "Sleep, my love."

Diego reached across her and turned off the bedside light. He felt her body relax against his and knew that she slept. But it was a long time before he did.

Chapter Four

In the predawn light of almost morning the bells of Santa Catarina began to ring. Annmarie stirred, then moved closer to Diego. His breathing was regular and she thought he was asleep until he moved his arms and took her hand.

"Buenos días, querida," he said and began to stroke her back.

While his eyes were still closed she studied the face that was unlike any other's. His high cheekbones, small straight nose, and almond-shaped eyes gave his face an exotically foreign look. His hair was crisp and crows-wing black; his skin was a deep sun bronze.

Slowly she dropped her gaze to what the blankets exposed of his body. His shoulders were broad and there was only a small patch of hair on his chest.

"What do you think?" he asked with an amused chuckle. "That I'm an ugly fellow who has little hair on his chest?"

"You're not ugly and I don't like hairy chests."

"Thank heaven for that." Diego kissed the top of her head. "What would you like to do today?"

"You don't have to fight?"

Diego shook his head. "Not for several days."

"Why do you do it?"

"¿Torear?" He shrugged. "It's what I do, what I have always done."

Diego wanted to tell her why he fought because it seemed to him important to have her understand. But how could he tell anyone, especially this young American woman, why he or any other man fought the bulls? How could he explain the feeling of pride a young man experiences the first time he dresses in the suit of lights? How could he make her understand the dedication, the passion, the excitement—and yes, the fear—of those last moments when you are alone in your room, when you cross yourself and pray to the Virgin of Guadalupe for the courage to fight bravely and well?

He was thirty-two. He'd been fighting since he was sixteen and with luck he would fight for another five or six years.

Annmarie pulled the blanket up around their shoulders. "I want to know," she said. "Please help me understand, Diego."

Diego kissed the top of her head. "You have to be Latin to know what bullfighting means to us." He shifted to better accommodate her in his arms and tried to form the words to tell her why a man becomes a matador.

The lure of money was one of the reasons, and so perhaps was the glory. But there was something so much more important than money or fame, and that was the deep satisfaction that came from doing something so difficult and dangerous. There was such a wonderful feeling of exhilaration when you had faced the onslaught of a wild creature that outweighed you by almost a thousand pounds, whose deadly horns came within a hairsbreadth of your body. Of doing it with grace and dignity and emerging triumphant from the battle.

"To be a matador is something almost every boy in Mexico and Spain dreams about," he said. "Just as every American boy wants to be a baseball player or a football hero. A Mexican boy grows up hearing about the bulls, especially if he's raised on a ranch the way I was. My older brothers played with the *becerros*, the calves, and when I was only five or six they would give me a shirt and I would pretend to be a matador.

"My uncle came to visit us when I was fifteen. We had a fiesta the day he arrived and he saw me with the *becerros*. Afterward he talked to my father and said that he would like to train me. My mother protested but I think she understood how much it meant to me, and finally she gave me her blessing."

Diego smoothed the hair back from Annmarie's face. "My father is dead but my mother still lives in our small town near Guadalajara. I will take you to meet her before you leave Mexico." He tightened his arms around her and continued, unable to bear thinking about her leaving. "I came to live on my uncle's brave bull ranch here, near Santa Catarina. He died last year and left me the ranch. That is where I'll go when I retire."

Annmarie looked up at him. She took one of his hands in hers. It was smooth, slender and fine boned, with short, rounded nails. "You're a gentle man," she said. "I can't understand why you'd be in such…such a violent, such a bloody sport."

His body tensed, as it had on the night he'd met her. "Then let us talk about big-game hunting," he said coldly. "About your American hunters who kill so they have trophies to hang on their walls. Or about men who spend hundreds of dollars on expensive equipment so they can hook a large and beautiful fish and play it for three or four hours before they bring it in." His voice was angry. "Or about small animals that are slaughtered so that a rich man's wife will have its fur to wear. Or prizefighters who beat each other to a pulp. Or—"

"Please…" Annmarie put a finger against Diego's lips. "Don't be angry. I want to understand, but it's so difficult. I don't condone those things, either."

Diego let his breath out. "I'm sorry." He kissed her. "I didn't mean to make a speech."

"Maybe we'd better get up."

"Or maybe not." Diego put a finger under her chin and, lifting her face to his, said, "You're very beautiful this morning."

"Diego…"

He stopped her words with a kiss that grew and deepened, and when she sighed against him he tightened his arms around her.

"Querida," Diego said against her lips. "Do you know what you do to me? I touch you and I am eighteen again and my body is wild with desire."

"That's how I feel, too," Annmarie whispered. "I didn't know, Diego, not until last night, that I could...could feel what I did. I didn't know a woman could feel that way. I've never..." Too embarrassed to go on, she sought his mouth again.

Diego rolled over to raise himself over her, but when he did he fell back, barely smothering a groan.

"It's your leg, isn't it?" Annmarie's face was filled with concern. "Oh, Diego, I forgot about your leg."

"It's all right. Don't worry."

"But—"

"No, don't say anything, just kiss me, Anna-maria."

His lips were firm and demanding against hers, and before she could protest he lifted her over him and held her close to his naked body. She felt the strength of his masculinity against her leg and shuddered with apprehension and desire when he urged her against him.

Diego cupped her face and rained kisses on her forehead, her closed eyes, her nose and her mouth until she thought she would faint with desire. Only then did he lift her up over his body.

His heart swelled with passion and with love. Her long mane of blond hair fell forward to partially cover her breasts and small sounds of pleasure emanated from her parted lips. He grasped her hips and tried to hold himself back, but a fever was raging in him, a fever that only her love could quench.

Annmarie moved cautiously, shyly, wanting to please but not sure what she was supposed to do. But suddenly her caution and her shyness evaporated and her body caught fire, and when Diego began to caress her breasts she cried out her pleasure.

They moved as one person. Their cadence quickened, faster and faster. Diego grasped her hips again, holding her body tight to his.

"Anna . . . Annamaria," he whispered.

She collapsed over him, trembling with pleasure as his body exploded. He took her mouth. He kissed her hard and deep while still the shimmering delight of passion shook their bodies. He held her, breathing in her scent. His hands roamed her back and pressed her close to his quivering body.

"I'll never let you go, my Annamaria. Not after this. *Mi amor, mi querida gringa, mi muchachita.*"

She clung to him as he told her in Spanish how much he loved her and how she was the only one for him.

Diego knew in his heart that though he said the words in the sweet aftermath of passion, he meant every one of them.

Rose was in the dining room when they went in for breakfast. She asked Diego how his leg was and raised an eyebrow when he ordered fresh orange juice, papaya, scrambled eggs, ham, pancakes and *café con leche.*

"I'm going to the orphanage this morning," she told Annmarie. "How'd you like to come with me?"

Annmarie looked at Diego.

"I have some things to do," he said. "But I'm going out to the ranch this afternoon. I thought you might like to go with me. You too, Rose."

"Thanks, Diego, but Vince and I have plans." She turned to Annmarie. "How about it? Would you like to see the orphanage?"

"Yes, of course. Thank you for asking me."

Rose pushed her chair back and got up. "Just knock on my door when you finish breakfast." She smiled at Diego and said, "See you later, matador."

"You don't mind going to the orphanage?" he said when Rose left.

"Mind? No, I'd like to see it."

"But don't get involved."

"Involved?"

"With the children." Diego hesitated. "I mean don't get emotionally involved. The kids there need so much." He covered her hand with his. "I just don't want you to be sad."

"I'm only going for a few hours, Diego. I'm not going to get *involved*."

An hour later Annmarie wasn't so sure. They entered the orphanage from the street into a dark, stone hallway. To the right there was a small chapel with four wooden benches and an altar draped in tired red velour. The Virgin's face was chipped, a part of her nose was missing.

As they moved down the corridor a black-robed nun hurried forward to meet them, and Rose said, "*¿Cómo está, Sister?*. I'd like you to meet my friend, Annmarie Bannister."

"Mucho gusto." The nun shook Annmarie's hand. "Come in. The older children are in school but the young ones are playing in the courtyard."

"Thank you, Sister," Annmarie said as she followed Rose and the nun into a yard filled with almost thirty children. The grass had worn thin and there was only the bare, cold ground. The children looked up, then some of them, mostly little girls, ran over.

"Hola, Señora Rose," they chorused, and looked shyly up at Annmarie.

"This is my friend, Annmarie," Rose said. "She's come to visit." Taking a package out of her purse she handed it to Annmarie. "I bought some hair bands yesterday. Will you give them out while I talk to the sister for a minute?"

"Sure." Annmarie looked at the children and in her night-school Spanish said, "Let us go to sit on the bench and I will give you the hair bands."

A cluster of little girls followed her. Annmarie sat down and opened the package. There were a dozen headbands and at least sixteen or seventeen little girls with anxious eyes. She began to give out the bands. The last one went to a rather fat little girl with short straight hair and a sore on her cheek. The child stretched the blue band down over her forehead and the other little girls giggled. One of them, a pretty girl with long black hair who hadn't received a band, stuck her lip out. Her chin trembled and two large tears formed in her big brown eyes. Annmarie looked at her, then at the not-too-pretty girl with the band stretched across her forehead.

"Maybe it would look better on a girl with long hair," she said, and held her hand out for the blue band.

The child with the sore on her face didn't speak. She pulled the band off and handed it to Annmarie, then she pulled her dress over her face and began to weep.

Annmarie stared at the child, then with a smothered cry she pulled the little girl onto her lap and began to rock her back and forth. "I'm sorry," she whispered against the short dark hair. "I'm sorry, baby."

She stayed until it was time for their lunch, then she left and returned an hour later with more headbands for the little girls and little toy cars for the boys.

Rose shook her head. With a grin she said, "So they've hooked you, too. I knew this would happen." She put her arm around Annmarie. "Same time tomorrow?" she asked.

Annmarie nodded. She knew that she couldn't stay away if she'd tried.

That afternoon she and Diego drove out to his ranch. Ten miles from Santa Catarina he turned off onto a narrow road that led through rolling hills and green pastureland.

"The bulls are over the rise to your left," Diego said. "You can't see them from here but we'll take a look later if you like."

"Do you spend a lot of time here?"

"Not as much as I'd like to. I have a manager, Pepe Rodriguez. He runs things for me."

"And this is where'll you come when you retire?"

Diego nodded. "It's pleasant here; I really wouldn't want to live anywhere else." He reached for her hand. "Tell me about your home."

"I have an apartment." Annmarie looked out over the rolling hills. "My parents sold the house I grew up in last year when they started the divorce proceedings." Because she didn't want to talk about it she looked around her, at the rolling hills, the fields and pastureland.

"That's the house," Diego said, "there through the trees."

It was a big, rambling Spanish-style house. Scarlet bougainvillea made a brilliant splash of color against one of the white walls and part of the red tiled roof. As they drew closer Annmarie could see that the iron gate was open and that there was a flower-filled patio with a fountain in the center.

When Diego stopped the car he came around to Annmarie's side and said, "Come, let me show you my home." He paused and, looking down at her, said, "Do you know the expression, *Mi casa es tu casa*?"

"No, I'm sorry, I don't."

"It means, my house is your house." He took her hand. "Come into your house, Annamaria."

She looked at him and felt the breath catch in her throat. Before she could speak a heavy, middle-aged woman hurried to meet them. She wore a clean white apron over her long black skirt. As she approached she said, "*Hola*, Diego, I did not know you would be here today. Have you had your lunch? Why didn't you let me know you were coming?"

"I'm sorry, Juanita." He took Annmarie's hand. "This is *Señorita* Bannister. I wanted her to see the ranch."

He turned to Annmarie. "Juanita is my house-keeper. She's the one who keeps the place running."

Annmarie put her hand out. "How do you do," she said.

"Mucho gusto." Juanita pumped her hand enthusiastically. "Come in. It is warm in the sun. Would you like a cool drink? A lemonade, perhaps?"

"A lemonade would be fine, thank you." Annmarie looked around her. A rough stone fireplace dominated one wall, a row of bookcases lined another. There were two soft leather sofas on either side of the fireplace; deep, comfortable chairs, a dark mahogany coffee table and other smaller tables. Black iron wall candelabra with fat white candles stood on either end of the fireplace mantel. A bullfight poster from Seville, Spain, hung above it.

Annmarie turned and smiled at him. "It's a man's room," she said. "I like it."

That pleased him. "Come," he said, "let me show you the rest of the house."

The dining room was as big as the living room. There was a table long enough to seat twenty comfortably, and high-backed chairs with cushioned seats. When she'd seen the kitchen—a large, bright room with a dining alcove that overlooked a garden—Diego led her down the outside corridor.

"These are all guest rooms," he said, indicating the doors. "Once in a while I'm able to convince my mother to visit, and occasionally my brothers come with their families." He opened a door at the far end of the corridor. "This is my room," he said.

This too was a man's room. The bed was king-size, the furniture dark and heavy. Sliding glass doors opened out onto a small terrace where there was a chaise, two lounge chairs and a round table.

"That is where I have my breakfast when it's warm," Diego said.

"It's very—" Annmarie smiled up at him—"masculine," she said.

Diego nodded. "Everything about this house needs a woman's touch."

Annmarie looked at him, then quickly away. "You have Juanita. She seems capable."

"She is capable." Diego hesitated. "I have a week after the fiesta before I leave for Spain. I'm going to spend it here at the ranch." He took her hands in his. "I wish you would spend it here with me, Annamaria."

"I . . . I couldn't do that."

"I thought all women in your country were liberated," Diego said with the suggestion of a smile.

"Not this woman."

"I care about you, Annamaria. I want to be with you."

"I want to be with you too, but you'll be leaving Mexico soon and so will I."

"You could come to Spain with me." Even as Diego spoke the words he knew he was being foolish. She didn't understand about the bulls, and soon she would go back to Florida. He didn't need or want any kind of commitment. And yet . . .

He had known other women; beautiful, sophisticated women, in Mexico and in Spain. Women who wore designer clothes, whose nails were polished, whose hair and makeup were always perfect. This young woman's nails were plain. She wore almost no makeup and her hair was like flyaway corn silk. But she pleased him as no other woman ever had.

"I don't know what you do to me," he said. "I look at you and my body catches fire. I touch you and I want to carry you to some dark and quiet place where I can kiss you until we're both trembling with passion." Diego reached for her and pulling her close whispered, "And I will, Annamaria. Before the day is over I will have you in my arms again."

She wanted to make a joke of it, to say something funny, like "Promises, promises." But she couldn't. All she could do was to look at him and say "Diego, please—" without even knowing what it was she pleaded for.

But he stopped her words with a kiss so fierce that she trembled against him. When he let her go she clung to him, afraid that if she didn't she would stumble and fall.

"If we don't get out of here in the next two seconds I'm going to make love to you," Diego said in a voice hoarse with passion. Then, without another word, he took her hand and led her out of the room, out to the patio where they sipped the lemonade that Juanita had prepared. They talked of pleasant, inconsequential things and didn't speak of the longing they felt to touch each other.

That night they had dinner at a small restaurant off the main plaza, and afterward they walked back to the plaza where the band played—not well but with great enthusiasm—in the center kiosk. Children, shrieking with laughter, darted back and forth among the stands that sold balloons, popcorn and tacos, and splashed each other from the water in the fountain. Young ranch hands, dressed in tight-fitting pants with silver-trimmed belts, their boots shining and their faces self-conscious, strolled in one direction around and around the plaza eyeing the girls of Santa Catarina who walked in twos or threes in the other direction, whispering behind their hands and casting fleeting glances at the boys.

When the hour grew late the musicians packed up their instruments and left. Parents gathered up their children and the crowd drifted away. The girls of Santa Catarina returned to their homes, and the boys climbed back into their pickups or went to catch the last bus leaving town.

When the bells in the big church that faced the plaza chimed the hour of twelve, Diego put his arm around Annmarie's waist. "It's time to go home," he said.

Chapter Five

Home. A strange word for a small room down a cobbled street in a country where she barely spoke the language. Yet in a way Annmarie found difficult to understand, she felt more at home in this one room with Diego than she had ever felt, either with her parents, or on her own.

She'd only known Diego for a short time. She knew little about his country and almost nothing about him. Yet she felt closer to him than she'd ever felt to anyone before.

All of Annmarie's life there'd been a part of her that had always felt like an outsider. It was as though she stood on the outer fringes of life, peering in at all the excitement and happiness that other people experienced. Now, for the first time in her life, she felt a wonderful sense of belonging.

Except for one relationship during her senior year at college, Annmarie had little experience with men. She knew in part that was because her parents' marriage had been so bad and she'd grown up amid an atmosphere of tension and endless arguments. The memories of the shouting matches were as clear as day—*Tell your father we're eating at seven whether he's here or not, Tell your mother I damn well won't be here!*

Like a spectator at a tennis match, Annmarie would turn her head from one to the other, nervous and anxious, her stomach in painful knots, fearful of saying anything that might add to their wrangling.

When she was older Annmarie had told herself that if she ever married, she wouldn't live the way her parents had. But to her, marriage wasn't a pleasant prospect and she'd decided years ago that she would rather live alone forever than marry and bicker for the rest of her life; hurt and be hurt, as her parents had hurt each other—as well as her.

Marriage was difficult enough when two people came from the same backgrounds; it would be even more difficult when two people were as different from each other as she and Diego.

But Diego hadn't mentioned marriage, commitment or any other kind of relationship. He'd only asked her to stay with him at the ranch before he left for Spain. He'd even mentioned her going to Spain with him. But although Annmarie told herself that she didn't want a serious relationship, the thought that Diego might think of her as only a *gringa* who was here for a vacation, someone he could be with for as long as the fiesta lasted, hurt her terribly. So did the knowledge that the time they had together would end when the fiesta ended.

These thoughts tortured Annmarie as she and Diego walked back toward the hotel through the cobbled streets of the now quiet town. There was a part of her that knew she should break their relationship off before it went any further. The longer it went on the more difficult it would be when they parted. Soon the fiesta would be over. Diego would go to Spain and she would return to Florida. Wouldn't it be better to end it now before the involvement became even deeper?

Annmarie was still trying to form the words to tell Diego how she felt when they reached the door of his room. She took a deep breath but before she could speak, he stopped her with a kiss, then opened the door and led her into the darkness.

"What is it?" he asked gently. "What is troubling you, Annamaria? Are you angry because I asked you to stay at the ranch with me?"

"No, Diego. It's not that." She hesitated. "But anything like that is impossible."

"Why is it impossible when we are as we are? When, more than anything in the world, I want to be with you?" Diego tilted her face up. "It doesn't have to end here in Mexico, Annamaria; you could come to Spain with me. I fight in Madrid first, then we'll go down to the Costa del Sol because I have *corridas* in Seville and Malaga. After that we'll move up the coast, to Alicante and Valencia and Barcelona. We'll walk along *las Ramblas* and I'll buy you armfuls of flowers." Diego kissed her again. "You must come with me," he said.

Annmarie shook her head. "I have a job, an apartment. I can't just . . . just go away like that." She hesitated. "I've never lived with anybody before, Diego."

"I didn't think you had. But we have found something special, Annamaria. I know this has happened suddenly, but that doesn't make it any less real. I feel things with you I've never felt before. I think it is the same for you.''

Diego brushed her lips with his. "We need time to get to know each other, Annamaria. I don't know how we can have that time unless you come to Spain with me."

He saw the question, the doubt in Annmarie's face, and because he was afraid of what she might say, he kissed her. He didn't want words now, he only wanted her. The terrible need, the excitement, had been building in him ever since that moment in his bedroom at the ranch. The uncertainty he saw in her expression only fueled his resolve to possess her.

He kissed her, slowly, deliberately, holding her so that she couldn't move away. A part of him knew that he was taking advantage of her inexperience, of the fire that his lovemaking had kindled in her, but with the thought that he had awakened her, his body flamed. He couldn't kiss her hard enough, deep enough, and when her lips parted and softened he picked her up and carried her to the bed. Quickly he laid her down and, clasping her to his body, he rolled her beneath him.

"Diego..." Frightened by his intensity, Annmarie tried to pull away from him, but Diego held her. He opened the buttons of her shirt and pushed her bra aside to touch her breasts.

"*Ay, mi Anna, mi Annamaria,* how I love to touch you like this." He bent to suckle the peaked and tender tips.

Annmarie gasped a protest, but he tightened his hands on her hips, holding her while he caressed her with his tongue. Only when her body began to relax did he let her go, then he undressed her and tossed her clothes over a chair. He grunted with pain when he removed the boot from his bad leg, but ignored it and brought his naked body over hers.

"I can't wait," he said hoarsely, and turning her toward him joined his body to hers.

Somewhere in the back of Diego's brain he knew that his urgency alarmed her, but he couldn't stop himself. He had to possess her, now, tonight, because he was afraid that soon she would leave him. Blood rushed to his brain and he cried her name as his body exploded into a million particles of stinging sensation.

Diego collapsed over her, dizzy with reaction, his heart thudding against his ribs. "I'm sorry," he murmured. "I didn't mean to do that."

Tentatively Annmarie lifted her hands to caress his shoulders, to sooth him to calmness.

At her touch, something softened and broke inside Diego. He buried his head against her breasts and clasped her to him as though he would never let her go.

His body shook with reaction. He was tired, more tired than he'd ever been in his life. He told himself he would close his eyes for a moment or two, just before he drifted to sleep.

Diego awoke and reached out his hand for her. "Annamaria?" he whispered, then opened his eyes and sat up, afraid that she'd left him. When he heard the shower he ran a hand through the thickness of his hair and swung his legs off the bed. The bad leg hurt and he massaged it before he got to his feet.

The bathroom was filled with steam. Because he didn't want to frighten her he called her name, then pulled back the shower curtain and got into the shower with her.

She turned a startled gaze on him. "I thought you were asleep," she said, not quite meeting his eyes.

"I was." He took the soap from her. "Let me bathe you."

She started to protest, but he turned her gently and began to wash her back.

Her skin was like cream, soft to the touch, pinked from the hot water, slippery when he slid his soapy hands down her back to her sweetly rounded bottom. Diego drew her against him and clasped her around the waist, loving the feel of her soapy softness. He moved his hands to her breasts, caressing their roundness.

Annmarie whispered his name and turned. A dollop of soap hung suspended from one rosy nipple. Very gently Diego flicked it away and watched her shiver.

He cupped her face in his hands. "Forgive me, Annamaria. It wasn't good for you and I'm sorry."

Hot color crept into her cheeks. "It doesn't matter."

"Of course it matters." He began to massage her shoulders with the soap, then around to her breasts again. Her lips parted and the breath caught in her throat. For a moment she leaned against him, letting the water cascade over her. Then she stepped back and said in a voice so low he could barely hear, "Let me bathe you," and began to lather his body.

Diego had never known this particular kind of joy. There was an exquisite pleasure in her touch, in the gentleness of her hands. His body swelled and grew with need, but he held himself back. He didn't want her to stop, he didn't want her ever to stop.

At last he turned the water off and taking Annmarie's hand helped her out of the shower and made her stand while he dried her, as gently as though she were a child, lingering over the sensitive places of her body until her legs began to tremble. Then he picked her up and carried her to the bed.

Their bed.

She raised her arms to welcome him and he came down beside her. Tenderly he kissed her lips. "This time it is all for you, Annamaria."

"Diego?"

"Yes, my darling?"

"Sometimes I'm almost afraid of the way I feel when I'm with you...." The words trembled on her lips. "Sometimes I feel so much that it frightens me."

"I know, *querida*. I know because it is the same for me." He smoothed the damp hair back off her face. "Are you frightened now?"

She caught her lower lip between her teeth. Her eyes were wide and very blue. She touched his face. "No," she whispered. "Not now."

It seemed to Diego in that moment that his heart overflowed with love, for he knew that this small, shy woman had captured his heart.

He warmed her with kisses. He touched her with hands made gentle with love and told her how beautiful she was and how she pleased him. She grew warm and pliant in his hands, and when she did he whispered a line of kisses down her body, thrilled by her small gasps of pleasure, her sighs, her moans.

"Oh, Diego..." She fastened her hands on his shoulders to push him away, then hesitated. She whispered his name and each whisper set his blood on fire.

When her cry came it touched the core of him, shaking him as it shook her. He soothed and caressed her trembling body before he lifted himself over her. He joined his body to hers and when he felt her softness, his throat constricted with a feeling he'd never experienced before. He moved against her, holding himself back, waiting until she began again. Only then did he let himself go, and when he did, it was better than anything he'd ever known.

Their breaths and murmured whispers mingled when they climbed the heights of passion and fell, both weakened and strengthened, back to the safety of each other's arms.

Diego knew then, as surely as he knew the sun would rise in the morning, that he loved her.

Diego hadn't told Annmarie until they were having breakfast that he was going to fight today. When he told her, her face paled.

"Your leg," she said. "You can't, Diego."

"It's much better. I'll wear a tight bandage; that will help." He took a deep breath and letting it out, said "I hope you will come."

Annmarie looked at him across the table, then she nodded. "Yes, I'll come."

He asked her to come with him to the *sorteo*, the selecting of the bulls that each matador would fight that day, because he wanted her to know and understand the whole process of the *corrida*.

And again she agreed.

The others were already there when they arrived; the other two matadors, the *banderilleros*, and Diego's manager, Manolo Hurtado.

"This is how the bulls we will fight today are selected," Diego told her. "The three bulls that appear to be the best are chosen, then paired off with the other three so that the division is as equal as possible—the heaviest with the lightest, the one with the smallest horns coupled with the one with the largest horns."

Annmarie watched while the names and numbers of each of the three pairs were written on a piece of paper and thrown into a hat. Then the three balls were drawn according to the seniority of the matadors. Diego drew first. He opened the ball of paper, looked at the two bulls whose numbers they represented, frowned slightly and nodded.

When they left the plaza he handed her three tickets and said, "I must talk to Manolo for a while. I

won't see you until after the *corrida*. I hope you don't
mind being alone this afternoon."

"I thought we could have lunch together."

Diego shook his head. "Bullfighters don't eat before a *corrida*."

Annmarie looked at him. "Is that because if surgery is necessary the stomach must be empty?" she
asked softly.

"It's only a precaution," he said.

A precaution. She looked away. In a voice that
shook a little she said, "I'd planned to spend a couple of hours at the orphanage today. I told Rose I'd
meet her there."

"*Bueno*, then I will see you back at the hotel after
the *corrida*. Vince has suggested that the four of us
have dinner tonight. Is that agreeable with you?"

"Yes, of course it is, Diego." She kissed him goodbye, keeping a smile on her face when she walked
away. It was only after she turned the corner that the
smile faded and her hands curled into nervous fists.
When she'd looked at the bulls in the corral this
morning she hadn't been able to stop thinking of the
fact that Diego would face two of them this afternoon, a piece of cloth his only defense against the
deadly horns.

She would force herself to go to the *corrida* even
though it terrified her. Diego wouldn't stop fighting
the bulls, but if she was frightened enough, repelled
enough, perhaps she would have the strength to turn
and walk away from him.

These were the thoughts that troubled Annmarie as she went down the narrow cobblestone street to the Casa de Hogar, the orphanage.

The same nun who'd opened the door the first time she'd visited answered her knock. When Annmarie asked if she could stop in the chapel before she went in, the nun nodded. "Of course. Take as much time as you like."

The chapel smelled of dampness and dust. The kneeling bench wasn't padded, but Annmarie knelt and looked up the battered statue of the Virgin. She tried to form the words of a prayer, but the words wouldn't come. Instead she found herself whispering, "Please, please, please." She bowed her head, resting it against her hands. "Don't let anything happen to him," she prayed. "Keep him safe from the bulls. Protect him with your love."

She said the same words over and over again, until tears stained her hands and the words became a litany for Diego's safety.

Finally Annmarie raised her head. Her knees hurt. She turned to stand and when she did saw the little dark-haired girl sitting on the bench behind her. "Hi," she murmured, and knuckled the tears away. Then in her stumbling Spanish managed to say, *"¿Como estás, Maya?"*

"Bien." The small round face was solemn, the dark eyes serious. *"Estás triste,* are you sad?" she asked.

"Yes, a little." Annmarie smiled. "I am happy to see you again."

"*Tu también*, you also." A bell sounded and Maya stood. "It is time for lunch," she said, and made a face.

"Don't you like your lunch?"

"No. It is *frijoles y arroz* and I don't like that." With a sigh the small girl started out of the chapel.

"Maya?"

"Yes, *Señorita*?"

"If the sister says it's all right, would you like to have lunch with me? In a restaurant, I mean."

"A restaurant?" The girl's dark eyes widened and a smile brightened her face.

"Yes." Annmarie took Maya's hand. "Let's go and ask her," she said.

Sister Dolores hesitated only a moment. "Yes, of course you may take Maya to lunch. It will be a wonderful treat for her." She turned to Maya. "Wash your hands and face and comb your hair," she told the child. "Hurry now, *Señorita* Annamaria will wait for you."

Rose waved when Maya ran off, and when she approached Annmarie she said, "I haven't seen you for a day or two. I suppose you've been busy with Diego."

"Yes. He gave me three tickets for the *corrida* this afternoon. Can you and Vince go with me?"

"Sure. I couldn't keep Vince away from the bullfight even if I wanted to." Rose hesitated. "Are things getting serious between you and Diego?"

"Yes, I suppose they are. But they shouldn't."

"Why not?"

"The fiesta will be over in a few days. Diego will go to Spain and I'll soon go back to Florida."

"And it'll be *adiós* and toodleloo?"

"Yes, except that he...he's asked me to go to Spain with him."

"Aha!"

"What's that supposed to mean?"

"Nothing. Just aha!" Rose grinned at her. "Are you going?"

"Of course not!"

"Oh?" Rose looked at her sympathetically, then after a moment's hesitation said, "I suppose living with a man like Diego would be hard. You'd always be worried about him and you wouldn't really have a home, would you? You'd be travelling most of the time, staying in hotels, never really settling down. Doesn't seem the right kind of life for a woman like you."

"No, it doesn't." Annmarie frowned, not sure why Rose's words—"a woman like you"—angered her. She saw Maya running toward her, and glad to end the conversation with Rose, she said, "I'm taking Maya to lunch. Would you like to come with us?"

"No, thanks. I'm having lunch here with the kids." Rose straightened Maya's headband. "You two have a good time."

"We will," Annmarie said, taking Maya's hand.

They went to a patio restaurant and sat out under a spreading poinciana tree. The tablecloth was pink and white, the silver was polished. The waiter held Maya's chair and when she was seated he placed a pink and white napkin across her lap.

"What would you like to eat?" Annmarie asked the child. Because Maya was too dumbstruck to speak, Annmarie said, "How about fried chicken with mashed potatoes? Would you like that?"

Maya nodded. She sat up straight with her hands in her lap. She looked around her, too frightened to move, so Annmarie talked in her hesitant Spanish. She told Maya all about Florida, about Walt Disney World and Mickey Mouse, and anything else she could think of to get the child to relax. When the chicken came she tucked the napkin under Maya's chin, then picking up a chicken leg said, "Chicken tastes better when you eat it with your fingers."

Little by little Maya relaxed. By the time a large piece of chocolate cake was placed in front of her she was chattering away in Spanish too rapid for Annmarie to understand.

When they went back to the Casa de Hogar Annmarie went in to tell Rose she would see her back at the hotel. Maya still had hold of her hand and Annmarie found herself reluctant to leave. Finally she broke away from Maya long enough to speak to Sister Dolores.

"I'd like to have a small party for the children on Sunday, if that's all right with you," she said. "Maybe after lunch I could bring an ice-cream man in and we could all have ice cream and cookies."

"That would be nice," Sister Dolores said. "But very much trouble for you."

"It's no trouble at all. I'll make the arrangements today. Will two-thirty be all right?"

"Of course." The nun smiled. "That will be very nice indeed, *Señorita* Annamaria. It will be something for the children to look forward to."

When Annmarie left, Maya followed her to the door. "I'll see you on Sunday," Annmarie said. "We're going to have an ice-cream party here. Won't that be nice?"

Maya nodded.

"I have to go now."

Maya looked up at her, waiting.

Annmarie stooped and took the child in her arms. "Give me a nice hug," she said, and when Maya did, Annmarie hugged her back. She stood up, still reluctant to leave, then made herself say goodbye.

Annmarie went out, closing the door behind her, and tried not to think of the child she'd left behind.

Chapter Six

The sound of the clarion rang clear in the late afternoon. The first notes of "Cielo Andaluz," that most stirring and solemn of *pasosdoble*, sounded. The matadors stepped out into the arena.

Annmarie forced herself to watch everything, wanting desperately to learn and to understand. She looked at the people sitting around her, their faces as excited as fans watching a World Series or a Super Bowl game. She saw the richness and the pageantry of the *fiesta brava* and tried to feel the same thrill that those around her felt. But all Annmarie felt was fear.

The first bull, the smaller of the two that Diego would fight today, raced into the ring. One of the helpers waved his cape and the bull charged. The man darted behind the *barrera* and the animal slammed into it, ripping at the protective wood with razor-sharp horns.

Diego stepped into the ring and called the bull to him to perform those first dangerous passes that would test the charge of the bull. Annmarie cringed when the bull charged close, so close to the slender body in the green and gold *traje de luces*.

When it came time for the *banderillas*, the crowd whistled, demanding that Diego place the brightly colored sticks himself. He took them, held them high

and poised above his head, and began his zigzag run.
The bull charged and in a motion almost too swift to
see, Diego placed them in the bull's hump of neck
muscle and jumped back. He performed this three
times and the last time he broke the sticks so they were
less than a foot long. Then, step by step he advanced.
The bull charged. Diego ran forward, then cut suddenly across the charge. The bull lowered his head to
hook and Diego, his body exposed and vulnerable,
raised the short sticks and plunged them into the bull
before he spun away.

Annmarie did not think she could bear to stay, neither could she bear to leave.

When it was time for the final *faena*, the last act of
the drama to begin, she tightened her hands in her lap.
She wouldn't look away when Diego fought. This was
his life, his profession and it wasn't going to change—
not for a long time. This was the fear she would have
to live with day in and day out if she loved him. There
were many differences between them, but this was the
major one. This was what made it impossible.

The sword boy handed Diego the sword and *muleta*, the small red cape. Diego took off his hat and
went to stand before the president's box to ask permission to kill his bull. The *faena* began.

Annmarie saw the skill, the flowing grace of movement as Diego called the bull to him. Time and again
he brought the animal so close that the blood from the
picador's lance stained Diego's suit of lights. The
small red cape swirled in fluid, graceful motion as the

bull passed, again and again, while the music rang out in the afternoon sunshine.

She didn't look away when it came time to kill. Diego lowered the red cloth. The bull's head went down, and Diego, sword poised, went over the horns for the kill. The bull staggered, then dropped. The arena erupted with applause and shouts of *"¡Olé, matador! ¡Olé! ¡Olé!"*

"Fantastic!" Vince jumped to his feet. "I've never seen better. He's great, isn't he? Absolutely great!"

Beside her Rose said, "Are you all right?"

"Yes, I'm fine."

Diego walked to the side of the ring, near where she sat. He looked up and Annmarie smiled.

She smiled all through that long afternoon.

Diego's second bull was difficult. It didn't move as fluidly as his first bull had, but stopped midway through each pass to raise and slash widely with dangerous horns.

Sweat ran down Annmarie's body, and her stomach tightened with nausea. Still she watched as with each frightening pass Diego drew the bull closer and yet closer.

At last it was over and she stood with the others when he received his awards and began to circle the plaza. Straw hats and flowers sailed into the ring. *Botas*, leather wine bags, were thrown and each time Diego removed the cap, and with his throat arched back, drank just enough to make the crowd roar its approval. A woman tossed a red high-heeled shoe into the ring. A helper picked it up off the sand and handed it to Diego, who raised it to his lips before he threw it back.

When his tour of the plaza ended he went to stand in the center of the arena. Holding the dozens of red carnations that had been thrown into the ring, he crossed his arms over his chest in a gesture that said "I embrace you all," then bowed and walked back to the *barrera*. He glanced quickly up to Annmarie as though to assure himself that she was there, then turned his attention to the ring as the next matador's bull exploded out of the gate.

At last it was over and Annmarie left with Rose and Vince.

"We won't have dinner until about eight," Rose said. "You look tired, Annmarie. Why don't you rest for a while."

Her body ached with tension. "Yes," she said, "I think I will."

"It was a great afternoon," Vince said. "You surprised me, Annmarie. After that first *corrida* I didn't think you'd be able to take another one. Good thing you're beginning to like it, especially since you and Diego are turning into a twosome." They turned into the entrance of the hotel. "How about a drink?" he asked.

Annmarie shook her head. "No, thanks. I really am tired." She looked at Rose. "I'll see you about seven-thirty," she said.

"Sure. You're okay, aren't you?"

Was she? Annmarie wasn't certain when she went into her room and closed the door behind her. She felt numb, unable to think or to feel. Like an automaton she undressed and showered. Then she lay down on the bed and stared up at the cracked and scarred ceiling.

Scarred. Like Diego's body. She'd seen some of the scars like flashes in a dream that hadn't registered on her brain until now. Once, as they began to make love, she'd glimpsed a jagged scar that crisscrossed his stomach from hip to groin. Another time she'd seen a smaller, two-inch scar in the upper part of his thigh. And the new scar on his leg. How many of them did Diego have? How many more would he have before he stopped?

Annmarie closed her eyes. She didn't understand why a man would stand before the horns of a bull and risk his life. She didn't know how a woman who loved such a man could live with the fear she was forced to face each time he stepped into a bullring.

A woman who loved a man.

Hot tears stung Annmarie's eyes.

She would never understand Diego's profession. She didn't think she would ever understand his country. There were too many differences between them— differences that were insurmountable.

The tears dried on Annmarie's cheeks. She felt cold, drained of all emotion, empty. She'd made a decision.

The four of them drove into the mountains to a restaurant tucked in among a stand of pine trees. Annmarie wore a simple but elegant black silk dress and pearls, sheer black stockings and high-heeled pumps. She'd pulled her pale blond hair back off her face and twisted it into a bun at the back of her neck.

She looked stylish and beautiful, but somehow remote, Diego thought as he slipped a hot pink *rebozo* off her shoulders. He felt uneasy and wasn't sure why. He'd been pleased today that Annamaria had come to the *corrida*. She'd appeared less apprehensive than the first time, and whenever he'd looked her way she'd smiled at him.

They had drinks before dinner while a mariachi band played lively, vigorous music. Rose and Vince laughed and talked a lot. Annmarie listened politely, but added little to the conversation.

Diego ordered wine with dinner and smiled when Vince told him how wonderful he'd been that day.

"We had good bulls to work with," Diego said. "Andrés Gallo was the best I've ever seen him. And did you see the *derechazo* Jaime Beltran did?"

The two of them began to discuss *corridas* and matadors they'd seen in the past, men like Arruza, Cordobés and Luis Miguel Dominguin. Diego became absorbed in the conversation and it wasn't until they were almost through with dinner that he became aware that Annmarie had had a great deal of wine. She sat very straight in her chair, the same kind of smile on her face that she'd worn earlier today in the bullring, twisting the stem of her wineglass back and forth over and over again.

When they began to talk of other things, Rose said, "Annmarie's hooked on the orphanage. She took one of the kids out to lunch the other day."

Diego looked at her curiously. "You didn't tell me," he said.

Annmarie shrugged. "You were busy. I didn't think you'd be interested."

He reached for her hand. "Of course I'm interested."

"Maya's still talking about the chocolate cake she and Annmarie had for dessert," Rose said. "Sister Dolores said you're going to have an ice-cream party for the kids on Sunday afternoon, Annmarie."

"Yes." Annmarie took another sip of wine. "It's the last day of the fiesta. Everybody else will be celebrating, I thought they should too."

"Sunday is the last *corrida*. I wanted us to go together," Diego said with an edge to his voice.

"I've ordered the ice cream for two-thirty. We should be finished by three-thirty. You can pick me up at the orphanage or I'll meet you at the bullring. Whatever suits you." Annmarie raised her glass. It was empty. She frowned and looked at the empty bottle.

"Guess we need some more wine," Vince said, but before he could signal the waiter, Diego shook his head. He picked up Annmarie's *rebozo* from the back of the chair. "You're tired," he said.

"Yes." Annmarie bowed her head and it was as though all of the energy and all the smiles she'd tried so hard to manage all day had faded and died.

When they left the restaurant Vince and Rose sat in the front seat, Annmarie and Diego in the back. The air was cool and she rolled a window down so that she could feel it on her face. Diego put his arm around her and she leaned her head against his shoulder, feeling more tired than she'd ever been in her life.

She was almost asleep when they came down from the mountain and the car rattled along the bumpy cobblestone streets of the town. She sat up and looked out on a scene that was slowly becoming familiar. She smelled corn roasting on the street-stand braziers and tacos frying in black iron skillets. She heard music and voices raised in song coming from a cantina.

"Fiesta!" Vince said from the front seat. "Eat, drink and have yourselves one hell of a good time. It'll all be over on Sunday." He looked back over his shoulder at Diego. "You're fighting again on Saturday, aren't you?"

"Yes, Saturday."

Annmarie turned away from the window and closed her eyes.

When they said good-night to Rose and Vince, Diego took her to her room and undressed her. She didn't want him to but she was too sleepy to object. "I drank too much wine," she said.

"Yes." He kissed her forehead and helped her into bed.

"You know this has to end," she said.

"Go to sleep," he said, and lay down beside her. Soon her breathing evened, and she slept. But it was a long time before Diego did.

Some time later, as the first faint edges of a gray dawn lightened the sky, Diego felt the brush of her lips against his. He opened his eyes and saw her face close to his. Her lips were slightly parted, her eyes still heavy with sleep. Before he could speak she kissed him again, snuggling close against his body as she did, her hand against his back to urge him closer to her.

Like kindling too close to a flame, Diego's body caught fire. He brought her into his arms and whispered her name against her lips.

They came together quickly, urgently, there in the half-light of the room. He looked at her face when their bodies fused. Her fair hair had loosened around her shoulders, and her eyes were closed, her breath short with desire.

She laced her fingers through his dark hair, to bring his face close for a kiss so demanding he felt his body shake with need.

Her movements were frantic, desperate. He tried to slow, to make it last, but she wouldn't let him. He hadn't known she could be like this—so demanding, so exciting. He looked at her, wanting to tell her how magnificent she was, and saw the tears streaming down her face.

"*¿Querida?*" he whispered. "*Querida*, what is it?"

But Annmarie didn't answer. She forced him on, higher and higher, until it was too much, until she cried his name and his body exploded with rapture.

He kissed her. He licked the salt tears from her face and gave them back to her on his tongue. He tried to ask her why she was crying, but she couldn't answer. She only continued to weep and to cling to him, until finally her body relaxed against his and she went to sleep.

Chapter Seven

Diego wasn't there when Annmarie awoke at seven-thirty that morning. She looked at the clock on the stand next to the bed, then groaned and held her head. She'd never before experienced a hangover, and if that's what this was, she never wanted another one. She hadn't meant to drink so much wine; she didn't even *like* wine, but somehow all the tensions of the day had caught up with her last night. The wine had dulled the sharp edge of panic she'd felt when she watched Diego fight yesterday; it had muted the pain that came when she knew that soon she would leave him.

She didn't know how other women—wives and sweethearts and mothers—coped with the fear of watching the men they loved expose themselves to the terrible danger of the bullring.

Love? She could admit it now—she had fallen in love with Diego. But there were too many differences between them in culture and attitude. Marriage was difficult, at best; with them it was impossible.

Annmarie sat up in bed and hugged her knees. The fiesta would be over on Sunday. She would stay until then, partly because she'd promised the children a party, partly because she couldn't bear to leave just yet. But on Monday, or Tuesday, she would leave Santa Catarina—and Diego.

He'd asked her to spend a week at the ranch with him, and in her mind's eye she could see his room. She pictured lazy mornings in bed, having breakfast in the sun on the patio, nights of making love. She thought too of Spain, of castles on hillsides and Don Quixote, of whitewashed houses with red roofs and beautiful women in colorful dresses dancing the flamenco. She thought of what it would be like to go there with Diego.

At last, her mind still a jumble of troubled thoughts, Annmarie bathed and dressed. She went into the dining room, half hoping, half fearful that Diego would be there. But he wasn't. The only people in the room were a large family of tourists from Chicago who asked her what there was to see and do..."in a burg like this."

Annmarie suggested a few places, then sat at a table by the window. She ordered orange juice and black coffee. By the second cup of coffee she began to feel almost human. When one of the Chicago tourists asked her about the fiesta she said, "It'll be over on Sunday. But there are still two more bullfights. You might enjoy seeing one."

"A bullfight!" a lady with blue hair shrieked. "Good heavens, I'd probably root for the bull."

Annmarie finished her coffee in silence.

The town had come fully awake by the time she left the hotel. Produce trucks rumbled through the cobbled streets and began to unload their daily wares: fat white scallions with bright green ends, radishes and tomatoes, tangerines and mangoes, avocados and cactus fruit.

Dogs barked and sniffed the refuse. Children darted in and out of stalls or whimpered when their mothers dumped them in empty orange crates while they set up their stands. Older sisters wiped noses and washed potatoes in tubs of water. Crying babies were given a bare breast to suckle. A husband and wife shared a plate of food and a cup of hot chocolate.

The tortilla women set up their stands on the corners and started their braziers. Ranch women arrived from the hills with armloads of flowers—pinks, baby's breath, wild roses and yellow daisies. All around, over the bustle and the hurry, was the vibrant sound of life.

At eight-thirty the children from the Santa Clara School paraded through town in their blue and white uniforms. The little girls, prissy and self-confident, wore their black hair in long, swinging braids. They walked carefully in line, frowning at the boys who jostled and jabbed each other until one of the nuns stepped in to jerk a few shoulders and hiss a few words. The little girls smirked in satisfaction.

Indian dancers, dressed in traditional costumes, were performing in front of the old church when Annmarie crossed the square on her way to the orphanage. Again she thought how different everything was, how strange, how foreign.

Rose was already at the *casa* when Annmarie arrived. "I didn't expect to see you here so early," she said. "How do you feel?"

"Like 'Drums along the Mohawk' has taken permanent possession of my head." Annmarie pressed fingertips to her forehead. "I don't ever drink that much," she said.

"I didn't think you did." Rose's expression was kind. "It's Diego, isn't it?" Before Annmarie could answer, Rose said, "I watched you yesterday when he was fighting. You sat there with a fixed smile on your face and I knew you hated every minute of it."

Annmarie took a deep breath. "Yes," she said. "Yes, I hated it."

"I don't suppose it's any of my business, but you've fallen in love with Diego, haven't you?"

"Yes, Rose. And I wish to God I hadn't."

"Because of what he does?"

Annmarie nodded. "I hate his profession. I'd never be comfortable with it." Annmarie hesitated, not wanting to say too much, yet feeling the need to talk to someone. "But it's more than that, Rose. I told you that Diego had asked me to go to Spain with him—I'm just not ready for that, for any kind of a commitment."

"But if you're in love with him—"

"I am in love with him, but love and commitment and marriage scare me to death." Annmarie took a deep breath. "My parents are in the process of a divorce right now. They've been married for twenty-five years and the marriage was hell for both of them. I've grown up with that, Rose. I don't want any part of it."

"But you and Diego aren't your parents. Their bad marriage doesn't mean the same thing would happen with you and Diego."

"Doesn't it?" Annmarie's expression was bleak. "My mother and father had all the right ingredients for a good marriage, Rose. They grew up in the same town. They went to the same high school and college together. They had everything going for them—similar backgrounds, same religion, everything. Their marriage should have worked but it didn't. And if theirs didn't work, how could I expect marriage—if that's what it ever comes to between Diego and me—to work? His realm of experience is so different from mine. We barely speak the same language."

"But if you love each other..." Rose hesitated. "Maybe that was the problem with your parents, Annmarie. Maybe they just didn't love each other. I don't want to sound profound, but I honestly think love can transcend cultural or any other kind of barriers. If I were you, Annmarie, I'd give love a chance. I'd go to Spain with Diego and take it from there."

"I have a job, an apartment," Annmarie protested. "I can't just...just go dashing off to Spain with a man I've just met."

"Can't you?" Rose shrugged, then, turning away she said, "It takes courage to love, Annmarie. I suppose it takes a double dose of courage to love a man in Diego's profession. But real love only comes along once in a while. When it does, it seems like such a terrible waste to throw it away."

When Annmarie didn't answer, Rose said, "But nobody can tell you what to do. It's your decision, yours and Diego's. But he's a good man, Annmarie. It'll be a damn shame to walk away from him."

Rose had little to say after that. She left after lunch but Annmarie stayed on until late afternoon. She helped out in the kitchen and bathed a new baby that had arrived only a few days before. She played with the children, and tried not to think about anything but the moment.

The air was cool when she left the orphanage. She turned up the collar of her sweater and put her hands in her pockets. Instead of going back to La Quinta she cut across the square and sat on one of the iron benches facing the old stone church.

She sat there for a long time, deep in thought until, with a flurry of activity, a wedding party came out of the church. The bride was young. Her long black hair was partially covered by a wisp of veil. She laughed excitedly and clung to her groom's arm as they ran down the steps amid a shower of flowers and rice to a car that was adorned with bright crepe-paper streamers.

Behind the bride and groom came ushers in white jackets and bridesmaids in frilly pink dresses, then what must have been the bride's and groom's parents, along with dozens of exuberant children, and girlfriends who looked with speculative eyes at suddenly nervous boyfriends.

Photographs were taken amid hugs and kisses and shouted congratulations. Then the bride and groom jumped into the waiting car. She tossed her bouquet out the window, her girlfriends jumping to catch it, and with laughter, waves and blown kisses, the newly married couple drove away. And finally, in groups of two or three or four, the wedding party drifted off.

The bells in the church began to toll the time, and a sudden gust of wind swept across the plaza, whirling bits of colored streamers and forgotten flowers across the stone courtyard.

Diego heard the bells and it seemed to him there was sadness in their sonorous tones. But he knew the sadness was in him. He thought of last night when Annamaria had awakened him with kisses, and of how they'd made love, and that she had wept in the midst of their passion.

Suddenly Diego felt cold and chilled because he knew she was going to leave him. He wished he could make her understand how he felt about his profession, and he told himself that she would if she were a Mexican woman. But that wasn't true, of course. His mother had never understood. She'd protested when he'd told her that he was going to be a matador, and she had wept. He didn't know if she wept still, but he suspected that she did. God knows, she still protested.

Diego turned up the collar of his jacket. His leg hurt but he didn't want to think about that, or about the bulls.

"Cancel out on the *corrida* Saturday," Manolo, his manager, had said a few minutes ago. "You look tired. Everyone will understand that your leg hasn't yet healed. Romero and Gutierez can fight a *mano a mano*."

"No," Diego had said. "I'll be all right, I can do it. When this one's over I'll take a rest. I won't fight again until Spain."

Spain. On the spur of the moment he'd asked Annamaria to go to Spain with him because he couldn't bear to part from her. Even though everything had happened so fast, he knew that he loved her—and yes, by heaven, yes, that he wanted to be married to her!

The breath caught in Diego's throat. *Por Dios*, he wanted to marry her! That thought terrified him, but not as much as the thought of losing her did. He would ask her on Saturday night after the *corrida*. He knew she had many doubts about their relationship, but he would convince her that even though it had happened quickly, the feeling that he had—and which he was sure she had—was a forever feeling. He and Annamaria belonged together; he couldn't imagine his life without her.

Diego stopped for a moment beside the fountain in the plaza to rest. He leaned down to massage his leg and when he straightened he saw Annamaria sitting on one of the benches.

She looked as she had the first night he'd seen her, when she left the *posada*. The collar of her sweater was turned up around her neck, her long blond hair blew about her face. She looked very alone, there on the park bench with bits of colored paper swirling around her. Diego stayed where he was for a few moments, then he went to her and said, "I wondered where you were."

"I've been at the orphanage." She looked toward the church. "There was a wedding a little while ago."

Diego sat down beside her and reached for her hand. "You're cold," he said.

"Yes."

"It's warmer in Spain."

"And in Florida."

He tightened his hand around hers. "Annamaria..." he started to say, but she stopped him.

"No," she said. "Don't say anything now."

"We've got to talk."

"Not now."

"Saturday, then, after the *corrida*."

"All right." She looked at him. "I didn't know until Vince mentioned it that you were fighting again. You shouldn't. Your leg hasn't healed yet. You probably shouldn't have fought yesterday."

"It's all right. Just this one more *corrida* and I can rest until...until I get to Spain." He'd almost said until *we* get to Spain.

Diego looked away from her, at the eighteenth-century church. The facade was Gothic in feeling, yet full of the charming freedom native to the Indian artists who'd built it so many years ago. It was a beautiful church, a church built for weddings.

He wanted to ask her then. He wanted to tell her he loved her and wanted to marry her. But he didn't. He only held her hand and sat with her until the birds came to roost in the laurel trees and the bells began to toll the hour of the evening mass.

Chapter Eight

The woman's throaty voice drifted like hazy smoke across the room. She sang of love; of old and new and lost love, her voice blending like rough velvet with the accompanying guitars. The lights were low, the flames from the fire cast wavering shadows on the dancing couples.

Diego's hand was warm against Annmarie's back. She closed her eyes and surrendered to the moment, letting her body flow with the music of the guitars. She didn't understand the words, only the passion with which the woman sang, a passion so rich in emotion Annmarie felt tears sting her eyes and her body soften and mold to Diego's.

They danced as one person, lost in the music and in each other. For them there were no fancy, intricate steps, no twists or turns or structured poses. They were two people caught up in the music, feeling and moving to the sensuous rhythm of the guitars.

When at last the song ended they stood for a moment, still clasped in each other's arms. As though she were awakening from a dream, Annmarie opened her eyes and looked at Diego. His face, bronzed by firelight, was like no other face in the world. With his eyes and his high cheekbones he looked part Aztec warrior, part Spanish grandee.

Annmarie touched his face. "I love the way you look," she said.

He kissed her fingertips. "And I love you."

When they went back to their corner table their waiter brought their steaks and a bottle of red wine.

"I'll be sorry to leave Santa Catarina," Diego said as he looked around him. "The restaurants in Spain are perhaps the best in the world, but there's a charm, a warmth here that I enjoy and that I will miss." He touched his glass to hers. "Have you ever been to Europe?"

"I went to England for two weeks at the end of my junior year at college. It was an English-literature tour."

"Did you enjoy it?"

"Yes." Annmarie smiled. "But it was in December, over Christmas vacation, and I was very cold."

"You wouldn't be cold in Spain. The sun shines every day there, especially in the south along the Costa del Sol." Diego looked at her over the rim of his glass. "We could swim in the Mediterranean, lie on the beach and let the sun seep into our bones. Afterward in our room I would kiss you from the top of your head down to your thumbs."

"Toes," Annmarie said with a smile.

"Toes?" He nodded. "Ah, yes, I forget it is different in English." He reached for her hand. "Come to Spain with me, Annamaria."

She took a deep breath and held it. "I...I don't think I can."

"You wouldn't have to go to the *corridas*. I'd understand if you didn't, if I knew you would be waiting for me when they were over."

"Diego—"

"No, don't say anything now. We have a few more days." He reached for her hand across the table. "My brother Carlos phoned me from Guadalajara this morning. He's bringing my mother to visit."

"That's nice, Diego. How long will she stay?"

"Only for a few days, I imagine. She wanted to see me before I leave for Spain. I want you to meet her while she's here, Annamaria. I think the two of you will like each other."

"Does she speak English?"

"Yes, a little."

"When will she come?"

"I'm not sure. Perhaps tomorrow. I've asked Juanita to prepare a special dinner Saturday night. You must come, of course, and Vince and Rose. We'll have a small fiesta. My mother will like that. She loves parties."

"Will she go to the *corrida* on Saturday?"

"No, of course not."

Annamaria looked at him questioningly.

"My mother has never seen me fight."

"I see." She hesitated, then couldn't resist saying, "I thought it was only *gringas* like me who didn't like bullfights."

"It's not that my mother doesn't like the *fiesta brava*," Diego said defensively. "It's that she refuses to watch *me* fight. On Saturday at four o'clock she will be in the kitchen with Juanita, cooking our dinner and pretending to herself that it is a day like any other day."

"She must suffer a great deal when you fight."

A muscle jumped in Diego's cheek. "Yes, she suffers. But because she loves me she has never tried to change me."

"That must take a special kind of woman."

"I suppose it does." He looked at her across the table, his gaze steady and challenging.

They finished their dinner in silence, pretending to listen to the music of the guitars. But they avoided each other's glances.

They danced once more before they left, but it wasn't as it had been before. They danced stiffly, like strangers, and when the music stopped they stepped away from each other.

Silently, together yet apart, they walked through the quiet streets back to La Quinta. When they reached Annmarie's door she said, "I'm . . . I'm awfully tired tonight, Diego."

"Of course," he said, his face frozen and still. He took the key from her and unlocked the door. Then he kissed her forehead, said "Good night, Annamaria," and went down the quiet corridor to his own room.

Annmarie went in and closed the door. For a moment she leaned her back against it. She felt hollow inside, drained of all feeling, lost and more alone than she'd ever felt in her life.

She saw Diego only briefly during the next few days. He moved out of the hotel and went back to the ranch so that he would be there when his mother arrived. Once, when they met in the dining room, he asked her if she would like to ride out to the ranch with him. She said she couldn't, that she'd promised to go to the orphanage.

On Saturday morning Diego returned to La Quinta to dress there before the *corrida*. On his way, driving in from the ranch, he stopped at the corral of the bullring to look at the bulls he would fight that afternoon.

He leaned on the corral fence, watching the six animals. He wasn't happy with the first bull. The horns, though large, were oddly shaped, and the animal seemed skittish. His second bull weighed almost twelve hundred pounds. The horns were set well apart. The shoulders were heavy and well muscled, the hind quarters were lean. He thought this one would be brave and as he looked at it he felt the excitement building in him.

When Diego left the corral he got back into his pickup to drive to La Quinta. That was when he felt the wind. He frowned, for wind was a matador's enemy; it billowed the cape, disconcerting, distracting the movements of the bull.

When he drove by the church on the square and saw people leaving from early mass, he parked and went into the church. There were only a few people still there, women whose heads were covered by dark *rebozos*, whose roughened fingers caressed their beads. He thought of his mother and knew that she had gone to mass this morning in the small church near the ranch to pray for his safety.

Diego touched the holy water with his fingertips and crossed himself. He looked at the candles flickering in the gloom and tried not to listen to the sound of the wind.

Annamaria had agreed to meet him for breakfast this morning. The *corrida* wasn't until four that afternoon and he wouldn't be able to eat later. When he got to La Quinta she was sitting in the sun in the corridor throwing down scraps to a small black goat that was tethered in the garden.

She got up when she saw him and said, "Good morning. Has your mother arrived yet?"

"Yesterday afternoon." He wanted to kiss her but he didn't think she wanted him to, so instead he put his hand on her shoulder and said, "You look very pretty this morning. Are you hungry?"

"Starving."

They took a table by the window, and when they had ordered, Diego said, "I've missed you."

"I've missed you, too. But I know you had things to attend to. You must be glad to see your mother."

"Yes." He hesitated. "I've told her about you."

"Oh?"

"She's looking forward to meeting you tonight." He hesitated. "Are you coming to the *corrida* this afternoon?"

"No, I . . . I'm going to spend the day at the orphanage."

"I see."

"I have a lot of things to do," she said quickly. "Things to arrange for the party at the *casa* tomorrow."

"Then I'll see you at the ranch tonight. You can drive out with Rose and Vince, can't you?"

"Yes. What time?"

"Seven." He frowned. "What about the *corrida* on Sunday afternoon? I'd planned on your going with me but perhaps you'd rather not."

"No, I'll go with you."

Diego took a sip of his coffee. "I leave for Spain a week from Monday." He looked at her. "We have to talk, Annamaria."

She swallowed hard. "Yes, I know."

"Tonight, after the party." He covered her hand with his and kept it there while they finished breakfast. When they left the dining room he said, "I'm going to see my manager now. I'll come back later to rest before the *corrida*. I wish you would rest with me."

With a slight smile Annmarie said, "Isn't there an unwritten law that says bullfighters shouldn't...exert themselves before a *corrida*?"

"Making love with you is not an exertion." Diego put his hands on her shoulders. "I think I will die if I do not kiss you," he whispered. And he did, there in the sunlit corridor, with only the black goat to see them.

Annmarie's lips parted under his as she swayed toward him. I've missed you, she wanted to say. I miss the sound of your voice, the warmth of your arms around me in the night. But she said nothing. She only held him and prayed a silent prayer for his safety.

Diego let her go. "I'll see you tonight," he said.

Her lips still tingling from his kisses, Annmarie nodded. She rested her face against his for a moment longer. *"Suerte,"* she whispered. Luck.

He held her close, then he let her go and went quickly across the garden to his pickup and drove away. Annmarie stayed where she was, leaning against the corridor railing. Then she went into her room for her purse and a shopping bag, hurrying so that she wouldn't have to think about how he'd looked when he left her.

On the way to the orphanage she went to the *neveria*, the ice-cream store, and ordered fifty Popsicles and fifty ice-cream bars to be delivered to the orphanage at two-thirty on Sunday afternoon. Then she went to the small supermarket on Hidalgo Street and bought a dozen boxes of cookies.

She stayed at the orphanage until four-thirty. When she left she went to the street of the bullring and stood across from the arena. She listened to the excited roar of the crowd, the shouts, the screams, the *olé*s. She felt chilled by the wind and thought that wind must be a dangerous thing for a matador.

Finally she turned and went back down the cobblestone street toward La Quinta.

The patio was filled with lantern light and the music of mariachis.

"Sounds like the party's already started," Vince said. "I'm looking forward to tonight. I bet Diego is too. Must be a relief for him to let off a little steam after the *corrida*. It's a shame you weren't there today, Annmarie. You should have seen what Diego did with his second bull."

"He had a fine animal to work with," Rose said. "It was an *indulto*, which means the bull wasn't killed."

"The bull was wonderful and so was Diego. It was a fantastic fight and now I'm ready for a fantastic party." Vince glanced at the two women sitting beside him. "It's a treat to escort you two good-looking ladies. Blue is your color, Rose. You look like a million bucks. You too, Annmarie. You're as pretty as I've ever seen you."

It helped to have Vince say that, because she hadn't been sure about the dress. She'd bought it in a small shop just off the square yesterday. Made of a rough, off-white material, the dress hung straight from shoulder to ankle in smooth, flowing lines. It had long sleeves and a V neck that was trimmed with macramé tassles. It was simple and Mexican and it had felt right on her.

Diego greeted them at the entrance to the patio. "It's cool tonight," he said, "so we've decided to have the party inside." He took Annmarie's arm. "Come in, I want to introduce you to my mother and brother."

Doña Elena Cristina Ortiz was a small woman. Her black hair, only slightly touched with gray, was pulled back off her face and held in place with a high Spanish comb. She wore a long black silk dress and diamond earrings.

"Mamá," Diego said in Spanish, "I would like you to meet my friends, the Señora Rose Cameron, Señor Vincent Stolarski, and the Señorita Annamaria Bannister."

"Mucho gusto," Doña Elena said. "My English is not good, but I try." She smiled at each of them, but her dark eyes lingered a moment longer on Annmarie.

"This is my brother, Carlos," Diego said.

Carlos Ortiz, a few years older than Diego, was two inches shorter and twenty pounds heavier. He shook hands with Vince and kissed Rose's hand before he turned to Annmarie and said, "Diego has told me much about you. I see he did not exaggerate. You will sit next to me at dinner, yes?"

"No," Diego said. "Behave yourself, Carlos, or I'll tell Gabriela." He smiled at his brother and to the others said, "Gabriela wanted to be here, too, but she has only recently presented this brother of mine with their eighth child."

"Eighth?" Vince stuck his hand out. "Congratulations."

"He has never learned that enough is enough," Diego said.

"One of us must keep the family name alive, *mano*. We have all given up on you." He smiled at Annmarie. "But perhaps if the right woman came along..." He let the words hang in the air, then with a laugh said, "Let us have an *aperitivo*. Yes?"

A bottle of champagne was opened to celebrate the new baby. When the others began to talk about the afternoon's *corrida*, about how brave Diego had been, Annmarie went to sit beside Diego's mother.

"You do not like to talk of the bulls?" Doña Elena asked.

"No, I'm afraid I don't."

"You did not go to see Diego fight today?"

"No, *Señora*, I didn't."

"It is because you are *norteamericana*. You don't understand about the bulls."

"No, I don't suppose I do."

"I understand, but I do not go when Diego fights." Doña Elena waited, and when Annmarie didn't speak she said, "Is that why you did not go today? Because it was Diego who fought?"

Annmarie looked into the eyes that gazed so intently into hers. She didn't think there were many people who could fool Doña Elena and decided not to try. "Yes," she said. "That's why I didn't go."

Doña Elena nodded. "I have never seen Diego fight. I never will. I cannot bear to see him endanger his life, because I love him." She paused, then said, "Is that why you do not want to see him fight? Because you love him?"

"Señora Ortiz, I..." Annmarie looked at Diego's mother, and then away.

"Are you in love with my son, *señorita*?"

Annmarie, held by the intensity of the Doña Elena's gaze, said, "Yes, I'm in love with Diego."

"So?" Doña Elena paused. "It is obvious, of course, that he is in love with you. Then, why, my dear Annamaria, has my son been so unhappy these last two days?"

"Everything has happened so fast, *señora*. Diego and I are very different. We've been brought up differently. Our cultures, our..." Annmarie's voice trailed off. "Even our language is different. There are times we don't even understand the words we each say."

"But when you love, you must listen with your heart." Doña Elena took Annmarie's hands in hers. "That is what love is, my child, listening with the heart. How many people who speak the same language do not understand each other? If you and Diego truly love each other that is all that matters. Has he asked you to marry him?"

"No, we haven't discussed marriage."

"Then it is time you did. Diego is almost thirty-three." Doña Elena smiled. "The ranch would be a nice place to live, a nice place to raise children." She patted Annmarie's cheek and said with a chuckle, "And do not fear, not all my sons are like Carlos. Nor are all women as prolific as Gabriela." Her voice sobered. "I hope you will not let Diego leave Santa Catarina without you, Annamaria."

Before Annmarie could answer, Juanita called out that dinner was ready, and Diego came to take the arm of his mother and of Annmarie to escort them in to dinner.

Doña Elena sat at the head of the table, with Carlos on her right, Diego on her left. The mariachis played at one end of the room while Juanita served platter after platter heaped with cheese enchiladas, chilis *rellenos*, *carne asada*, fish cooked in the style of Veracruz, *frijoles*, and fresh tortillas.

Over the noise Diego turned to Annmarie and said, "This is a fairly typical family celebration. I hope you're enjoying it."

"It's a wonderful party, Diego." She looked toward his mother and with a smile said, "Your mother's certainly enjoying herself."

"Mother loves an occasion like this. I saw her talking to you before. Did she tell you what a fine fellow I am?"

"Of course!" Annmarie laughed, then slowly her laughter faded, for it seemed to her that over the sound of the music, the talk and the laughter, she could hear Doña Elena saying, *When you love, you must listen with your heart.*

Diego covered her hand with his. "What is it, *querida*?"

Annmarie shook her head. "It's nothing, Diego. Nothing."

But it was something, of course, and Annmarie knew that before the night was over she would have to tell Diego.

Chapter Nine

The music of the mariachis faded to a softer melody when Annmarie and Diego left the patio to take the path down to the pastures. The leaves stirred in the breeze that brought with it the smell of rich earth, clover and night-blooming jasmine. In the distance they could hear the barking of dogs and the lonely howl of a coyote.

"I love it here at the ranch," Diego said. "This is where I come when I'm tired. This is where I will come when I stop fighting."

Annmarie heard the sadness in his voice. "And you'll raise bulls for other men to fight."

"Yes, for other men." Minutes passed before Diego spoke again. "But there will be *tientas* here at the ranch. That's when we test young cows to see how brave they are. Neighboring ranchers come, matador friends, relatives, and after the serious business there's music and dancing, and occasionally one of the *aficionados* takes a turn with the cape."

Diego pointed off to his right and Annmarie could see the family bullring, deserted in the half-light of the moon. For a moment it seemed to her that she could see Diego there, the magenta and yellow cape whirling gracefully about his body, and the animal, white horns shining in the moonlight.

When they reached the bullring, which was half the size of a regular ring, Diego let go of Annmarie's hand and put one foot up on the fence rail. He knew they needed to talk but he was reluctant to begin.

At last he turned to her. "Last week I asked you to come to Spain with me," he said. "I didn't mention marriage because in a strange way I thought that would make you hesitate even more than my asking you to come with me. I told myself that if we began this relationship without ties or commitments you might not be so afraid. But I was wrong, Annamaria. What we have is not temporary, it is for a lifetime."

"Diego—"

"No, let me finish. I love you and I want to be married to you. Everything may have happened quickly but that doesn't make it any the less real. I know that you are afraid because of the bullfighting, but that won't last forever. I have told myself that I'll retire in five or six years. Now I'll make that promise to you."

"It isn't just the bullfighting," Annmarie said. "We're different, Diego, in the way we think, the way we've been raised."

Diego's face tightened. "Isn't it strange," he said. "You see only the differences, I see only the similarities." He leaned his arms on the corral fence. "I don't say that a marriage between us will be easy. Perhaps it won't be, especially for the next few years when I'll be traveling much of the time. I've got contracts lined up in Colombia and Venezuela after the season in Spain. You could stay here at the ranch, of course, but

I would rather you travel with me. It's not an easy life Annmarie, but I'm asking you to share it with me. I'm asking you to marry me." He took her hand. "Will you? Will you become the Señora Annamaria Ortiz?"

She looked at him and it seemed to her as though the night had stilled. This was the moment, the moment of truth, and she wasn't ready for it.

The call of a whippoorwill broke the stillness of the night.

Listen with your heart, his mother had said.

"Marriage..." Annmarie took a deep, shaking breath. "Marriage is so permanent, Diego, so difficult. When it's bad it can be terribly painful. I know because I've seen it in my parents' marriage. You and I...we've only just met. There are so many things I don't understand about you and your country." She touched his face. "I don't think I want to talk about marriage, not now, Diego, but...I'll go to Spain with you if you still want me to. I'll take more time off from my job and we...we could just see what happens. I mean, if we still feel..." She saw the expression on his face and her voice trailed off.

Diego shook his head. "No, *querida*, I want a lifetime love, not a short-term affair." He cupped her face between his hands. "What we have is a rare thing, Annamaria. Can't you trust the way we feel about each other?"

"My mother and father trusted the way they felt about each other and their marriage was a disaster."

"We are not your mother and father, Annamaria. Because they failed in their marriage does not mean we will fail." He put his arms around her, holding her so close he could feel the beating of her heart. But he didn't kiss her. When he let her go he looked at her and said, "I'm waiting for your answer."

His face was shadowed by the moonlight. She wanted to touch him again but she knew that if she did, she would be lost. "I can't," she whispered. "It's too soon. Marriage is too final." Tears streaked her face. "I'm sorry, but I can't."

The children were atwitter with anticipation. The boys were rowdy and rambunctious, the little girls were giggly. Every five minutes a five-year-old named Pablo, whose two front teeth were missing and whose hair stuck up at odd angles, demanded to know when the ice cream was coming.

"You're rude," prim Aurora said.

Annmarie glanced at her watch. The ice cream and Popsicles were supposed to have been delivered at two-thirty, and they were almost an hour late. She looked down at Maya, who always sat as close to her as she possibly could, and at the other children. "The ice cream will be here any minute now," she said with more conviction than she felt.

"Of course it will," Sister Dolores said. "It is only delayed, that's all. It will arrive eventually."

Eventually. Diego would be here any minute to take her to the *corrida*. She didn't want to disappoint the children, but she wanted to go with him because this would probably be their last day together.

Last night they had walked back from the corral to the house without speaking. They could hear the mariachi music and when they reached the patio Diego had looked at her and said, "One more dance, Annamaria?"

Without waiting for her answer he had taken her in his arms, there on the moonlit patio, and they had danced to the music of a Mexican waltz. When the waltz ended Diego had said, "For the rest of my life I will miss you and be sorry that we could not be together."

Then he'd let her go, but before they went into the house to join the others he'd said, "There is no reason to cancel our plans tomorrow. I'll pick you up at the orphanage at three-thirty."

Annmarie looked at her watch. It was three-thirty.

"When's the ice cream coming?" Pablo asked, just as the front-door knocker sounded. He yipped in delight as he and a passel of small boys and girls raced to the door. Pablo reached it first. He opened it, then, hands on his hips, looked up at Diego and past him to the empty street. "Where's the ice cream?" he demanded.

"Isn't it here?" Diego stepped inside. He looked over at Annmarie. "What happened?" he asked. "I thought the party would be over by now."

"The ice-cream man never came." She shook her head. "I'm sorry, Diego, but I can't go to the *corrida* with you. I'm going to have to go out and find ice cream somewhere.''

"No, let me see what I can do." Diego looked down at Pablo. "You and a couple of your friends want to come with me?" he asked.

Pablo's eyes widened. For the first time all day he was speechless. He looked up at Diego, then at Sister Dolores. "Yes," she said with a smile. "You may go with the *señor*."

"I'll be back as soon as I can," Diego said.

It was almost fifteen minutes before another knock sounded. This time it was Sister Dolores who opened the door, and when she did Pablo and three other boys bounded in ahead of Diego and two men pushing ice-cream carts.

"This should do it," Diego told Annmarie with a grin.

A chorus of thank-you's rose in the air. Annmarie looked at her watch. It was ten minutes to four. "We can leave now," she said.

But Diego shook his head. "Pablo told me he's never been to a bullfight. I thought we'd take him and any of the other children that want to go. I spoke to the officials at the bullring; they've agreed to delay the *corrida* until we get there." He looked at Sister Dolores. "I hope that's all right with you, Sister. It's the last day of the fiesta and I thought the children would enjoy it just as much as the rest of Santa Catarina. You're invited too, of course."

"I accept your invitation, Señor Ortiz. I haven't seen a *corrida* since I entered the convent."

Annmarie was speechless. She helped Diego hand out ice-cream cups and bars and Popsicles. She watched him take a three-year-old girl on his lap and help her spoon chocolate ice cream into her mouth. His voice was soft, his hands were gentle.

Annmarie felt something clutch at her heart. She wiped Maya's chin and saw that her hands were trembling.

Fifteen minutes later the whole group of them marched up the street toward the bullring; fifty-some children, all of them chattering like magpies, a black-garbed nun, Diego and Annmarie. Diego carried the three-year-old. Annmarie held Maya's hand.

When they reached the bullring Diego handed the man at the gate a wad of tickets, and they paraded, two by two, into the arena to the first three rows of seats.

The clarion sounded. Pablo leaned forward, his eyes alight with anticipation.

"I expect this to be very interesting," Aurora said in her prim little voice.

The *alguacil* came into the ring on a beautiful black horse and Maya clapped her hands. The matadors stepped out into the sun and the children gasped.

All through the *corrida* they oohed and ahhed and shouted *"Olé!"* Even Sister Dolores jumped to her feet once or twice to scream, *"¡Bravo! ¡Bravo!"*

Annmarie looked on in wonder at Diego surrounded by little boys who listened attentively as he explained some of the intricacies of the *corrida*. And suddenly she understood that their pleasure at this was

as natural to them as watching a rousing good baseball game was to children in the United States, for this
was part of their heritage.

It was toward the end of the *corrida* that Diego
looked at Annmarie. He smiled at her over the head
of the little girl who'd fallen asleep in his arms, and
when he did it was as though something in Annmarie
stilled and waited, because his whole heart was in his
eyes.

Slowly, painfully, something inside her that had
been frozen for a long time, softened, leaving in its
place a warm and loving glow. She wanted to reach out
and touch him, but because she couldn't she smiled, a
tremulous smile that she hoped told him everything
that was in her heart.

When the *corrida* was over they walked back to the
orphanage with the children. At the door Diego said,
"I'm going to be away for a few months. I'll come to
see you when I get back and if there's another *corrida*, we'll go again."

He ruffled Pablo's hair, and grinned when it spiked
up against his fingers. "I'll see you again, *mu-
chacho.*"

The street seemed very quiet without the children.
Diego wanted to take Annmarie's hand but he didn't.
He'd seen something in her face today that had rekin-
dled a flare of hope. But his fear that he might have
imagined it kept him from speaking. They walked on
in silence until he said, "I thought we'd have an early
dinner," and led her into a restaurant on one of the
side streets.

A waiter took them to a corner table in the dimly lit room. When they had ordered Diego said, "It was a nice afternoon, wasn't it?"

"Yes, it was, Diego, thanks to you." Annmarie looked at him over the flickering candle. "You're a nice man," she said.

Diego waited.

"I was wrong. There are no differences, no *real* differences between us."

"Annamaria...?"

Her eyes sparkled with unshed tears as she reached for his hand. "Your mother told me to listen with my heart. I think that's what I did this afternoon." Her hand tightened on his. "If you still want me...if you still want us to be married..."

He thought his heart would burst with happiness, but all he could say was "Anna...Annamaria." Then he got up and came around the table and swept her into his arms.

There was another wedding at the old stone church facing the square. The bride wore a pale blue dress and daisies in her hair. She clung to the groom's arm and smiled at him when they came out of the church amid a shower of rice and rose petals. The bells in the tower rang and the pigeons nesting there flew out and up, circling over the laurel trees, pale against the blue of the sky.

Rose and Vince came arm in arm after the bride and groom. They were followed by Doña Elena and Diego's brother Carlos, friends and *aficionados*, and a gaggle of children from the Casa de Hogar.

"It was a splendid wedding," Carlos said as he kissed Annmarie's cheek. "You're a beautiful bride." He shook his brother's hand. "*Felicidades, mano.* May you have a long and happy life together, and many children."

"But not as many as you," Diego said with a laugh. He squeezed Annmarie's hand and looked at her with eyes that were filled with love.

"You're off to Mexico City tomorrow?" Rose asked.

Annmarie nodded. "The day after that we leave for Spain. We'll be there until spring when we—"

"¡Señora Ortiz!" The fat little priest who'd married them hurried down the stairs holding a rolled-up paper in his hand.

Annmarie glanced at him, smiled, then turned back to Rose.

"Señora Ortiz," the priest said again.

Annmarie looked at Diego's mother, unaware that the others were smiling until Diego said, "Darling, the *padre* is talking to you."

"Oh?" Just for a moment she looked surprised, then with a happy laugh she stepped forward to take the marriage papers from the *padre*. She knew that indeed she was the Señora Annamaria Ortiz, and that she couldn't have been happier.

* * * * *

Barbara Faith

I was born in Cleveland, raised in Detroit, and when I was twenty-one I went to Miami Beach for a two-week vacation that lasted seventeen years.

A month after I arrived there I went to work for the *Miami Beach Sun*. After that I did hotel and supper club publicity, and for ten years I worked in broadcasting, first in radio programming, then as editor of the company publication. In my spare time I took night classes in creative writing and Spanish.

I sold the first short story that I wrote in class to the *Alfred Hitchcock Mystery Magazine*, which convinced me that the business of writing was a cinch. But writing wasn't a cinch, of course, and a very long time passed before I sold another story.

But it didn't matter; I was hooked. And finally I decided to take a chance on myself. I quit my job, and armed with determination, a typewriter and not quite three thousand dollars, I set off for San Miguel de Allende in Guanajuato, Mexico, to study writing at the Instituto Allende.

That's where everything came together. I met my husband-to-be. I began to learn something about the culture of Mexico, and I wrote two not very good novels. I'd begun to learn my craft, but except for the sale of a Christmas story to *Mademoiselle*, I hadn't set the writing world on fire.

When my husband and I moved to California, I wanted to quit trying to write and get a job. He wouldn't let me. No matter how many times I failed, he said, "Try again." That's a lot of what it takes—somebody who believes in you—who doesn't mind a manuscript spread all over the kitchen table instead of a pot roast.

I finally sold my first novel in 1978, and my first Silhouette Intimate Moments was published in 1983. I'm happy to say my career has been zooming right along since then.

Alfonso and I love to travel, so most of my books have a foreign setting. Because I've lived in Mexico and love the country and its history, some of my books have been set there. We've traveled extensively in Europe, especially in Spain, and that country, too, has been the setting for a book. We've also been to Morocco and Egypt, to Japan, Taiwan and Hong Kong, and these places have also become backgrounds for books.

For me, the three best things in life are romance, writing and travel. It's just wonderful to be able to combine them all.

Barbara Faith

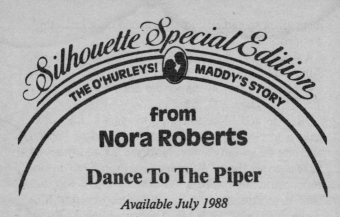

Silhouette Special Edition

THE O'HURLEYS! MADDY'S STORY

from
Nora Roberts

Dance To The Piper

Available July 1988

The second in an exciting new series about the lives and loves of triplet sisters—

If *The Last Honest Woman* (SE #451) captured your heart in May, you're sure to want to read about Maddy and Chantel, Abby's two sisters.

In *Dance to the Piper* (SE #463), it takes some very fancy footwork to get reserved recording mogul Reed Valentine dancing to effervescent Maddy's tune....

Then, in *Skin Deep* (SE #475), find out what kind of heat it takes to melt the glamorous Chantel's icy heart. Available in September.

THE O'HURLEYS!

**Join the excitement of
Silhouette Special Editions.**

SSE 463-1

Take 4 Silhouette Special Edition novels and a surprise gift
FREE

Then preview 6 brand-new books—delivered to your door as soon as they come off the presses! If you decide to keep them, you pay just $2.49 each*—a 9% saving off the retail price, *with no additional charges for postage and handling!*

Romance is alive, well and flourishing in the moving love stories of Silhouette Special Edition novels. They'll awaken your desires, enliven your senses and leave you tingling all over with excitement.

Start with 4 Silhouette Special Edition novels and a surprise gift absolutely FREE. They're yours to keep without obligation.   You can always return a shipment and cancel at any time.

Simply fill out and return the coupon today!

* Plus 69¢ postage and handling per shipment in Canada.

Silhouette Special Edition®

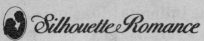

A Trilogy by Diana Palmer

Bestselling Diana Palmer has rustled up three rugged heroes in a trilogy sure to lasso your heart! The titles of the books are your introduction to these unforgettable men:

CALHOUN

In June, you met Calhoun Ballenger. He wanted to protect Abby Clark from the world, but could he protect her from himself?

JUSTIN

Calhoun's brother, Justin—the strong, silent type—had a second chance with the woman of his dreams, Shelby Jacobs, in August.

TYLER

October's long, tall Texan is Shelby's virile brother, Tyler, who teaches shy Nell Regan to trust her instincts—especially when they lead her into his arms!

Don't miss TYLER, the last of three gripping stories from Silhouette Romance!

***